State University
of Murder

Praise for Lev Raphael's
Nick Hoffman Mystery Series

"Deliciously wicked…the perfect book to take away for
a weekend in the country…a genuinely funny modern
comedy of manners."

—*Washington Post Book World*

Lev Raphael offers "a delightful take on death in
academe."

—*San Francisco Chronicle*

A "witty and devastating backstage view of college life."

—*San Diego Union-Tribune*

Raphael "elegantly skewers ivory-tower pretensions,
petty politics, incompetencies and hypocrisies."

—*Booklist*

"Bright, breezy, and laugh-aloud funny."

—*Alfred Hitchcock Mystery Magazine*

Also by Lev Raphael

State University of Murder

A Nick Hoffman
Mystery

Lev Raphael

Perseverance Press / John Daniel & Company, 2019

A Perseverance Press Book
Published by John Daniel & Company
A division of Daniel & Daniel, Publishers, Inc.
Post Office Box 2790
McKinleyville, California 95519
www.danielpublishing.com/perseverance

Distributed by SCB Distributors (800) 729-6423

Book design by Eric Larson, Studio E Books, Santa Barbara, www.studio-e-books.com

Cover photo: Perboge / iStock

10 9 8 7 6 5 4 3 2 1

LIBRARY OF CONGRESS CATALOGING-IN-PUBLICATION DATA
Names: Raphael, Lev, author.
Title: State University of murder : a Nick Hoffman mystery / by Lev Raphael.
Description: McKinleyville, California : John Daniel and Company, 2019. |
    Series: Nick Hoffman mystery series
Identifiers: LCCN 2018059490 | ISBN 9781564746092 (softcover : acid-free paper)
Subjects: LCSH: Hoffman, Nick (Fictitious character)—Fiction. | College teachers—
    Fiction. | College stories. | GSAFD: Mystery fiction.
Classification: LCC PS3568.A5988 S73 2019 | DDC 813/.54—dc23
LC record available at https://lccn.loc.gov/2018059490

For the plotmeister

——— ———

My thanks to Mary Chartier, Owen Deatrick, and L.J. Dragovic, MD, for their generous help with many legal, police, and medical questions

Do not open your heart to evil. Because—if you do—evil will come…Yes, very surely evil will come… It will enter in and make a home within you, and after a while it will no longer be possible to drive it out.

—Agatha Christie, *Death on the Nile*

Part I

UNIVERSITIES HATE SCANDAL more than Dracula hated sunlight, so there were major changes at the State University of Michigan after a mass shooting that had targeted me and my partner Stefan.

Well, cosmetic changes, anyway, which were meant to *seem* major. That's how university administrators respond to a crisis that can damage their "brand" when they haven't been able to keep malfeasance from making headlines: with the appearance of action rather than the real thing. Committees are formed, mission statements are concocted, press releases are issued, and the public is promised dramatic results.

And so thanks to a crazed gunman, our university acquired what it proclaimed in a rah-rah press release was an inspiring and transformative new slogan: *People Power!*

Rumor had it on campus that despite approval by lick-spittle deans and other administrators, various faculty members had complained to our tyrannical, image-obsessed President Boris Yubero that this catchphrase, developed by a hip, expensive New York PR firm, sounded suspiciously "radical." Hadn't it been used in the Philippines or somewhere else to overthrow a government?

The slogan irked Stefan, who was an introvert and not given to complaining. He was our department's writer-in-residence, though, and words mattered to him deeply. Stefan wasn't one of those usage bullies who erupts when people split an infinitive, but he hated bureaucratic cant.

"What the hell does People Power mean on a college campus? Nobody has real power here except administrators."

"Power," I said, "and the best parking spots."

President Yubero—who claimed descent from Spanish grandees—had apparently swatted objections down in the spirit of Humpty Dumpty lecturing Alice: "It's going to mean whatever the hell I want it to mean." That attitude was typical. He was a millionaire hedge fund manager who had donated heavily to GOP campaigns locally and nationally, served as ambassador to Singapore under President George W. Bush, and had been anointed by the arrogant, secretive Board of Trustees in a closed-door session without any transparency at all. Faculty had complained that he had no connection to education whatsoever, but the board praised his "dedication to core American values." If that sounded old-fashioned, it fit a man who was a dead ringer for obese and walrus-mustached President Taft.

When Stefan and I returned from our long summer trip to Europe after the end of May's traumatic events, we also discovered that our department, which is where the shooting took place, had been rebranded by the Board of Trustees in an attempt to erase all memory of the carnage. We were no longer teaching in the Department of English, American Studies, and Rhetoric (EAR for short), but now worked in the somewhat more euphonious English and Creative Writing Department.

This name change was not discussed by anyone but the trustees, and privately. The department found out just before the beginning of the fall semester. Of course, some faculty members had objected to being "erased"—but without a union, and demoralized in general due to the rising tide of adjuncts teaching courses that used to be taught by tenure-track professors, it didn't matter.

"Everyone with tenure is a dinosaur, anyway," Stefan said.

"We're all doomed. I don't know why a sane person would start a university career now."

"Well, SUM likes having *some* of us around. We're decorative, like an organ grinder's monkey."

Stefan grinned. "Can I use that line in a story?"

"Absolutely. My lines are your lines."

Stefan and I had faced other realities after coming back. As if my colleagues and I were some unruly, possibly subversive mass of factory workers in old Soviet Russia that needed an ever-watchful commissar to guarantee our loyalty, President Yubero himself had picked our new department chair.

This was a gigantic break with precedent. The department wasn't allowed the time-honored chaos of feuding, backbiting, and vote-trading that usually went along with the lumbering search, interviewing three candidates after arguing about who would make the cut, and then final selection—which of course had to be approved by the Dean of Humanities—all that before a department chair ascended the shabby throne. Like little kids deprived of one more viewing of their favorite memorized DVD before bed, the department sulked and seethed. More than usual, that is.

You'd think that an outbreak of violence would have fostered some kind of solidarity among the survivors, most of whom avoided each other for numerous reasons, but it only made people feel more embittered, more besieged. And of course the ravenous new hires just wanted to forge ahead, stomping anything in their path like Godzilla in Tokyo.

Yubero's choice for our department chair was audacious, probably directed by that same PR firm, and it was also humiliating. He picked a celebrity who outshone even the Harvard, Yale, and Stanford Ph.D.s we had managed to entice to SUM. The new chair was a telegenic French academic who was a third cousin of the French president.

Napoléon Padovani had the kind of lean, six-foot-two frame photographers loved to drape barefoot across antique sofas even when the accompanying article was meant to be serious. He was so handsome and so well known as a bon vivant that he'd been profiled in magazines ranging from *The Atlantic* to *GQ, Vanity Fair, Men's Health,* and *People*—which meant that we knew far too much about him already.

We knew that he published not just in his native French but also in German, Swedish, Polish—and even Albanian. There were interview clips of him on YouTube speaking fluently in all those languages, an improbable and intimidating assortment even for a European.

"Why would anyone learn Albanian?" I asked Stefan, but neither of us had an answer.

We knew about Napoléon's morning kale-protein shakes, his exercise regimen (and personal trainer, who he had actually brought over from France), his divorce from a Danish supermodel and affairs with an array of French actresses, his ridiculous abs, even the hair products he used on his improbably thick and lustrous black curls. We knew he wore Charvet ties, Ferragamo shoes, and Lanvin suits. We'd seen numerous photo spreads of his "modest" family château in the Dordogne.

Hateful at a distance, he was despicable in person in the eyes of our ragtag, querulous department, which was so historically derided on campus as a nest of misfits that the recent shooting hadn't generated much sympathy for us from other departments. That's how bitter, divided, and ugly a place the State University of Michigan was. In department meetings, Padovani was so proper, so precise, and so amiable, faculty bristled at his manner. No matter how you dressed or comported yourself, he was so effortlessly, impeccably regal that he made my peers feel as if they'd showed up unwashed and wearing yoga pants, a torn tank top, and flip-flops.

Like many upper-crust Frenchmen, Padovani had weaponized his sense of style. He was like an elegant version of a skunk—that overpowering charm could be felt for miles.

"Do call me Napoléon," he confided with a glowing smile

to all of us at one time or another, "when you feel you can." It was bizarre and a little alarming—what else *would* we call him? Excellency? Your Magnitude?

But Stefan and I found ourselves actually admiring him at first. After reading him in the original French, Stefan said Padovani's work on Anthony Trollope's heterosexual panic was "fun."

"You know," he cracked, "French literary criticism, the best kind, it reads like science fiction."

"Well, I'm just happy Napoléon is a Trollope fan." Those big fat novels were my comfort reads.

On top of that, I had briefly chatted twice in Swedish with Padovani. Because of my deep interest in mysteries and thrillers, I'd been studying Swedish in an attempt to read Swedish crime writers like Henning Mankell, Stieg Larsson, and Camilla Läckberg in their original language. It was going very slowly, but I loved even the sound of Swedish, and Padovani hadn't come off as condescending.

This was not something to share with my colleagues because I would have become the target of envy and scorn, accused of sucking up or worse: being a quisling. Universities are obscenely hierarchical, and within departments there's always a kind of smoldering anarchy just barely held at bay. With the right conditions, even the most docile group of professors could easily devolve into the schoolkids from *Lord of the Flies*. That's why op/ed pieces by right-wingers about professors trying to indoctrinate their students are so laughable—most academics are too obsessed with their petty privileges and perceived insults to even care what their students think.

Given that I didn't loathe the new chair whose office was down the hall from mine, I had just been nodding and saying a soft "Wow!" when people fulminated to me about Padovani's excesses and violations of sacred practice. I never offered up any teeth-grinding examples of my own mistreatment, since I didn't have any. Besides, most of my colleagues were so used to lecturing their students that they were quite happy to rant at anyone in eyeshot, with minimal encouragement.

But even if we had been allowed to choose the department chair of our dreams, nothing could have made up for the biggest shock of all. Because of the attack on our "home," beautiful and historic nineteenth-century sandstone Parker Hall, SUM's administrators decided to move the department lock, stock, and egos to another building: Shattenkirk Hall. New name, new location. There was a certain psychological sense to this decision, and at least we hadn't been moved to an underground bunker. I wasn't thrilled about giving up my spacious, high-ceilinged office with its beautiful, almost pastoral view, but I also knew that every time I walked into Parker Hall it would likely trigger memories of having been trapped and attacked there by a psychotic gunman, so I was very open to relocation.

Not so the rest of the department, which reacted as if they were the Cherokee Nation forced by Andrew Jackson to set out on the Trail of Tears and suffer disease, starvation, and death—though they were merely exchanging offices with the Physics Department just a five-minute walk away. Admittedly, the new base of operations was something of an eyesore: three small, grim, squat floors of white tile and streaky white linoleum, very institutional, cold, and clinical. It had been the gift of some alumnus who won the Nobel Prize, and the Board of Trustees had okayed the plans way back when, even though it was wildly out of synch with the rest of the university's much warmer, more traditional styles of architecture. It looked more like the headquarters of a pharmaceutical company than anything remotely connected to higher education: everything was blisteringly white inside—but it was our new home, like it or not. I had a big enough office for myself and an adjoining one just as big for my assistant because I administered a program for visiting authors, thanks to a large bequest from a former student of mine.

The first-floor classrooms were bleaker than anything else on campus and the offices in the small building, which was all ours now, were generally smaller than our old ones. On each floor they formed a square around the elevator bank, with windowless conference rooms, storage rooms, and a combination mail room/lounge. The ring hallways were narrow, barely wide enough for two people to walk side by side and it all felt claustrophobic the more time we spent there. The ceilings were low, the windows were small, and the lights were too bright. Some professors joked that it was really a gigantic laboratory experiment and we were the rats.

It was as if we were being punished for having been attacked.

Of course it was worse for the adjuncts who were relegated to dank, airless basement offices that stank of cockroach spray. And that probably gave many of the tenured faculty some passing relief: at least somebody else was worse off than they were.

Despite my office having a large window with a view of mature maple trees outside, I disliked my new situation for the way it left me vulnerable. Both my office and my assistant's office were within sight of the twin elevators on the second floor, and I always felt exposed to the students and faculty getting on or off. I could have closed my door, but that would have made the office feel even more suffocating—despite my having had the walls painted a cheerful apricot, bought wooden blinds, laid down a bright orange-and-black kilim rug, and hung new prints from a Matisse exhibition I'd seen in London. It was the best I could do to make the office seem less sterile and forbidding.

But given my new accessibility, I shouldn't have been surprised when Viktor Dahlberg burst into my office from my assistant Celine's office and yelled, "I hate that fucking prick!"

That was the beginning of two weeks of chaos and death.

I wasn't sure, but I guessed he meant our esteemed chair. I leapt up from behind my desk to close the door behind him, even though my assistant was in the copy room at the moment. Viktor Dahlberg thudded into one of the captain's chairs in front of my desk, breathing heavily as if he had actually been in some kind of altercation. But his deep blue suit and matching tie looked unruffled and I didn't see any marks on his long narrow face or elegantly manicured hands. His thick, prematurely gray hair was smoothly slicked back as always, which made his square jaw and cleft chin even more pronounced. Viktor had the air of a James Bond villain: elegant, brooding, and imperious.

A full professor who taught screenwriting and other film-related courses, Dahlberg was someone I'd never gotten to know because the film faculty in the department didn't mix with the creative writing faculty or anyone else for that matter. Possibly they resented their own small department having been shut down years ago and then having been forced to amalgamate with those of us in English. Their screenwriting classes were now part of the Creative Writing major, but that was a tenuous connection.

Cost-saving was the official reason for the amalgamation, though at SUM, the axe usually fell on a department or program because of a private vendetta—despite official explanations. Some of the film people carried themselves like aristocrats in a country that had abolished titles: sneering but wounded. Dahlberg wasn't like that, though. Tall, slim, around forty-five, with eerily light blue eyes, he was one of the quieter members of the program and was vaguely friendly in a "How are your classes this semester?" sort of way. Settling into the Mirra chair I'd bought for myself because SUM-issued chairs were so uncomfortable, I felt like a therapist when I prompted him with "Tell me what's going on."

"Napoléon is taking away my summer program, the one I created five years ago!"

Based in the old university town of Lund in southern Sweden, Viktor's program was very popular with students partly for the location, but mostly because students loved Dahlberg's enthusiasm and concern for their work. They also loved that his family came from that part of Sweden, too—it made the experience more authentic. Even though Swedes were among the best speakers of English in Europe, I understood that Viktor's command of Swedish and his ancestral ties combined to steamroll any obstacle that ever came up there, bureaucratic or otherwise.

Viktor had foresight. He had wisely designed it from the beginning as a four-week program, which was two weeks shorter than most of the other summer programs based in Europe and thus more affordable. The traditional six-week programs taught by two professors were on their way out because of shrinking enrollment, despite efforts by desperate, incompetent department chairs to keep them alive.

"But why? Why would Napoléon take your program away?" I asked.

In a soft but resonant tenor voice that you'd expect to hear on stage, Viktor explained. "He says we need new blood. After only five years?" Viktor clenched his fists so tightly, he looked like a drunk about to get into a bar fight. "He says other faculty need the chance to teach it. And he had the nerve to tell me this in Swedish! *Jävla hundjävel!*"

This was a Swedish curse I'd never encountered before, but whatever it meant didn't matter. Viktor's venom gave it the power of a knife to the gut.

I asked, "Who else would want to teach it?" Summer programs were a lot of work and if you took family or even a spouse with you, the pay didn't add up to much. The flip side was being in Europe and having weekends for cheap flights anywhere on the continent. Or quick train rides, for that matter.

"*He* does, of course. He wants it." And now Viktor slumped heavily in the chair as if he'd been tricked by some inquisitor into revealing a fellow rebel's name. "Napoléon speaks fluent Swedish, you know that. And he demanded that I give him all my contact information at the University of Lund and everything else I've put together: itineraries, tour guides, the works. *Everything* from the last five years."

"Can he do that?"

Viktor nodded. "Our emails belong to the university. Even if I deleted everything, someone in IT could probably find what I trashed."

Until Dahlberg had joined the department over a decade ago,

our students had typically chosen programs in London, Dublin, or Paris. But the rise of terrorist attacks in Europe had made Sweden increasingly attractive because it seemed safer, and students who didn't want to be plunged into a large foreign city gravitated to the Lund program. It was exotic but not stressful.

"Has Napoléon taught screenwriting?" I asked. "Does he know Swedish film the way you do?" Dahlberg offered a film survey course there as well as screenwriting, and brought in Swedish experts as guest lecturers. He also took students to the studio where the Wallander mystery series was filmed and toured Ystad, the center of action in the series. Students loved going behind the scenes.

"Nick, does it matter? *För i helvete*, for fuck's sake, he can change the focus any way he wants to." Dahlberg's face crumpled and I thought he was about to cry. Then he breathed in deeply and said, "I've given my life to that program—I love that course—I love Sweden—I'm not letting him take it away from me."

I didn't know if it was true, but I'd heard that Viktor had created the program after his wife died and was in effect married to the program now—it gave him more satisfaction than anything else he taught. But I doubted there was anything Viktor could do to hold on to the summer program he had been so nurtured by for the past five years. I doubted that anyone in the administration could overrule a chair about something like this, and the Study Abroad Office wouldn't get drawn into what on the surface looked like a staffing issue. They just cared about enrollments.

"Han är en jävla idiot," Viktor growled.

I knew that one just fine: He's a fucking idiot. And the way Viktor said it and the look on his face made me back my chair up just a little, though he didn't seem to notice. I didn't know if he was about to totally lose his temper, but I felt that he could, easily.

"You know what's worse, Nick? He's also sadistic. Napoléon knew it would hurt me. When I didn't know how to respond, I could see he was *delighted*."

I wanted to say that I was sorry, but that would have been

totally inadequate to the moment, yet what else was there to say? Administrators give and administrators take away. Twenty-five percent of SUM's budget went to administration—and to student amenities like up-to-date workout centers in every dorm and beautiful, well-stocked coffee bars in every branch of the campus library.

"He's a devil," Viktor spat.

Getting up to leave, he paused and narrowed his eyes as if trying to make out a road sign just a bit too far away. "That asshole deserves to die," he said, and with eyes fixed and back straight, he didn't look at all like a college professor, he looked like a hitman.

2

STEFAN AND I HAD sold our house and moved because it had been invaded last spring by a SWAT team that brutalized both of us and arrested Stefan under false charges. They'd been sent there by a stalker, who had also broken in a couple of days later while we were away. Despite having dealt with murder and chaos before at the university, all of this had hit me much harder. It devastated both of us.

Hemingway wrote in *A Farewell to Arms* that the "world breaks every one and afterward many are strong at the broken places." It was too soon to tell if we would become strong—it still is—but we were definitely broken. So I went out and bought a gun. I picked a 9mm Ruger American Pistol because of its low recoil, safety features, the three-dot sights, and how it felt in my hand—smooth, natural—and the way it made me feel: *strong*. I took more lessons at our local firing range to get truly comfortable with it, but doubted that was enough. So what was the answer?

Even though we both had good salaries and Stefan had published a real money-making book after years of trying, looking for jobs at another university was too overwhelming a prospect. We were not a university power couple. He was the star and bringing someone new like that into a department could cause friction and even flames. And if he did get an offer from another university, I would likely just be a "spousal hire," part of the package and therefore resented by other faculty, but at a lower level of animosity than I was resented at SUM. After all, my main achievement was publishing a secondary bibliography of Edith Wharton, a book listing and describing everything that she had written and that had been written about her, in whatever languages. A useful book for researchers, but not the academic version of clickbait. Since then, I'd only co-authored books with other Wharton scholars, and hadn't really had the most brilliant career even though Whartonites emailed me all the time to praise my bibliography—and ask for my help. I've devoted more time to teaching than adding books to my online department profile.

Then there was the complication of the Nick Hoffman Fellowship I directed, which was designed to bring a well-known author to campus each year for a month to do a reading, give a lecture, and teach some workshops. A former student who had made it big in a dot.com apparently enjoyed my classes so much that he left two million dollars to the university in his will with several restrictions: the fellowship would be named after me, not him, and I would be the director, not anyone else in the department or university. Former administrators had tried to control it by talking to me about my being on a committee, but I'd squashed that idea. The other significant stipulation in my student's will was this: If I left the university for whatever reason, the money wouldn't go with me to a new university but would be redirected to a leukemia charity. I was sure that SUM's phalanx of lawyers would contest that provision of the will with endless litigation in a modern day version of *Bleak House*. I didn't want to see that—it would have made ugly headlines and tarnished the memory of my student.

I'm not ashamed to say that I enjoyed how the bequest had improved my status at SUM, even though it made other faculty members jealous, since there weren't any endowed chairs in our department or even any "named" professorships. I relished the little bit of status and power it afforded me: even best-selling authors had been contacting me and applying for the fellowship, which was very generous at $25,000 for a month's work.

And even if that hadn't been a factor, Stefan and I didn't have enough saved to retire early and relocate to our vacation condo on Lake Michigan—or leave the state altogether and go back to New York City where both of us had been born and raised. In the end, moving somewhere else in town was easier, inevitable, and urgent.

Our previous home was a house we'd lavished a lot of time and money on, but it was unlivable now, forever stained and degraded, as if black mold had spread inside each and every wall. The sale had been easy enough and we'd found a very different sort of house just a mile away in the same neighborhood. This one was on a hushed cul-de-sac and surrounded by enormous weeping willows that seemed to both grace and protect it. It was in the Art Moderne style: two smooth stucco cream-colored stories with an asymmetrical façade, flat roof, and porthole front door flanked by large panels of glass brick. The rounded lines were meant to evoke the luxurious sleek ocean liners of the 1930s like the *Normandie* and the *Queen Mary*. That's what the real estate agent had said, anyway. She didn't laugh when I asked if it came with life preservers, maybe because she knew our stories as well as everyone else in town did.

The new house had standard features of the style: a curved living room wall of glass brick, a cast-concrete fireplace mantel, and a cantilevered balcony along the front of the house with a railing made of steel. The whole house gave you a feeling of solidity which I found comforting, but it also felt somewhat of a disguise. This wasn't a house I would ever have imagined living in, but the timing was right, ditto the price. We'd bought the house from owners who decided to retire to Palm Beach and the sale included a houseful of pristine or restored original Art Moderne furniture that was more decorative than comfortable. We sold most of the furniture we'd amassed over the years and put the rest in storage.

Our new house was decorated in bold reds and oranges inside except for the black and white leather furniture in the living room, and the black slate floor in the dining room, which had two window walls. Nobody but the deer could spy on us back there when we had dinner because a protected wetlands area lay right behind the house, beyond the small fenced backyard, lined with flourishing low-maintenance hemlocks and holly. I was actually relieved to give up serious gardening. This was now our hideout, our redoubt. I felt safer inside. Mostly.

Having a gun helped.

There was a lot to like about the house. The remodeled kitchen with its rose quartz counter tops, deep red Viking appliances, and sleek white Italian cabinets was filled with light. The master bath had been updated with a giant soaking tub, and a rainforest shower that was smarter than my smart phone, and the walls were tiled with tiny squares of Italian rose marble. Marco, our Westie puppy, loved the move, excitedly tracking what I supposed were scents of previous cats or dogs who had lived there before us, snuffling along the white oak floors and updated rugs as if chasing ghosts. The noise was welcome and comforting.

We needed distraction because a move anywhere couldn't change the fact that Stefan and I were both still traumatized by having had that SWAT team storm through our old house, even though they hadn't done serious damage to it, the way you read about in the news. Thousands of these raids happen every year, primarily targeting minorities, but nobody was safe, not even two Midwestern college professors like us. Especially not two gay men living together, even married. Since the raid, Stefan had developed early morning migraines. He'd consulted a local specialist and had become reliant on Imitrex injections to stop the attacks and Xanax to get back to sleep after frequent nightmares in which he was being chased and tortured.

I'd never had trouble falling asleep or staying asleep in my life, but now I had what was called "maintenance insomnia": I'd wake up after sometimes as little as an hour and have trouble falling back asleep. I'd tried sleep therapy for the problem and followed "sleep hygiene" religiously: regular bedtime, no PC or tablet for an hour before bed because of the bright light from the screens, just calming music and meditation, and I would read an actual book for only half an hour in bed. Then the lights always went out at the same time. It was a structure that was supposed to work—but maybe for people who hadn't been victimized and weren't dealing with PTSD.

On those tough nights, I had taken to padding down to my study to read so I wouldn't disturb Stefan, and Marco followed me, grumbling a bit, but he curled up in my lap or on the floor near me and quickly went back to sleep. I'd never enjoyed historical fiction very much, but was finding solace in Bernard Cornwell's novels set in Anglo-Saxon England. They charted fascinating conflicts between the Vikings and the English when England was still a handful of mini-states like Northumbria and Wessex. The gory battle scenes didn't faze me as they might have before last May's troubles.

But lack of sleep at night meant mid-day naps were essential for me, and both Stefan and I felt years older when we compared morning notes about how poorly I'd slept and how much pain he was in from his migraines. And anxiety about future migraines, too. He didn't even find going to Mass or talking to his spiritual director helpful. One small mercy: He wasn't one of those people who asked, "Why is God doing this to me?" since he didn't envision a heavenly bureaucrat bent on torment and confusion below. His conversion from Judaism to Catholicism had given him ballast, but not going to church, Stefan was somewhat adrift now, and he'd also stopped writing. I didn't probe him about any of this. He was usually so introverted that direct questions could make him angry, and circuitous ones with an agenda angrier still.

We'd both been knocked off center, but we still loved teaching and mentoring. That hadn't been stolen from either one of us. Stefan worked closely with creative writing students who were doing a senior thesis, and I taught independent study courses with students on authors not covered in other classes, like Sinclair Lewis. A favorite author of mine, he was the first American author to win a Nobel Prize, but grossly neglected in academia despite brilliant satires of American small town life and bourgeois complacency like *Main Street* and *Babbitt*. And of course I was always happy when a student caught the Edith Wharton bug and thought of devoting a semester of independent study to something like her later novels that were so much less known than *The House of Mirth* or *The Age of Innocence*.

We still found solace, as we always had, in food and wine. Stefan was the better cook and that didn't just give him pleasure, it was profoundly therapeutic. And so when I arrived home after my visit from Viktor Dahlberg, I wasn't surprised to find Stefan in the kitchen, caramelizing sliced onions and simmering Cremini mushrooms in sherry.

"Beef Stroganoff?" I asked, reaching down to scratch Marco's neck. Happily recognized, he went back across the kitchen to loiter near Stefan, hoping some scrap would come his way. His black nose twitched.

"Da, tovarich." His Russian accent was like something from a cartoon, but he wasn't smiling as he carefully floured beef chunks to brown in a Le Creuset pot that was one of the first kitchen items we'd ever bought. The aroma was wonderful.

In recent months, Stefan had changed his workouts at our health club because of having been victimized. He had a young, passionate trainer now who he worked with five times a week, and had taken on the bulk and heft of a wrestler, which made his always-refined movements in the kitchen intriguing to watch. Picture a shorter, beefier version of Harrison Ford at the end of the Indiana Jones series. Stefan had "craggy and commanding" not just written across his face, he radiated it in a way that some people might have found intimidating. He was barefoot now, wearing black-and-white checked Nordstrom lounge pants and a black University of Dresden T-shirt taut against his chest and biceps. He had taught there one semester and still talked about spending more time in what used to be East Germany. Someday.

"I opened that Australian Shiraz for dinner," he said, "and there's some Karlsson's Gold in the freezer."

I took out the rounded bottle of earthy-tasting potato vodka, poured myself a shot, topped it with a pinch of salt and some cracked pepper, and knocked it back.

"You might need another," he said. "The department's about to implode."

"What now?"

"Check your email."

I went to the kitchen island where we kept an iPad, quickly logged on to my university account, and found a new email from our new illustrious chair:

Friends!

From next semester forward, the adjuncts among us will be welcome at all faculty meetings and will be invited to vote on any and all issues if they so choose. The current divisions between tenured and non-tenured faculty are antiquated, frivolous, small-minded, and claustrophobic. It's time to do more than say that we value the contributions of our adjuncts, it's time to prove it. I understand that previous department heads have prevented adjuncts from teaching certain upper-level undergraduate courses, but they will now be allowed to teach any courses that tenured professors teach, if qualified and interested.

It will be my pleasure to supervise this transition.

Please remember, my office is always open to you.

> *With every best wish,*
> *Napoléon Padovani*

"Holy shit," I muttered, and poured another shot of vodka.

Stefan turned from the stove and leaned back against a nearby counter, beefy arms crossed, an unexpectedly dreamy grin on his face. "That's right. He's making everyone in the department supposedly equal, to the extent he can."

Adjuncts were grossly underpaid for doing the same work that tenured faculty did. But this move of Napoléon's would at least recognize their talent and experience, while it was going to infuriate those tenured faculty members who enjoyed having second-class citizens in their midst to look down upon. Stefan and I had talked about this inequality for years, but hadn't been able to do anything to change it. Ancient Rome would have collapsed without its millions of slaves; SUM would likewise founder without a steady supply of desperate, cheap labor.

Stefan turned back to the stove and said over his shoulder: "There's going to be trouble."

Just on the surface, I knew that other professors disliked the new chair's salutation of "Friends!" It struck them the way grammar bullies got agitated by the use of "nauseous" for "nauseated." Me, I thought it was meant a bit derisively, and didn't mind that. Despite the sudden turnover in faculty through early retirements and people finding jobs elsewhere, the new crop of professors was just as status-crazy as their predecessors and just as quick to take offense. I guess in a climate where higher education was routinely attacked in the press for being elitist and out-of-touch, it was easy to become defensive and stay that way.

"There already *is* trouble, but not about this bombshell." I sat at the island on the red leather stool, beginning to feel the vodka, and started to tell him about the encounter with Dahlberg in my office.

"Wait." The beef was all browned, the mushrooms ready. Stefan turned the burner higher under the pasta pot and opened the bag of extra-wide egg noodles, added some salt to the already-simmering pot and a bit of olive oil to keep it from boiling over, and slowly poured in the noodles. Marco grumbled. Any kind of package we opened in the house might have a toy in it for him. Given how devoted we were, you could say that he was spoiled, though I prefer thinking of him as "celebrated." After all, he was a rescue dog, had been abused, and so he deserved extra love.

"Wait," Stefan repeated, after he let me recount everything that Viktor had shared with me. "Viktor said all that to you? Why you? He never talks to you."

"I know, I was just as surprised as you are."

Stefan and I didn't socialize with anyone in the department: if we had people over for dinner or brunch, it was couples we knew from our health club, local journalists or authors, and a few neighbors. I had sometimes thought about inviting Viktor out for coffee to chat about Sweden and try some of my Swedish out on him, but had never actually done it. It had even crossed my mind that if we were to become friends, I could join him in his Lund summer program some year, which I thought could be reconfigured to include a literature component. That seemed unlikely, though. Viktor knew about my fondness for Swedish crime novels since I'd taught a course devoted to the subject, and he hadn't reached out, either—it was as if we were members of feuding clans and a meeting would have broken a taboo. Yet today he did reach out. And made me feel very uneasy, too.

"I don't know," I went on. "Maybe Viktor just needed to vent, and I was available. But there was an edge to what he told me."

The meat had finished browning and was "resting" in a glass bowl. Now Stefan added beef broth and Worcestershire sauce to the pan, scraped the bottom with a wooden spoon, and turned up the heat. Then he set the table carefully with large, wide flower-patterned Williams-Sonoma pasta bowls—the set was a housewarming gift from my cousin Sharon—and poured us each a glass of wine at our seats. Marco followed every step of his, almost tripping Stefan at one point, then wagging his tail and prancing around as if it had been some kind of game. Stefan pulled up iTunes and started a CD of beautiful cello and piano sonatas by Beethoven. It was a sentimental favorite because we'd heard it first on a flight from Brussels, where my parents had been born.

"An edge?"

"I never pictured him as someone capable of violence before, but now, well…"

The beef went back in the pot along with the mushrooms. Stefan brought a small bowl of sour cream to the table. As soon as it was hot enough, he drained the noodles and served each of us a healthy portion of Stroganoff over them. After I'd stirred in a spoonful of sour cream, tasted, and complimented him, I ate for a while in silent appreciation. Marco never got table scraps but was perpetually hopeful anyway and sat between us, watchful but not annoying. I marveled at how adaptable he was.

I felt that despite years-old comfort of being with Stefan— who was now my partner in marriage thanks to the Supreme Court—and eating a delicious meal together, I wasn't really myself. This was partly because the house on some days felt like a stage set. A cutting line about a horrible woman in *The House of Mirth* came to mind just then: at dinner one night in Monte Carlo she was "engrossed in establishing her relation with an intensely new gown." That was us—or me, anyway. I didn't feel that I had established a relation to our new house, and it was truly disorienting. For all that I loved travel abroad, being home and being rooted had always been one of my joys. My cousin Sharon said it was because I was a Taurus, like her. Yet in spite of its obvious charm and all the renovations, this new house felt weirdly makeshift. I still felt like a guest in my own home and sometimes even like an intruder, one of those hapless figures who's unknowingly entered a haunted house.

Of course *I* was the one who was haunted.

"This is delicious," I said, trying to push the image of Viktor's clenched fists from my mind.

Stefan set down his knife and fork. "I'm really glad it's so good." He gestured at our meal, and then as if thinking aloud, and bringing his half-full wineglass to his chest like you'd hold a warm drink in the winter, "If someone like Viktor who's usually so calm is that angry, then he's not the only one."

"Well, nobody else has a summer program being taken away from them—that we know of."

Stefan took a long drink and refilled his glass. "It's a really cruel thing to do."

"Agreed." But it was Napoléon's email that suddenly loomed over us.

"Napoléon's taking over course assignments," I said. "Isn't he? Isn't that what this email really implies?" Matching faculty to classes—balancing what the department needed with what people wanted to teach each semester—had traditionally been the responsibility of the department's associate chair for undergraduate studies. In one email, Napoléon hadn't just undermined the rigid hierarchy in the department, he'd also made a major power grab. Was the talk about giving adjuncts more access to courses merely a cover?

"For sure," Stefan said, turning his focus back to the steaming, savory beef and looking down into the bowl as if he were a fortune teller reading tea leaves or a crystal ball. "And that means he's going to make lots of enemies...."

3

MARCO WAS SNORING gently in his dog bed as we cleaned up, ground Jacobs Krönung beans for coffee, and set out some pistachio French-style macarons from Whole Foods for dessert. I envied Marco's ability to fall asleep in seconds, though I often wondered now about the dreams which made his legs twitch and produced low growls or even low-key *woof-woof* sounds. Were they ever bad dreams? I know mine were, far too often.

Over coffee, Stefan mused, "I think we're safe."

I nodded because I understood what he meant: that despite Napoléon creating intense animosity so soon after taking charge of the department, and despite what felt like an authoritarian manner, we ourselves were likely to remain untouched. But just thinking this way made me feel like we were minor nobles in some medieval kingdom pondering the fate of our peers under a new, unpredictable liege lord, fearful that we just might be punished for some as yet unknowable, imagined crime.

And that word "safe" was a chimera, wasn't it? The newspapers and talk shows made that pretty clear every time someone was shot or beaten by the police because of excessive use of force, and no one ended up being sentenced to prison for the violence. I knew this viscerally. Two white, privileged professionals like us had learned we were just as vulnerable as some black kid walking down the wrong street at the wrong time. SWAT team raids were occurring at the daily rate of one hundred, and only a fraction of them were for situations that involved active shooters or hostage situations. Most of them were for drug raids, and the SWAT teams often failed to find drugs. Our cities were becoming war zones and horror stories were common: just recently in Georgia, police had used a flash-bang grenade in a raid and severely injured a one-year-old in his crib. There was nothing surprising about this story, and not enough public outrage.

Nobody was truly safe, anywhere, ever—and nothing could protect you from that knowledge once you took it in, or it forced its way into your consciousness. There was a line in Joan Didion's novel *Play It as It Lays* which summed up our new reality: "In the whole world there was not as much sedation as there was instantaneous peril." I had grown up in New York, as Stefan had, and neither of us had ever been mugged or personally dealt with any sort of crime until we came to this bucolic Midwestern campus.

So how could we predict what Napoléon might do if he took a sudden dislike to Stefan or to me, or dreamed up some new organizational scheme for the department that disadvantaged us? After all, it was common practice at SUM for new deans, provosts, and presidents to initiate some kind of change just for the sake of change, even if that meant repeating the mistakes of a distant predecessor. Nothing could stop them from ruthless and sometimes senseless "initiatives." SUM's faculty was not unionized and administrators at all levels looked at us *de haut en bas*, from a great height, seeing all of us as vastly inferior and annoying—unless we brought in grant money, that is. The sooner we were all gone and the place run by cheap labor, the better.

I'd heard the rumor that one department chair had even raised the possibility of farming out all of his department's online classes to teachers in India who'd be happy to earn just one thousand dollars per course, far less than even our adjuncts made. The idea had been quashed—for now. But like many universities, SUM was now being increasingly run as a business or corporation, not as an institution of higher education. That kind of thinking was actually first valorized back in 1888, when Princeton's then-incoming president had announced: "College administration is a business in which trustees are partners; professors the salesmen; and students the customers."

Stefan had been patiently waiting for a response while I was lost in my musings.

"I hope so, Stefan. I hope we're safe. At least Napoléon can't mess with the Nick Hoffman Fellowship, given all the iron-clad stipulations, and—"

"—do you know who you'll be bringing in this year?"

I didn't. There were many dozens of applications. I needed a visiting writer who wouldn't be self-important and dour. That's where my administrative assistant, Celine Robichaux, was invaluable: she scoured the Internet for people's video interviews, studied their Twitter feeds and Facebook pages to make sure we weren't bringing in a dud. She wanted to see them where they revealed themselves the most, no matter how fine their books were.

"Somebody funny, I hope." That seemed crucial.

Life under President Obama had been made much easier for us since our Canadian marriage was now recognized and legal and we could file joint federal and Michigan tax returns, but those new freedoms and benefits existed in a parallel universe to the one in which the country had become militarized down to every local police force longing for military-style weapons and armored vehicles that could withstand land mines. We'd been liberated in one world while being victimized in another. No wonder I found myself drawn to those Bernard Cornwell novels. Their protagonist was a man caught between the Christian and pagan worlds, hungry to reclaim his inheritance, and aware that Fate ruled everything. The books were beautifully written and perfect escape reading for me because the hero always rose from defeat.

Stefan was about to say something when the doorbell rang and I almost spilled my coffee. I was easily spooked now by unexpected noises, from car horns down to email notifications on my tablet or phone—and sometimes I even yelped out loud, which embarrassed me. After all, I'd grown up in New York but the things I'd feared most were doing badly in school and disappointing my parents. Now, I lived with real fear, fear that was way too easily triggered.

The doorbell rang again, insistently, and we exchanged a sour look. Despite a large NO SOLICITING sign near the front door, there were enough people selling services or salvation who still ignored it. Marco was surprisingly fond of company for a rescue dog and didn't bark at strangers, so he wagged his tail as he softly padded after me to the front door. That, at least, was a sound I loved.

I was wrong about who was there. Through the porthole window I could see one of our colleagues, Ciska Balanchine, the newish associate chair who also taught in the Women's Studies Department. We had not yet gotten to know her even though she lived two streets over, in a small mock-Tudor house.

I scooped Marco up and let her in.

She was generally muted and serene, almost as if she had just been given two hours of massage therapy (or was on anti-depressants), but tonight she was frowning and squinty-eyed. "I need to talk," she said as I closed the door behind her. Her low voice had an edge of something sinister to it.

Stefan had already left the kitchen and he met us in the living room. Marco raced ahead and planted himself on one of the boxy black leather chairs with chrome arms grouped by the fireplace. Stefan took the other one, which left the matching big white leather couch for me and Ciska. She was in her typical uniform of black slacks, collarless blouse, flats, and black-and-white Chanel scarf. She looked more at home in that streamlined room than either one of us did.

Somewhere in her thirties, Ciska was as tall, pale, and remote-looking as a high-fashion model, with the poise and posture to match. She had curly black hair and large, dark, inexpressive almond-shaped eyes. Her last name was Russian, but I think she was ethnically part Dutch, and with her very long neck and exotic oval face, she could easily have been a model for Modigliani. I had looked up her first name once because it was so unusual, and discovered it was a derivative of Franciscus and supposedly connected to the kind of axe the medieval Franks used. A violent name for such an aloof and low-key woman.

"I've always wondered what this house looked like inside," she said, tenting her hands at her chest and locking her French-manicured fingers together. I watched her take in the white oak flooring, the rug with oversized red and orange roses, and the framed Matisse poster of an odalisque over the mantel. Then she grinned crookedly. "That's a rum thing to say, sorry." Ciska had lived in England for many years and it popped up now and then in her diction, and seemed to inflect her perfect posture and general hauteur, too. She crossed her legs, uncrossed them, then crossed them again. Marco was watching her with his ears up and must have been picking up on her anxiety.

I assured her that we had wondered, too, and she gave me a weak smile. There were only a few Art Moderne houses in Michiganapolis—perhaps because flat roofs aren't a great idea in a climate with snowy winters—so that made each one noteworthy.

Stefan asked her if she wanted fresh coffee or a drink but she shook her head, then said, "Actually, yes, please. Something strong." Stefan went over to the chrome-and-glass bar cart and poured her some Oban.

"Cheers." She took it from him with a smiling return to her usual untroubled grace. I suddenly felt that there was some faint undercurrent between the two of them apart from whatever had brought her to our house on this particular evening. Unless I was just hopelessly misreading someone I didn't really know… but Stefan looked more comfortable with her than I was, which was odd. Almost as if they were continuing a conversation that had been interrupted.

"You've seen Napoléon's latest email," she said, with a twist on the last word that made it sound like something toxic.

We nodded.

"I am the associate chair for undergraduate studies, but he didn't consult me at all about how we would be handling course assignments, didn't give me a heads-up. He doesn't give a toss about my opinion." She knocked back her scotch and held out her glass for a refill. Stefan complied, and she went on: "I feel undermined and disrespected."

Stefan murmured something consoling that I didn't quite catch. I hadn't thought of how Napoléon's email would affect Ciska, given that anyone in her position was traditionally in charge of assigning courses. I'd found her fair and reasonable so far, unlike some previous associate chairs.

"And this business of addressing us as *friends*? It's so unctuous! I'm not his friend, I don't want anything to do with him." She shuddered, almost spilling her scotch.

"It *is* creepy," I said. And then a line from *Hamlet* popped into my head: "One may smile, and smile, and be a villain." I blurted out, "Has he threatened you—?"

Chin up, she said, "Not really, but we had an…interaction, you might say. He invited me to dinner when he first arrived, back in the summer. He said he admired my latest book—he read it in French, of course."

Stefan and I had tried reading Ciska's *Relativizing Fraud*, which used impenetrable post-Structuralist jargon to write about famous contemporary literary scandals like James Frey's fake memoir *A Million Little Pieces* and David Leavitt's plagiarism of the venerable British author Stephen Spender.

"That's great," I said. "His opinion of your book, I mean." I wondered if it made more sense in French translation than in English, but kept the thought to myself. The whole field of academic publishing was filled with arcane studies whose audience was mostly other authors of arcane studies.

Ciska scowled and ran her fingers through her hair, fluffing up the curls, and it felt as if she had thoughts she wished she could dispel. She set her finished drink down on the chrome-based black glass coffee table, and was struggling to bring out the words: "The wanker made a pass at me, and when I said I was in no way interested? He told me that I would have a much brighter future at SUM if I—"

"—succumbed?" I said.

"Nothing quite as euphonious as that." She grimaced and reached for her empty drink, put the glass back down and waved off Stefan when he made to refill it. Face flushed, she shook her head, eyes blazing. "And he was quite explicit."

"But that's sexual harassment, isn't it?" I felt queasy. And I also found myself wondering if the rumors that she was a lesbian were true—not that it was any of my business. She had supposedly pushed the department very hard to hire Jasmine Alinejad, a colleague from Ohio State where they both had been teaching before SUM.

Alinejad was a mediocre half-Iranian memoirist who had published *Lena Dunham Should Wear a Chador* with an obscure press. The title was meant to be provocative, I guess. Or funny? She was short, prickly, given to beaded macramé shawls over shapeless black dresses befitting ancient Italian widows in a movie about The Old Country. The outfits contrasted oddly with her heart-shaped, girlish face—and perhaps that was intentional.

Nobody knew why Ciska wanted her at SUM, where she was teaching creative nonfiction and Shakespeare, but there was the obvious speculation. I'd seen them together in our small coffee lounge and hadn't picked up any vibes—in fact, they seemed pretty cold toward each other. That could have been a cover, though why would they have to hide their sexual identity in 2015 when even SUM had openly Trans and gender-queer faculty and staff? The university might not be especially welcoming to the LGBTQ community, but Stefan and I hadn't found it actively hostile either.

"Of course it's sexual harassment," Stefan said, voice raised while hitting the arm of his chair with a fist, startling Marco who gave out a low growl. "You have to report him."

Ciska sneered. "Bollocks! He's a superstar, he's the president's darling, and the whole Board of Trustees is in love with him, too. He's on magazine covers, who's going to believe me? Who's going to *care*? Do you know what happens to students here at the university even if they're actually raped?"

Well, we did, some. Though staffed entirely by women, SUM's Sexual Assault and Sexual Harassment office—which had the unfortunately silly acronym SASH—had made headlines across the state for weak, disorganized, deeply flawed investigations of complaints from students and even some professors. Each and every headline was greeted by empty boasts about how successful the office had been and assurances that the university was deeply committed to protecting its students and seeing justice served, blah, blah, blah. Two of my own students had actually transferred to other universities because the adjudication of their complaints had been grossly mishandled, taken far too many months, and they'd felt victimized by the very people who were supposed to help them.

"It's a nightmare," Ciska said softly, as if she were trapped in one herself. "There've been dozens of accusations of violence, sexual harassment, and sexual assault against football players and basketball players since I got here. They run wild and the Athletic Department does everything it can to cover it up. Nobody gets punished or even reprimanded. So when I look at Napoléon I see a facilitator, a denier, a predator. I don't like to use the word 'hate'—but I have to tell you, I *hate* that man. I don't know him well personally, but I know the type: arrogant, privileged, no sense of boundaries. Just like my father. Men like that revolt me. They're far too many of them here already, we didn't need one more."

It was very strange to feel angry *for* Ciska, even outraged, when my relationship with the chair had been so positive thus far. And I wondered if this had ever happened to her before, then thought, of course, she was an attractive woman, how could it *not* have happened, either at SUM or some other university?

"I find myself imagining ways he could die, you know, a car crash, fast-spreading cancer. Strangled, poisoned, stabbed." Ciska's face was hard and set, her eyes flashing, and right then I could picture her doing more than just *imagining* Napoléon harm. As slim and muted as she usually was, I could picture her as Tosca triumphantly plunging the knife into villainous Scarpia. She looked straight at Stefan, then at me, and I noticed that one of her eyelids was fluttering.

Stefan said, "Wow."

"I know it's crazy, but I'm not the only one," she added sharply, eyes turning icy as if *we* suddenly had become her antagonists. This was the second time in one day that a colleague had made me feel not just uncomfortable, but wary. "Not the only one who hates him," she continued.

I had to ask who else she meant, but she wouldn't say. And I didn't want to raise Viktor Dahlberg's visit with me earlier that day because I didn't think it a good idea to violate his privacy. I also was being careful not to say anything to make her even angrier. This was one of the longest conversations I'd ever had with Ciska. She'd always struck me as being an introvert, and I know from living with Stefan that rage in people like that could be explosive.

"Has he harassed anyone else in the department?" Stefan asked.

Ciska shook her head. "Not that I'm aware of, and there's no record of harassment in France, nothing that I could find on the Internet or social media."

"Then he'll say it was a misunderstanding," I brought out. "Won't he? If someone you talked to leaks the story—"

"I didn't tell anyone else," Ciska said in a monotone, crossing her legs at the knee. And then, apologetically, she added, "It's not as if it's as terrible as anything that happened to the two of you back in May."

Stefan graciously waved that away. "Your story is terrible enough."

Then Ciska looked so distressed I thought she might cry, and as if to comfort her, Marco leapt down from his chair, trotted over and jumped onto the couch and curled up in her lap like they were old friends and proceeded to go to sleep. Ciska was startled into uncrossing her legs, but then she seemed to relax and even stroked his back, with a look in her eyes that I could only call hungry.

I felt sure of two things: That she hadn't told the whole story of what took place between them. Something was holding her back from revealing the details. I was convinced that there was more to her interaction with Napoléon.

And that Ciska was determined on somehow getting revenge.

4

THE NEXT DAY threw the stark contrast between my private life and my public role in high relief. In addition to a basic composition course, I was teaching a dream course in international thrillers that semester, and my reading list was made up of books I'd read more than once because I was blown away by them, including Joseph Kanon's *Alibi* set in Venice, Leslie Forbes's *Bombay Ice,* Ken Follett's *The Man from St. Petersburg,* and Jo Nesbø's *Headhunters.* With only twenty-one students, the class was small for a literature course at SUM. That meant I'd learned all their names quickly and could call on them with ease and weave their comments into the discussion. They had learned each other's names, too, partly because the room was big enough for us to sit in a circle and talk directly to each other. That was a powerful counterweight to anonymity on a large campus.

In the years that I'd been teaching at SUM, English majors had become increasingly unwilling to read assigned books, which made no sense to me, because if you didn't love literature of whatever genre, why choose English as a major? But this class didn't have any shirkers. There were actually ten books on the syllabus, some of them long, and nobody complained because they were so gripping and well-written. The students were lively, came to class prepared, and always had intelligent things to say about the readings—even their writing was polished and insightful.

So I usually left class feeling a little high, once again reminded why I had become a teacher in the first place: to share my excitement about books. That helped put troubles at the university in the shade, temporarily at least. Not exactly balm in Gilead, but close.

Our new department HQ had one advantage: Java Joe's, a generic but large coffee shop on the main floor whose coffee was thankfully not as strong as Starbuck's. I had a Braun coffeemaker in my office, but sometimes stopped downstairs anyway for a specialty drink. Lines could be twenty to thirty people long at peak hours, but it wasn't crowded that 4 P.M. and I didn't feel like heading to my office where I might have another encounter like the one with Viktor. I got a mocha latte and sat down in the relative quiet, basking in the smooth rich aroma of different coffees and enjoying the company of students I didn't know. The anonymity was pleasant after an intense class. And so was the colorful interior of signs, Java Joe travel mugs displayed in neon colors, shelves of matching stuffed bears, and a glass case filled with sandwich wraps, brownies, cheesecake slices, and scones.

All of the dozen or so students sitting around me at small blue tile-topped tables wore headphones or ear buds. Lana Del Ray's *Ultraviolence* was on the sound system, but playing softly, unlike most other coffee shops in town that had taken to blasting their music. You could hear the faint sound of tapping on laptop keyboards and occasional alerts on people's cell phones, but otherwise it was a surprisingly peaceful place right then on our big, noisy campus. Everyone was in their own world, which was fine by me. Scenes like this were duplicated all over the mammoth campus of 50,000 students in 650 buildings spread across 7,000 acres.

I was old enough to be the father of any of these kids, and that struck me the most when I was outside of class. Like sitting here, or walking across a crowded bridge, or finding myself anyplace where students congregated in numbers large enough to seem anonymous despite the differences in their skateboards or backpacks or facial hair. I had never imagined having children, so it was curious to me that I even had that awareness. Maybe it was thanks to all the times I'd seen parents with their sons and daughters on campus tours, the parents looking like faded, worn copies of their kids. Eventually, when I really started thinking of retirement, I'd be old enough to be somebody's grandfather. It was mildly disorienting to even think in those terms.

I sipped my coffee now and mulled over the last twenty-four hours, the talks with Viktor and Ciska. I had never been harassed sexually, but I had been bullied by administrators, which was common enough at SUM. I wasn't really surprised by her experience, but it was still awful. I also wasn't surprised that Viktor's summer program, so special to him, was being snatched away. The university could be brutal at times. It was a unique combination of the vanity of professional sports, the hypocrisy of politics, the cruelty of big business, with a touch of organized crime thrown in. All of that was draped, of course, with lovely slogans and mission statements and pretty press releases.

Given Ciska's and Viktor's troubles, I felt almost guilty that I hadn't been shafted by Napoléon, that I even liked him. Or maybe it was more accurate to say that I appreciated him, his *Frenchness*, maybe even admired it a little—I did have Belgian parents, after all, and had never felt one-hundred percent American. Napoléon was also so different from previous chairs of the department and from all of us—and wasn't opening up who could teach which course an improvement over a coldly hierarchical system that nobody had challenged or attempted to change?

But I was dreading the next department meeting. There would likely be a heated discussion of the new arrangement about course allocation, if Napoléon's email had evoked such a strong response from Ciska, and given Viktor feeling that he had been robbed. Who else was unhappy for whatever reasons and how would they react? Department meetings had always been uncomfortable for me anyway, given the way people's secret network of wishes and fears could suddenly be revealed in a sharp retort, eye rolls, barely repressed sighs, or even just how someone sat there, brooding. Issues that people had, they simmered and erupted, but never truly got resolved, and grudges weren't just held—they were treasured.

The peace in the coffee shop was suddenly shaken by a loud call of "Nick! Wassup?"

I came out of my haze as brash Roberto Robustelli pulled over a chair and sat down at my table. A medievalist, he was one of the new professors hired after the shootings and apparently thought we had a lot in common because we were both from New York. He was from Staten Island, though, and I had grown up on the Upper West Side. We were worlds apart in other ways: he was the son of a cop, I was the son of an art book publisher. He relished attention, I avoided it as much as possible.

Around thirty-five, Roberto was short, slim, wiry, and hazel-eyed with a male model's cheekbones and jawline. His dense, wavy hair and large, thick eyebrows were coal black, and his widow's peak gave him a slightly devilish look. He always wore a spicy, woodsy cologne—possibly Lagerfeld—that I think would have given me a headache if we'd been in a less open space. He had a profane mouth on him that contrasted sharply with his typical preppy clothes: loafers, chinos, and a broadcloth buttoned-down blue or pink shirt.

Roberto studied me, looked me up and down as if I was some kind of bizarre but boring exhibit in a glass case. "So what d'you think of that cocksucker?" he asked jovially, and half a dozen heads turned our way. He leaned back, arms crossed, nodding repeatedly as if agreeing with me, even though *he'd* started the conversation. He wasn't a large man by any means but seemed to take up lots of space. It was a New York thing, I supposed, realizing as he sat opposite me that he actually reminded me of some of the hearty old gum-chewing cab drivers whose taxis I'd taken over the years while growing up in Manhattan. Or drunken braggarts at a bar, filled with equal parts alcohol and arrogance.

How was I supposed to respond to his question? If I asked who he meant, he'd scorch me for being naïve, but if I said anything about Napoléon it would imply that I agreed. I settled for a shrug.

"Yeah, me too, Nick. He comes across all liberty, equality, fraternity—but that's bullshit. He's just another power-hungry motherfucker. Columbia was full of them. I thought maybe being here in Michigan, well, it might be better, but I guess not. Just another bunch of assholes like in New York, but with lousier weather."

"Don't you think this is a discussion we should have somewhere else? Somewhere quieter?"

He threw up his large, hairy hands super-dramatically. "What for? I got nothing to hide. And it's pretty quiet here already."

Well, it was, except for him and the music. Lana Del Ray was singing now about "money, power, and glory." It was a good theme song for Roberto. He'd written a very popular book, *Chaucer for Dummies,* which had sold tens of thousands of copies at colleges and universities across the country. Academics rarely hit it big like that and he was more than cocky about his success, posting new reviews to the department listserv. The book and his Yale Ph.D. had gotten him hired away from Columbia University at the associate professor rank, with automatic tenure. I didn't know what to make of his book, but I'd heard that students loved his classes, that he was a lively, spirited teacher, and I had to respect that at least.

Just then, a student in what looked like flannel pajama bottoms and Beyoncé sweatshirt was on the way out, and while putting his backpack on, it hit the back of Roberto's chair with a crack. He whirled around and hissed as if he'd been assaulted, "Watch it, asshole!"

The student scurried off.

Should I admonish him? His fury was so sudden and inappropriate, maybe it was best ignored. I couldn't picture Roberto staying at SUM for long. Given his temper, he was bound to antagonize people. Surely he'd move on to another school after writing his next book, unless he leveraged offers from other universities to extort more money out of SUM. Stefan and I had never tried it, but it was common practice here, and I'd heard of some professors who every few years solicited offers from universities where they had connections in order to boost their salaries. I was frankly surprised that the strategy worked more than once, but I suppose the university was in one way very human: it didn't value someone as much as when other people wanted them.

"I went to see His Majesty this morning to get some answers about that bullshit email he sent."

Despite myself, I smiled at his slam on Napoléon's regal manner.

"You're not gonna believe what that son of a bitch told me." Roberto's voice was more conversational now, and around us, the students had gone back to their work or gaming, texting, or whatever they were doing. I sipped my coffee.

"What did he say?" I asked that with reluctance because I was beginning to feel like Lucy in the "Peanuts" comic strip: people in the department kept coming to me with their problems and complaints. Had I become some kind of gripe magnet?

Roberto leaned forward conspiratorially and practically growled his answer. "He wants me to teach basic composition like I'm some fucking loser, just another dumb wop."

His insult shocked me, but also didn't make sense. "Napoléon's French," I said, "not Italian."

"Bullshit. One generation living in France doesn't make you kosher for those arrogant bastards no matter how well you speak French. Me, teach comp? What an insult. And I'll tell you, with insults, I don't forgive and I don't forget."

I was hoping that nobody around us was filming this interaction.

"Let me tell you something else, Nick. No way am I cut out to slosh around in the sewers. If they can't write, it's not my problem. I'll wait till they can."

Didn't he know that I taught basic composition along with other courses?

"Teaching composition classes can be very satisfying," I said. "You see a lot of progress over the course of the semester. And it's the most essential course we offer."

"Whatever. The classes are too big and the work's too hard. I don't want all that shitty prose in my head and that's not what I was hired for. How the hell can I work on my own books if I have to read garbage every week?"

Robustelli's attitude was atrocious, but even though I found it repugnant, I wasn't going to argue with anyone that belligerent, not with an audience, anyway. And I couldn't help thinking there was something very odd about him sharing all this with me when we had never really talked about anything before.

He seemed to take my offended silence for some kind of complicity because he asked, "Am I right or what?"

I shrugged, hoping he would just disappear. This was not a conversation I wanted to be having with him, here or anywhere.

"That wasn't the end of it. The schmuck claims there've been student complaints about me in the classroom from juniors and seniors! He said as long as he's the chair, I will never teach upper-level courses again, just lower-level courses for non-majors because he doesn't want English majors to be 'exposed' to me. Like I'm some fucking virus? Nobody's gonna stab me in the back like that. I'm a Scorpio and I'm the one with the sting in his tail." He nodded sternly as if he were being interviewed about how tough he was.

I didn't know what Roberto had been told he would be teaching when he got hired, but I did know that most of the faculty felt something like what he had said about teaching freshmen how to write more clearly, correctly, efficiently, and with imagination, helping them break out of their high school straitjackets. It was not an assignment people were happy to undertake. Yes, it involved a lot more work than other courses, given how much student writing you had to read and grade, but so what?

It's not as if we professors had nine-to-five jobs, no matter what we taught.

Most of us in the department only had six to eight hours of class time plus two office hours every week, and those were usually free because students rarely came in unless they specifically set up appointment times. Most students were easily intimidated, and were also embarrassed and unwilling to ask questions one-on-one about the course or their papers in a private setting. I knew faculty members who studied a foreign language, worked on their journal articles, played video games, and even napped during office hours. In my own "spare time," I studied dossiers for the Nick Hoffman Fellowship that Celine brought me. Her one driving question: Was this someone we could trust to inspire our students?

But when you looked at those empty hours every week, and added in winter and summer breaks plus a week off in the spring, and even with a lot of student writing to read, it wasn't a grueling life, especially for people who never could have been successfully employed anywhere else. Academia attracted its share of original thinkers, people who loved to mentor, and enthusiasts of all types—but also narcissists and sociopaths who not only went unsupervised for the most part, but flourished in a hothouse environment. The pick of the lot ended up becoming administrators.

However, not letting Roberto teach English majors seemed gratuitously cruel.

"What kind of complaints?" I asked. "What have students said about you?" I wondered if he cursed in class the way he was doing here. I imagine some students would find it objectionable.

"That fucker wouldn't tell me, like he wants to throw me into a Kafka novel. And by the way, you might want to watch your back. I think that asswipe is gunning for you and Stefan."

"What?"

"Napoléon doesn't like, you know, queers— Anyone living an alternative lifestyle."

This was news to me. I'd never picked up discomfort or animus from the chair about us being gay.

"What makes you say that?"

He waved his hand airily. "You know the shit about his office is always open, well I heard him on the phone saying there were 'troubling elements' in the department and I'm certain he mentioned your names."

I didn't know what to say.

"I don't care who he's gunning for or why." My table-mate shook his handsome head. "I just gotta say that nobody fucks with Robustelli. *Nobody.*"

Was he actually talking about himself in third person? And he thought Napoléon was high-handed? Unbelievable.

"You could always quit," I said.

"Are you nuts? No motherfucker pisses on my parade. I'm just gonna have to take that bastard out before he starts thinking he's God."

Despite myself, I was curious. "How?"

Roberto grinned maliciously and I saw a vein pulsing in his neck. "People get hired, people get fired. They come, they go. Happens all the time."

And then he rose and strutted off.

In my years living in Michigan, I had lost my comfort around New York–style brashness. Michiganders tended to be much more subdued than people from my former home state, and were even loath to honk their car horns unless something egregious was going on. I'd gotten used to this restraint over the years, and had come to enjoy the way people were slower here to ignite. I'd never spent this much time talking to Roberto before, exposed to his raging ego, to his big-city bellicose bluster, and the experience left me feeling shaken.

My coffee drink had gone cold, and so had I.

5

BUT I CLEARLY wasn't done with troubled faculty for the day, because out in the grim hallway, which had white tiles halfway up the wall as if it were a hospital, I saw Atticus Doyle. He was slumped on one of the padded red benches that lined the lobby and that were the major splash of color aside from the multi-hued and full-color flyers of all kinds that clustered on bulletin boards. Shattenkirk Hall was also used for classrooms, so student-aimed flyers about jobs, events, and meetings were everywhere.

Eyes down, shoulders drooping, Doyle looked despondent and made me think of a line from Byron: "gorging himself in gloom."

Tall and hipster-slim, and still boyish at thirty, he dressed like a graduate student. Today he was wearing what might have been a vintage Led Zeppelin T-shirt since it was so faded, red skinny jeans that matched his red eyeglass frames, white Keds, and a red-and-black plaid flannel overshirt. Even though he'd been at SUM for what I thought was more than five years, we didn't know each other more than just to say hello and chat about our classes in the mail room, but I had to stop since his vibe was so dark.

I went right over and asked, "Doyle? Are you okay?"

His parents had named him after the lawyer in *To Kill a Mockingbird* and by request, everyone used his last name because he said he loathed the book. He loved teaching, though, radiated positive energy, usually had a joyful loping stride and a big, bright movie-star smile. Now he could have been a mourner at a cemetery staring into the abyss. I'd never seen him looking so miserable. He gazed up at me with bleak green eyes. Whenever I'd seen him before, they made his full, reddish-blond beard and curly blond hair seem brighter and more striking, but not today.

Doyle shook his head, and his angelic features—the soft mouth, the small straight nose, the glowing skin—were dimmed.

"You look like you could use a drink. I've got some scotch in my office.... Unless you want to go out someplace near campus? It's not too early and I'm parked in the lot across the street." That was dumb since he probably was, too. But his mood was making me edgy.

"Your office is fine." He rose from the bench as if he'd been planted there for hours, and wordlessly moved toward the elevator bank with me, sliding the strap of his burgundy WaterField messenger bag over his shoulder (Stefan had one in black). "I'll take the stairs, I always walk. I got trapped in an elevator once and I hate them."

Celine had told me a similar story about herself and I wondered how common that experience was.

"Okay, I'll meet you in my office."

On the way up, I thought about Doyle. His parents were both bigwigs in D.C., or so people said. One did something in Homeland Security, the other was a lobbyist. Doyle was a longtime adjunct who taught a range of courses because he'd published books in different genres, one of which had won a Midwest Book Award. By rights, he should have gotten a tenure-track position by now, but despite his accomplishments, he hadn't found a full-time job anywhere. One that paid what he was worth, that is. At SUM, he taught three courses a semester as an adjunct, which was a heavier load than regular faculty, and he earned barely half as much.

When he first joined us at SUM, he had mentioned to me in passing his surprise that adjuncts didn't have plastic nameplates on their office doors, the kind that slip into a screwed-in metal holder. I asked why, and he said he'd been told: "You could be gone next semester."

Well, I thought, the hell with that. So could tenured faculty. Any professor could retire unexpectedly, be hired away to another university, or get taken by a shark while vacationing in Australia. Denying the nameplates to adjuncts was petty and small-minded when the department apparently had a yearly budget of close to eight million dollars.

I hadn't been welcome in the former chair's office, given my propensity for getting mixed up in murder and challenging people at the university who thought they were my "betters," so I didn't complain about the practice. I'd gone online and ordered a nameplate for Doyle that looked just like the ones tenured faculty had: black with white lettering. He had emailed me that it made him laugh when he saw it suddenly appear on his door and he'd guessed it was my doing. After that, I went ahead and bought the same thing for each of the other eight adjuncts employed at the time since they didn't have one either. Then I dropped a note to the chair about what I'd done. No reply, but from that semester onward, all new adjuncts in the department had a nameplate as soon as an office was assigned.

It was eerily silent upstairs, and while Doyle settled into one of the low-backed chairs facing my desk, I closed the door and poured us some smoky Lagavulin in crystal scotch glasses my cousin Sharon had brought back from Galway. I turned on a few lamps, all with pastel shades, and the room filled with mellow light. Lamps were vital because the obnoxious fluorescent overhead lights all through the building were glaring enough for a morgue.

Doyle's hand shook as he reached for the glass and I asked myself what was haunting him: Cancer? A family death? Monstrous debt left over from graduate school? My parents had paid off my grad school debt as a gift. My taciturn father had simply said, "You shouldn't start a career in the red."

I took the nearby chair, and when Doyle didn't speak, I prompted him: "What's going on?" I felt almost fatherly at the moment because he seemed so lost and young.

"It's my class," he said. "They hate me."

"Which class?"

"Intro to Writing Fiction."

I was flummoxed. I'd never heard students say anything critical of Doyle. Reports about which professors were irascible or erratic, which ones were habitually late or disorganized, which ones talked down to students and even insulted them—all of that reached me sooner or later. With fewer than six hundred English majors and only thirty full-time faculty, it wasn't a big enough department for that kind of information *not* to spread.

The scotch apparently helped, because now he looked right at me and sat up straight, shoulders back. "Well, to be fair, they don't all hate me. Have you heard of the Justice League?"

"You mean that bunch of superheroes in Marvel comics? Sure. Wait—are you having your students read comics?"

"No, no, we're reading serious fiction. I'm talking about a new group on campus that's fighting for—"

I cut him off: "Whatever they're fighting for, that's a ridiculous name. How do they expect anyone's going to take them seriously? Please tell me they're not wearing costumes to class."

Doyle shook his head. "They're super serious. The group is all white, but they're not right-wingers or white supremacists, they're on the left and they say they're fighting for social justice on campus. Hence the name. Three of them are in my fiction class and they hate what we're reading. I put some terrific books on the syllabus that we could analyze and that would inspire their writing. That's what I hoped for anyway, but I'm being attacked about everything. They don't think *Beloved* should be on the syllabus."

"Are you kidding me? Toni Morrison's brilliant, what's wrong with reading *Beloved*?"

Now he grimaced. "It's me. *I'm* wrong because I'm white.

I can't know anything about oppression. I'm a hypocrite, abusing my white male privilege." He downed most of his drink and reached out to set the glass on my desk. He ran his fingers through his hair and I noticed for the first time how large and powerful his hands were, with thick fingers not remotely as delicate as his angelic features.

"Even if that were true—which it's not—you do know about writing. You've published as much as some of the tenure-track faculty here." I thought about it, and had to say, "More."

"Doesn't count, Nick. They've got a reason to pick apart everything on the reading list." He took another swig of scotch.

"Like what else?"

"Okay. I like to teach literary fiction and popular fiction for the contrast, right? Then we get to talk about genre expectations and everything that flows from that. But they don't like Charlie Huston's *Already Dead.*"

"You're kidding!" I had taught that novel myself in a Popular Literature course focusing on unusual crime novels. It was a funny, dramatic book that imagined a secret world of vampire clans with different turfs in Manhattan, and the narrator was a vampire private investigator. My students loved the voice and the way the book blended genres. "How can they not like a book with vampires *and* zombies?" I asked him. "They've grown up on *Twilight* and *The Walking Dead.*"

"First of all, there are dashes instead of quotation marks for dialogue, and they feel confused, but the main thing is, the Justice League students objected to my heteropatriarchal assumptions that Toni Morrison is a literary writer and Huston isn't."

I was certain that *heteropatriarchal assumptions* was their term, not his.

Doyle glanced over at his glass and nodded when I asked if he wanted another.

"They called me racist and said I was ghettoizing Toni Morrison."

I had to pour myself some more scotch, too, because what he was telling me sounded like something out of a ludicrous academic satire. It couldn't be real. What the hell was wrong with being classed as a writer of literary fiction?

"They said I'm an elitist." His free hand was clenched so tight I thought he might hurt himself.

"Because of teaching her at all, or putting her in a category?"

"Both, I guess. Oh, God, and the day I wore a T-shirt that said 'Poetry is Lit,' they called me a racist, they said I had no right to use that word."

Even though I felt too old myself to use the new slang word for "awesome" or "terrific" (and which also referred to getting high), I thought the pun I'd seen on T-shirts with that slogan was clever.

"I've been losing sleep, Nick, I can't eat much, I feel nauseous before class, and I've been horrible at home. Whatever my wife says, I snap at her. And she's been distant, coming home late, I'm sure she hates what I've become." Atticus looked away and dropped his voice: "And sometimes I think she must be sleeping with somebody because I'm so ornery and depressed. She gets phone calls at weird times, and she's acting, I don't know, like she has something to hide."

I had met his wife, Florice, at a party but we'd never spoken much. With a background in Art History, she was a docent at SUM's small art museum and also worked in SUM fundraising. She didn't use Atticus's last name but her own flowery one: Fleurisson. That alone would have made her unforgettable, but she was from Quebec and had a lovely accent. I remembered her as tall and imposing, very dramatic in emerald green, a blond version of Angelina Jolie. She and Atticus made a very photogenic couple.

I didn't know what to say in response to his suspicions about his wife, and I went back to what we'd been talking about: "So what happened in class today?"

Doyle flushed. "I hate confrontation. I grew up with parents who argued all the time. So I let other students deal with it."

"Does that work?"

His handsome eyes widened. "Actually, it does, yes. I have a lot of Honors students and they keep discussion from driving off the rails. They say the things I would like to say. The things I *should* say. Well, I do say them, eventually. But I've never been challenged like this before, by people *who don't make sense.* How do you reason with someone who's unreasonable? It's like a nightmare where you keep reaching for something and it always moves further away. The tension, it's wearing me out. I don't know what's next. It's bizarre. One of them says white people shouldn't be speaking about racial issues at all because it silences people of color and denigrates their history. He came to class with masking tape across his mouth."

"To demonstrate, what, solidarity? Why didn't he drop the course? He saw the syllabus the first day, right?"

"I think he's staying to make a point."

I'd read about this kind of classroom confrontation by students at small, ultra-liberal colleges around the country, but nothing like it had happened yet at middle-of-the-road SUM that I knew of. At least protestors hadn't invaded his class with signs and klaxons and prevented him from speaking. I didn't mention that, though, since I doubted it would cheer him up.

"They don't understand empathy," Doyle went on. "How did they get that way? How did they come through school this far and think a white professor can't understand the suffering of black people? Can't understand a black woman's novel? Do they think Morrison doesn't write for *everyone?*"

"Well, complaining about Morrison as a literary writer, that's totally screwed up," I said, imagining what could happen in one of my classes—or Stefan's—with students that were as myopic as Doyle's. "And calling literary fiction a ghetto—?" The folly of that almost made me shudder.

"I feel like I'm trapped in *Through the Looking Glass.*"

I quoted the Red Queen:"Sentence first—verdict afterwards."

"Exactly! I feel like I'm guilty of something every time I walk into that classroom. I'm white, I'm straight, I'm male, I'm doomed."

"How big is this group overall? How come I haven't heard of them?"

Doyle couldn't answer either question.

"What about Napoléon? Did you talk to him?"

Doyle finished his second scotch and set the glass down on my desk so heavily I thought it might crack. His eyes were narrowed and cold, his face was flushed, and he seemed to be reliving the moment when he said through clenched teeth, "Napoléon blew me off completely. He said I should know how to run a classroom without disruptions or the need for someone to rescue me from my own incompetence. I wanted to strangle that smug bastard—he was so blasé, so contemptuous. I could have been complaining about problems with the copying machine, that's how little he cared. But it got worse. He said that if I didn't know how to control my own classroom I didn't belong at SUM and he doubted he'd rehire me next year."

Here it was again: the new department chair disparaging and threatening someone else. I looked down at Doyle's restless hands and couldn't help but imagine them around Napoléon's neck.

"I know the tenured faculty look down on me like it's my fault there aren't enough full-time jobs." Before I could say anything, he added:"You and Stefan excluded, of course. And there are some others...."

I sensed that he wanted to say something more and was hesitating, so I just looked away to make him feel less self-conscious, and it worked.

"I don't like talking about this, Nick, but I have pretty serious PTSD from a car accident a few summers ago. I was on I-75, it was raining heavily, and a car going way too fast skidded into my lane, hit me pretty hard. I went into the median and the car flipped over. I blacked out and woke up upside down with the police there and firemen cutting me out of the car with the Jaws of Life. The air bags had come on but my concussion was so bad I had to take that fall semester off."

I gulped, unable to think of something to say. "I'm sorry" would be inadequate, and asking if he was okay was worse. I went straight to the point instead: "Class retriggers all of that for you?"

He nodded. "I was doing fine in therapy until this semester. Now I need a Xanax just to get through a two-hour class." He was glaring at me as if it were my fault. "I don't feel safe anymore. And Napoléon's made it worse. Much worse." His face was flushed again now, and tight. "I know it's terrible to admit this, but I truly hate him. Why couldn't he have been here in the spring when that guy went nuts and shot up Parker Hall—?"

Atticus turned red. "Oh, shit, I'm so sorry, I am so sorry, that was a fucking stupid thing to say...."

Yes it was, I thought. But he meant it just the same.

6

I HAD MORE THAN usual trouble sleeping that night, though Stefan's and Marco's light snoring had until lately been like white noise for me. My recent conversations with Viktor, Ciska, Roberto, and Atticus were circling in my thoughts like the hawks I sometimes saw riding air currents in our neighborhood, looking for prey down below. The anxiety and anger of my colleagues—and Robustelli's claim that Napoléon had it in for me and Stefan—had triggered my own, and underneath it all was the sense of dislocation and loss I could tune out during the day, but which lay in wait at night and disrupted my sleep.

I found myself thinking now about Nicole and Chuck, friends from grad school who both taught at the University of Texas in Houston. Their home near a bayou had been flooded several times in recent years after torrential rains, destroying their cars, ruining furniture including the harpsichord Nicole had built herself, and leading to months of remodeling and cleaning each time. Once they had fled to the second floor thinking the swift-rising waters would kill them.

Stefan and I hadn't faced the same kind of disasters at all, but in the emails I'd exchanged with Nicole, it was clear we were equally shell-shocked. We'd both felt helpless, invaded, crushed. They had also moved, yet were unhappy in their new home even though it was a safer neighborhood. One of the courses

Nicole taught was African-American Fiction, her favorite novelist being James Baldwin, and in a recent email she had quoted a line from *Another Country*: "Most people had not lived through any of their terrible events.... They had simply been stunned by the hammer."

I thought this was true right now. I had experienced the nightmare, but hadn't absorbed it—if anything, it had probably absorbed *me*. I had lost my taste for thrillers or movies where police or soldiers raided a house, even if there were terrorists inside. All that was too close to home. Pun intended.

In the morning there was an unexpected email for me from the chair, asking if I would come to his office that afternoon. I didn't have class, and the time he suggested was fine, so I emailed back a quick "yes." But I wondered what was up. Stefan suggested I email again about the purpose of the meeting.

"Wouldn't that seem like I'm defensive or anxious?"

He frowned. "You're just asking for information. That way you can't get surprised."

"How would he do that?"

Deadpan, Stefan explained: "By saying something surprising."

I had to laugh at that, but I didn't email. "I already said yes. I don't want to look ditzy with a P.S."

"Well, okay then."

Whenever either one of us got ready to go someplace, Marco would follow us around the house to observe us closely, seeing what we put on, watching what stuff we got ready to take with us. I was sure that he recognized the signs that meant he was not going for a ride with us—after all, we were his own private TV nature special he could watch whenever he wasn't snoozing. I wished I could take him to campus, it would humanize the place. I made some espresso before I left, downed it, gave Marco a liver treat and Stefan a see-you-later kiss. He wished me good luck, looking wary.

Napoléon's secretary was new and she shocked me: she looked like a serial killer. She was easily six feet tall, probably about two hundred pounds, and her eyes were zombie-dead in a bovine, doughy, red face that was framed by listless auburn hair. She wore a shapeless taupe suit and matching blouse with an old-fashioned jabot. Her meaty hands with bitten or radically trimmed fingernails were big enough to punch someone to death.

When she glanced up from her keyboard in response to my "Hello," she muttered, "Nick Hoffman, three P.M. meeting, go on in," with an affectless voice that was as chilling as her office. There wasn't a single family photo or anything personal there softening its bitter white-and-gray lines. Was she hiding something or did she expect to leave soon? Her desk nameplate read GRACE LOVEJOY, which seemed cruelly inappropriate.

Napoléon's well-appointed office was a relief after Grace's void. It was certainly not as cold, but was twice the size of mine, and I assumed that he must have paid for the furniture himself. The deluxe wraparound desk and wall unit with a hutch and computer station was made of some gleaming, exotic-looking reddish wood—maybe a kind of mahogany—and the glass-topped little table and two blue velvet-and-gilt Louis Quinze–style armchairs for visitors were far ritzier than anything I'd seen elsewhere on campus. There was a pleasant orangey scent in the air which might have come from furniture polish. The walls were hung with signed exhibition posters of luminous, dreamy Michigan scenes by the painter David Grath, so the office sent out mixed signals. The posters were welcoming, but the mammoth desk unit was like a barricade.

Enthroned in a high-backed burgundy leather chair, Napoléon himself was smiling, prosperous-looking, elegant as ever—and intimidating.

In his sky blue Ermenegildo Zegna suit like one I'd seen in a *Vanity Fair* advertisement, pale pink shirt and purple tie, he looked like a hip executive—or an actor playing one in a movie. Even the expensive-looking gold-edged leather desk set of trays and blotter and pen-and-pencil holder were like props. Why hadn't I noticed this air of masquerade about him before? Or was I seeing Napoléon differently now because of what other professors had told me about their interactions with him?

He didn't waste time on chatting. "Nick, how are you doing with this year's selection for the—" He paused, large perfect teeth gleaming in a showy smile. "—for the Nick Hoffman Fellowship?"

The question threw me off, and so did the pause. He couldn't have forgotten the name, so was he trying to make some kind of point? Was he being sarcastic? And why was he even asking, given that it was so early in the academic year?

I could feel tendons or muscles in my neck tightening. I shrugged to ease the tension, and tried sitting taller in the chair that encouraged lolling because it was so comfortable. I'd seen this kind of chair in magazines and movies like *Dangerous Liaisons*. They were called *bergères* and were originally meant for lounging. With their wide, deep seats and sloping backs they were a trap, I realized: sit back and you were stretched out and exposed, sit forward or even on the edge and you were unsettled. I was beginning to think they had been chosen for that very reason, not for their style.

I felt obliged to mention a few names that I was considering and he nodded thoughtfully at each one. Then he said, "I value your contributions to the department, but don't you think your choices are a bit parochial?"

The word "parochial" bothered me, and I tried to keep my voice level.

"How so? They're all well known, their work is terrific, and I hear good things about all of them as speakers and teachers." I didn't add that my administrative assistant, Celine Robichaux, would be vetting each one very closely. Someone like her could have been a private investigator, she was that thorough and dogged.

"Ah, yes, that may be. But don't you think we should aim

higher? Why limit ourselves to one country? The Booker Prize used to only consider novels in English by British, Irish, and Commonwealth writers. And now *any* novel in English can be eligible." He gave a very Gallic shrug, and waited for me to respond.

Napoléon was right about England's foremost literary prize, but that was in a completely different realm than my fellowship. *My* fellowship. After it was established, nobody at SUM had managed to interfere with how I handled it, and I could feel my cheeks go hot. In that quiet room I thought my breathing must be very loud. My neck was now as tight as if I'd been on a terrible overnight cross-country flight without a pillow. I fought the impulse to raise my voice or clench my fists. Making an effort, I asked as genially as I could, "Is there someone you think would be a better choice?"

"I'm glad you asked me that," he said, and the condescension made me breathe in slowly so that I didn't snap at him. He tipped his head to one side as if he were an alien trying to comprehend us poor benighted humans. Then he gave me a name: "I would propose to you Élodie le Bon." He sounded as cheerful as a headwaiter in a restaurant offering the day's special. He rested his right hand on an antique-looking, thin and pointed letter opener I hadn't noticed till then. The blade was easily eight inches long, had a silver fleur-de-lis handle, and looked sharp enough to open even the most tightly sealed packages, just like a box cutter.

"I've never heard of her."

"*Voilà!*" he said, and he chuckled, obviously delighted by my American ignorance.

"But why would I pick her?"

He looked at me with hooded eyes. "She is young, dynamic, well-respected in the French literary establishment. She's twice won the Prix Goncourt for literature, and you will find translated books of hers on Amazon, should you care to look. I myself can vouch for her excellence in every way." Then he smiled. "And I am happy to tell you that *elle a du chien.*"

I knew that French expression meant that a woman was charming and chic, but what the hell did it have to do with anything? Why was he telling me this? Did she and Napoléon have more than a professional relationship? Was that why he was pushing her candidacy? I kept mum, trying to figure out what to say. I did not have a good history with authority figures, dating back to my father, who was both aloof and intrusive when I was growing up. I either clammed up or became quip-happy and my European-born father had slapped me more than once as a boy, shouting, "Never speak to me as if I were a servant!" The first time, I was as shocked by what he said as by the mention of a "servant." It seemed so Victorian.

Napoléon might have guessed that I was disturbed by his comment about the French woman's appearance, because he added, "I am looking ahead to press coverage and photographs, of course. She is very photogenic." He fondled the letter opener, then picked it up and slowly twirled it with his thumb and first two fingers.

It was distracting me because I was trying to process what was happening, and failing miserably. Napoléon set down the letter opener on his blotter with its point facing me. Apparently noting my focus, he said, "This is a family heirloom, and there are rumors that one of my ancestors, a mad baroness, stabbed her husband with it in the middle of their conjugal pleasures."

He tented his fingers and was leaning far back in his chair now, eyeing me with clear enjoyment. His malicious smile made me feel that he was reading my mind.

"I must tell you, Nick, that Élodie has a super apartment in the Marais which she lends to friends and I'm sure she would be happy to let you and Stefan stay there some time." Though his English was excellent, he pronounced "super" the way French people did: *"soo-pair."*

Was he actually trying to *bribe* me?

If so, it was a great offer. Despite the threat of terror in France, the historic Marais district was one of our favorite places to spend time in Paris, with its ancient buildings, the Picasso Museum, hip clubs, great restaurants, and the Place des Vosges—possibly one of the most beautiful public squares in Europe. I suddenly felt paranoid: could Napoléon know I might be tempted by just that alone? Could he have accessed my campus email and seen emails to our travel agent? My assistant had told me last year that SUM had formed a super-secret committee tasked with security on campus that had access to people's phones and email, and the power to have anyone suspicious arrested. Power like that could all too easily be abused.

"You must love the Marais, there are so many of your people there. And I understand you're always happier among your own. There's nothing wrong with being clannish, as I see it. It's a force of nature, if you will."

"My people?"

"Israelites." That old-fashioned word felt like an insult, and I was pissed off by the way he said it, with his lips pursed as if he didn't like what the word stood for. I couldn't speak. I knew how endemic Jew-hatred was in French society going back at least to the nineteenth century and the Dreyfus Affair. Was I dealing with an anti-Semite? Or was he mocking me?

"Nick, there is no need to hesitate. Élodie le Bon would bring true distinction to your fellowship."

"And put the department on the map and get us some positive publicity?" My anger and revulsion had made me raise my voice, and I told myself, *Stay calm.*

He waved his hands like a priest happily addressing full pews. "That goes without saying. I am certain that the French press would give it as much attention as the American press undoubtedly would. An international figure like Élodie brings with her the celebrity and positive publicity we sorely need."

My fellowship was doing just fine without his interference, and I finally had to let loose: "It would make *you* look good, too, since you obviously need to do something dramatic and noteworthy in your first year as chair. You have to justify all the money they're throwing at you."

Napoléon sat up sharply, and if I were a romance writer, I would say that his eyes were suddenly stormy. "I am only thinking about what would be best for our little university. I have no selfish motives whatsoever. I am making you a generous offer, and you would be wise to take advantage of it." His voice was harsher than I'd ever heard it before, and it was as if the mask had come off.

But his rebuke and his warning didn't touch me.

I felt cold inside and that feeling was my own barricade. Now I saw the man who had managed to agitate and harass my colleagues after being chair for such a short time. Even though I currently had more status in the department than ever before, it still really meant very little. Napoléon couldn't fire me since I was now a full professor with tenure, plus I hadn't done anything unprofessional that would justify being let go; still, as chair of the department, he was my new overlord. And now that Napoléon had announced that he was going to determine course assignments, he could make my life miserable by never giving me a course I asked for.

He could also make sure my raises were meager and assign me to work on faculty committees I didn't want to be part of. When I put in for conference travel funds, he could deny my requests. Napoléon could do something even pettier and change my office or assign me to early morning classes which no faculty wanted to teach. When I first heard about the fellowship I would be directing, SUM's provost, Merry Glinka, had been furious that someone as insignificant as I was had been singled out for the honor my former student had created, with money the university couldn't control. She would be happy to see me hassled and even humiliated.

I saw all of that with terrible clarity, almost as if I were one of

those people about to drown, except it was my future that sped by.
Napoléon could even try to punish me by undermining Stefan's
position as writer-in-residence, lobbying the dean of our college
for a new position in the department for a memoirist or fiction
writer and making sure the person who survived the search committee's meat grinder was someone whose reputation was better
than Stefan's. That wouldn't be hard to do, since there were so
many good writers in the country and not all that many academic
positions for those who wanted one. Whether that person ended
up staying here in mid-Michigan didn't matter. The insult would
be what counted. As a new star on campus, Napoléon could
attract big names. And our dean, Magnus Bullerschmidt, fat and
vengeful, would enjoy anything that discomfited me or Stefan,
even though he reportedly was furious to have been left out of
the decision to hire Napoléon.

Evidently annoyed by my long silence, Napoléon pressed me:
"Well, Nick, what do you say?"

Should I say something vague to try and placate him? He was
my chair and I would have to live with him for who knows how
long. But I hated the idea of backing down when I was right.
Or felt right, anyway. And had been bullied and disrespected on
top of it.

"I know the Board of Trustees would approve of such a
choice," Napoléon said sweetly.

The board? Those wealthy Republican stooges appointed
by the ultra-conservative governor? I didn't believe they would
concern themselves with something at this level. They always
flew first class on university business, or invented university
business and SUM paid their way. Their ambitions were more
self-interested—like redecorating their vacation homes in Char-
levoix and improving their golf games. Napoléon had to be
bluffing.

"I would like an answer," Napoléon said, frowning.

I felt like a schoolboy being upbraided by his principal.

"It's an original idea, Nick, surely you can see that? You *must* see that."

"Yes, it's original," I brought out, trying to sound mildly enthusiastic, and cursing myself for being a coward.

"Ah, good! We'll certainly talk more about this another time. But know I've already spoken with her, and she's awaiting your call, assuming of course you'll see the wisdom in proceeding. I thought I'd prepare the ground."

His tone made it clear that I was being dismissed. He stood up and reached across his gleaming desk to shake my hand. I struggled up from the chair, still dazed, to give him mine. There was a cold, derisive expression on his face as we shook that told me he wasn't fooled by my reply.

His secretary glanced up at me with those Death Star eyes of hers, and with her lips tight managed to say, "You seem like a very angry, unhappy person."

I ignored her. I didn't even stop at my office on the way to the elevators. I wanted to quickly get as far away as possible from Napoléon and his brooding secretary. Riding downstairs and hurrying to the parking lot, I was angry, but I also felt like a chump. After almost twenty years here, and despite everything I knew about SUM and how things worked, I had let myself be fooled by Napoléon's charm, and by the fact that he had been nice to me until today. It was all pretense. I'd thought someone like him would be a change for the better, but in the end, he was just another arrogant, overbearing department chair. Not as shabby or scattered as some, and better dressed and better known than his peers, but not a better person in the slightest.

There was a Swedish proverb that I for some reason remembered in that moment as I started up my new Lexus NX, which I'd chosen because it made me feel like I was in a small tank: "Lawyers and soldiers are the Devil's playmates" *(Advokater och soldater är satans lekkamrater)*.

Administrators deserved to be added to that crowd. And given first place.

7

WHEN I GOT BACK HOME, Stefan was sprawled on the white leather couch re-reading a paperback of *The Handmaid's Tale*, which was as red as the throw pillows in this room and some of the walls in other rooms. It was one of the books he was teaching in a class on dystopian fiction that included classics like *Fahrenheit 451*, *Brave New World*, and *1984*. I was reading some of them, too, to see what I thought all these years after first encountering them in high school and college.

I remembered that when *The Handmaid's Tale* was first published, we'd found the novel scary and implausible. Maybe out of wishful thinking. Now, three decades later, with our first Black president late in his second term, we had diverged. I leaned toward scary given the obscene ways he and the first lady had been attacked online and elsewhere, but Stefan leaned towards implausible because he felt the country had been changing in amazing ways. We both still agreed that it was gorgeously written.

Marco was curled up at Stefan's feet and sleepily wagged his fluffy tail at me. I made a mental note to schedule a grooming appointment for him since he was starting to look a little shaggy. Stefan said, "Give me a second, I'm just finishing a chapter."

On the black coffee table there was a bottle of Pink Pigeon, the sweet, spicy sipping rum from Mauritius in the Indian Ocean, alongside two stemless squat glasses. I took the empty one, poured two fingers of rum, my hands still a little shaky. I sat in one of the big black chairs that actually felt more comfortable than the one I'd been stuck in at Napoléon's office. It wasn't objectively true, but maybe that meant I was inching my way towards feeling more at home here, unless it was just a relief to be away from campus and sitting with Stefan. And Marco, of course. After adopting him, I had quickly come to believe something I'd seen on a wall plaque: A HOUSE IS NOT A HOME WITHOUT A DOG. Whenever he was at the groomer's, the house felt vacant, thunderously silent, haunted by his absence.

When Stefan breathed in deeply, I assumed he was done, and I asked, "How are your students liking the book?"

Literature classes in our department were way too big: forty-five students when they should have been half that size. But the university didn't really care about people. Money, Reputation, and Sports were SUM's Holy Trinity. I knew from my own experience that in classes as big as Stefan's it was hard to get discussion going, and many students didn't bother speaking at all unless called on, because there was always someone else who contributed.

"Mixed," he said. Stefan put a bookmark into the Atwood book, closed it, sat up, and set the novel to his right to keep Marco from sniffing at it and giving it a tentative chew. Our puppy had a fondness for paper of all sorts, so we always had to be watchful.

"Half of them think it's too slow, they want more action, like *The Hunger Games*." He shrugged.

"And the other half?"

"Well, they love it for different reasons. Because of the characters, or the writing, or the vision—or different combinations. The ones who love it are passionate, and so are some on the other side. And...why are we talking about the book right now?" Stefan asked. "How was your meeting with Napoléon? You look pale."

I sipped and savored some of the rum, which was creamier than I remembered and laden with vanilla, and then recounted bits and pieces of the surreal scene in Napoléon's office. It came back to me in a jagged and incomplete way, and telling him, I felt like I was sharing a disturbing and confusing dream. But I made sure he understood that I felt I had seen the sinister Napoléon underneath the mask of elegance and French charm he wore so well. That part seemed unreal even though I'd experienced it just a short while before, like those moments in a film when the apparent good guy reveals what he's really been up to and the audience goes, "Whoa!" because they've been cleverly deceived.

"Napoléon must be miserable," Stefan said decisively when I was done.

"Wait. What? Seriously? Are you trying to defend him? Are you going to give me that bullshit about 'He must be unhappy inside if he treats people so badly'? Spare me the amateur psychology."

His glance slid sideways, and I could swear Stefan was imagining what he'd do with someone like Napoléon in a novel. Our new chair *was* larger than life—and not nearly so natural, to quote Oscar Wilde.

Looking back at me, Stefan said, "He hasn't been here long, but I think he probably hates being stuck in Michigan. Hell, who wouldn't after living in Bordeaux? Maybe even worse for someone used to being profiled in major magazines and photographed by paparazzi. He's figured out that being a department chair really isn't a big deal and he'd rather be a dean here, no, *president.* That's real power and publicity."

"Wait a minute—his salary is outrageous, he makes close to two hundred thousand a year. I checked online." University salaries are public since SUM is a state university. "I think you're imagining all this. How could he be miserable with that kind of money? And if he is, why did he bother to come here? What's he really after?"

Stefan frowned intently, as if I hadn't been listening. "Think of it. He's a celebrity in France. But SUM isn't Ivy League or even at the top of the Big Ten. He's been demoted, in a way, if you take the larger view. The position is too small for him, so he's going to make the faculty pay for his mistakenly signing on." Stefan smiled when he added, "It's easy to be small-minded in a small town."

"Lousy word play, and fuck the larger view. That sure sounds like you're making excuses for him."

"Nope. *Ç'est un gros con.* From what you've told me about how he's treating people, he's a jerk and a douchebag and anything else you want to call him. He should never have tried to bully you."

I grinned. "I love hearing you curse in French." It was something Stefan had never done when we traveled in France because he was too aware of the Ugly American stereotype. And because he was a stickler for accuracy and suspected that the vulgarisms and slang he knew from books and movies might be out of date.

"I'm *not* excusing anything Napoléon's said or done." Stefan looked very serious. "He's a menace to comity, to collegiality."

"Not that there's much of either of those here...."

He nodded. "And he's making it worse. Just wait."

"For what?"

"He's for sure going to unleash more Big Plans to turn things inside out in the department. You know the deal: new boss has to leave a mark, not that it ever matters."

" 'Look on my works, ye mighty, and despair.' "

"Right. And there's a line in *Fahrenheit 451,* 'Those who don't build must burn.' I don't think he's here to build anything but his own ego, which means the worst for everyone else. Except…that email about course assignments did make some sense."

"But watch him go about it the wrong way! He's abusing his power already, so he'll probably do things like a typical administrator and make as many people unhappy as he can at one time. I'm not sure how, but he'll enjoy it."

That's when I remembered that Roberto Robustelli had implied that Napoléon hated gays, or something like that, and I blurted it out.

"Is anything that guy says believable?" Stefan asked.

We shared a dark silence until I said, "What's for dinner?"

"Despite the chair, I was feeling nostalgic about France and I took out Patricia Wells's *Bistro Cooking.*"

I perked up because I loved the recipes in that cookbook. "And—?"

"I bought some fresh fettuccine and we're having it with crème fraîche and those truffles I've been saving."

"Great!"

"I thought maybe a Muscadet with that?"

"Yes, sir!"

He picked up his book and Marco and I followed him to the kitchen. I opened the under-counter wine fridge to find the right bottle. Stefan would have no trouble working off the meal at our health club. Me, I'd have to swim extra lengths at the pool, but it would be worth the fatigue. And swimming was the best thing I could do now, anyway. I felt safe in the water, protected, happy to be in a world where the only sound came from my own backstroke and flip turn, or someone else's swift, steady movement from one end of the Olympic-size pool to the other. I wasn't especially fast, but my form was good, and the repetition was like meditation after a while, relaxing, healing, and quietly transformative. I almost always left the pool calmer, my skin tingling, and with a sense of well-being.

"I love this dystopian course," Stefan said as he set a pot of water to boil for the pasta.

I sat at the counter and nodded. "That's terrific." Both of us had been mentored well in college and we each understood how to work with students to help them write and think more clearly, and also read with insight. It was a challenging process, because it was too easy to try imposing your own vision, your own voice even unconsciously. You had to be vigilant and careful, and still have fun, because if you didn't enjoy yourself, it was unlikely the students would. And then you had to strike the right balance to make sure your needs for the course to go well weren't over-shadowing their own.

Stefan turned from the stove and grinned.

I'd heard plenty of stories from my students about professors in the department who were anywhere from insulting to borderline abusive in class. Some had favorites who they always called on, while disparaging the comments of students they didn't like for whatever obscure reason. Some even interrupted students who were reading aloud from their stories or essays and called it "a waste of time" or even "bullshit." A number of professors could make students of both sexes cry—yet their toughness attracted other students who had no trouble with a course being taught as if the students were a failing sports team that needed invective to improve its game.

Stefan's eyes widened as if he was picturing some classroom scene. As a writer, he often had these moments that mixed distance and reflection. "When the people who do talk get going," he said, "the discussions are really so smart and insightful. And it's not just the English majors. Reading's not dead, not entirely."

"Yeah, even if they do obsess about *Dancing with the Stars* or video games or whatever." As I picked up the wine, I remembered Napoléon's stiletto and almost dropped the bottle. I placed it carefully on the counter.

"Shit—I didn't tell you about his tic! He was messing with this knife while we were talking."

"A knife? What kind of knife?"

"I guess he used it as a letter opener. But it was a stiletto. And it was huge."

Stefan cocked his head at me.

"Okay, maybe not huge, but pretty damned long."

Stefan was unpacking the fresh fettuccine. "The whole time you were there?"

"Just some of it. Actually."

"Sounds theatrical," Stefan said, eyes wide again as if trying to picture it and again I wondered if he was actively considering "using" Napoléon or the stiletto in a book.

"It felt creepy. The whole university feels creepy."

We were on familiar ground with that observation, but I let loose anyway. What's the point of being married if you don't have a place to repeat yourself?

"Don't you think SUM's become even more corporate, more interested in big bucks from foreign students?" Chinese, Indian, and Korean students paid even more than full out-of-state tuition and SUM craved more of them. "It's like this giant whirlpool sucking in money without paying any attention to its core mission to teach and reach out to the community. What happened to caring about our land grant heritage? Caring about students?"

"On their way out, thanks to the state legislators who think college is just about job training."

"Then why the hell are we staying?" I think the rum was getting to me.

Stefan leaned across the counter, took my hands and said, "Because for better or worse, this is our home, and teaching and mentoring is what we do."

I thought of the line Cassie sings in *A Chorus Line* about wanting to stay in the biz: "God, I'm a dancer! A dancer dances!" That was us, superannuated, maybe, but passionate about what we did. And trapped in a milieu that didn't really value our contributions and hard work because we didn't bring in grant money and our enrollments were shrinking. Not a bad trap in some ways, given our salaries and the life we lived, but the toxic side of being at this university was a constant drain.

Stefan returned to the stove.

While I uncorked the wine, I said, "Sometimes I think the university is a dystopia."

Stefan took out a small saucepan to warm the crème fraîche. "How so?"

"It's supposed to be a haven of learning, right? The epitome of humanistic values, but look at the reality. We both wanted to teach, we have teachers in our families, but teaching just gets lip service here. Publishing is way more important, and money is always the bottom line. If you get good evaluations from your students, so what? And look at how adjuncts are treated—like serfs. It's despicable. It's feudal, and even with tenure, anyone can be mistreated. Cruelty rules the day."

"Power corrupts, absolute power corrupts absolutely, but academic power corrupts exponentially."

I set the kitchen table and poured the wine. "Exactly! It doesn't look like a place where that should happen, but it does, every single day. This wasn't the life I thought I'd have as a professor, contending with wannabe tyrants. No, sorry, they *are* tyrants, even though their kingdoms are small." I did not mention last spring's traumatic events, I didn't have to, since that was always present for us at some level of consciousness.

Stefan drained the pasta, checked to see that the crème fraîche was simmering, then chopped two marble-sized truffles into eighths, added them to the saucepan to briefly warm. In a few minutes, he tossed the pasta with the sauce in a majolica bowl we'd bought in Florence and we sat down to our feast after feeding Marco and toasting, "To Survival!" Marco circled the table, sniffing hungrily, since preserved truffles were a new thing for him, and the intense, earthy aroma had to be tantalizing. He eventually settled down near us to snooze.

"Would you even consider Napoléon's proposal for the fellowship?" Stefan asked after a second glass of wine.

"Never!"

"Good." Stefan smiled. "Just wanted to check."

When we were done and setting things in the red dishwasher, I remembered the weird feeling I had when Napoléon used the word "Israelites" and shared that and his "clannish" remarks with Stefan. How had I not started out with that?

Now it was *his* turn to almost drop something. He'd been gently washing the majolica bowl in the sink, but caught it before it fully slipped from his hands. He set it down carefully, shoulders tense.

"Napoléon really said all that crap?"

"Well, yeah."

"Un-be-lieve-able."

"Maybe I misheard him or I'm being too sensitive...."

"That's how bigots *want* you to feel." He inserted a soap packet and got the dishwasher going. When he turned to me, his face was set and angry and I could see a blood vessel throbbing in his forehead. "It's how they undermine your sense of reality. What he said was offensive. It's like he's out to demean everyone he talks to."

I nodded, reluctantly, unhappy to be facing time working with someone like Napoléon. How was I going to keep out of his way? How was I going to protect myself?

Stefan said, "You remember what Maya Angelou said?"

I knew exactly the quote he meant:" 'When someone shows you who they are, believe them the first time.' "

8

IT TURNED OUT that I wasn't paranoid when I had been imagining various ways in which Napoléon could go about harassing me. If anything, I wasn't paranoid *enough*.

The next morning, Thursday, there was a department-wide email:

> *Dear Friends!*
> *In reviewing the history of our registrations, I've discovered far too many courses with consistently low enrollments. We do not serve our students well or allocate our valuable faculty resources efficaciously when classes underperform. These courses are parasites. One of the first that I have identified is Jewish-American Literature, which has never reached its intended level of 25 students. I am suspending assignments to this course and it will not be offered any longer.*
> *Please remember, my office is always open to you.*
> *With every best wish,*
> *Napoléon Padovani*

Stefan and I ate a very grim breakfast, or more accurately, picked at it. It was one of my favorites, too: a creamy goat cheese frittata with *fines herbes*. It smelled rich and moist, but I couldn't really taste much, and while we sat there listlessly, it went from wonderfully inviting to just rubbery and sad. I could hear the fridge humming in the silence and the room felt cold though I didn't think it really was.

Napoléon was right that the course had never reached its limit of twenty-five students in my time at SUM, but it never fell below fifteen or so, which was an ideal number and allowed for deeper involvement by the students, encouraging them to talk with more freedom about the books and the subjects they raised. I had recently taught it—with seventeen students enrolled— and had hoped to do so again. For a while it was handled by a "spousal hire" whose wife SUM wanted to keep in Psychology because she had some sort of super-star reputation. Her husband was a wannabe wunderkind with no sense of his audience and taught it like a graduate seminar, using complex critical jargon that aimed way too high, and his students were reportedly miserable. The couple moved on anyway, as people often did because more prestigious schools than SUM made better offers.

Before that, it had been variously staffed by professors in Religious Studies, Sociology, or History, but in my version, it was a cross-genre survey from 1900 to the present, assigning both popular and literary authors from all kinds of backgrounds, like Orthodox Faye Kellerman to agnostic Phillip Roth. Most of the students were non-Jews and had very little insight into Judaism or Jewish history either in general or in America, so I supplied lots of background, which I enjoyed. My book list was diverse, discussions were fruitful, student papers strong, and my evaluations were some of the best I'd ever received. I was sure I'd be re-assigned, since it was so very successful.

"This is a hit job," I said. "On *me*." That was obvious. But it also felt like part of something much larger and more insidious.

Though he hadn't put down his fork, Stefan had stopped even trying to eat and fallen into a brooding silence, easy enough for a classic introvert, but I could hear his breath coming quick and shallow. Even Marco noticed he was upset, and sat close by him now, rubbing his head against Stefan's leg like a cat. Stefan reached down absentmindedly with his free hand to scratch the top of Marco's head. "I hate administrators," he brought out, eyes closed.

I agreed. In our time at SUM, we had seen way too many administrators across the university engage in what you could only call perverse tinkering. Majors and minors, programs, and whole colleges would be ripped apart, reorganized, or even scrapped. Buzzwords swarmed around each supposed improvement: "metamorphosis," "outreach," "rationalizing," "incentivizing," and the now-sacred standby: "diversity." It was all just an exercise in arrogance, fancy words that masked old-time chest thumping.

Sometimes only a few years passed before another administrator decided to reverse the change and trumpet a new set of buzzwords, creating more upheaval, even more confusion, and simmering resentment. It was as if they were applying the classic line about relationships from *Annie Hall* and had taken it as a mantra: "A relationship is like a shark.... It has to constantly move forward or it dies." They were supposedly moving forward as if it were vital not to stop, but it was usually just movement for its own sake.

"They can't really create," Stefan said scornfully. "They don't want to. Underneath, they want to destroy." He set the fork by his plate as if laying something important to rest. At moments like these, he had the charisma of an actor whose smallest gesture could mean worlds.

I thought of the immortal line in *Conan* where he's asked to describe what is best in life and Conan intones, "To crush your enemies. See them driven before you. And to hear the lamentations of their women." SUM was riddled with vengeful, single-minded berserkers like Conan, only they wore expensive suits and shirts whose cuffs were embroidered with their initials—and they spouted untruths as easily as they straightened their designer ties.

Since I joined the faculty at SUM, our own department had been overhauled multiple times. It went from offering rigorous survey courses which grounded students in literary history but were supposedly "retrograde," on to "genre tracks," and now almost everything was taught through a lens of race, gender, class, or sexuality in a way that seemed to diminish books themselves. But that was of course temporary—something new was bound to be introduced in yet another soul-crushing department meeting. Well, it was up to the department's academic advisor to explain to English majors how things worked, not my job. I just kept my head down and taught whatever I was assigned to teach in the way I wanted to, worked with students in independent study and on senior theses, and tried to ignore the irrational, sometimes frantic need for change that swept campus over and over like a fever that hemorrhaged common sense.

The ultimate effect of curriculum instability at SUM was to keep faculty in a constant state of anxiety: Where would the axe fall next?

"Napoléon's email was really something," I said, determined to finish my now-cool frittata. I forked some of it and managed to get it down.

"I know. Parasites…" Stefan shook his head, his mouth turned down at the ends.

"Parasite" is a classic anti-Semitic trope historically used with great effect by Nazis and Jew-haters everywhere. Finding it in Napoléon's email was grotesque and truly frightening. I'd grown up on the liberal, heavily Jewish Upper West Side in New York and hadn't experienced direct anti-Semitism in the city, though I knew it was lurking there. It was only since coming to mid-Michigan that I had felt like an actual minority. SUM was a public institution and couldn't stop fervent young local preachers from planting themselves on campus to shout doom and gloom and damnation at bridges, and anywhere else they could corral a crowd. I'd more than once heard Jews consigned to Hell by these pimpled, fulminating, red-faced evangelists.

I sat there drinking way too much coffee, contemplating our options.

Could anyone stop Napoléon? Because the course was only an elective for students outside of our own department, I couldn't imagine any other department chair caring one way or the other. What recourse did we have to a decision like this? The Faculty Senate was a joke and had no power. The dean of our college hated me and Stefan for historic reasons—like the time we had basically accused him of murder. And Napoléon was the darling of SUM's president, so appealing to President Yubero would be pointless. Even well-meaning "outsiders" might dismiss this as just an internal issue.

Jewish Studies couldn't help us either. It wasn't a department, it was just an available program on campus. De-centralized, Jewish Studies had no real home and drew faculty from varying disciplines, which meant it lacked clout. The tiny, soft-spoken, well-meaning director Maureen Moskowitz wasn't very assertive either. The loss of one course wouldn't make much difference to the Jewish Studies program overall, and even if she thought it did, I couldn't imagine her being able to change Napoléon's mind.

"What about Hillel, or, uh, community action?" Stefan asked.

I guessed he'd dismissed Maureen as I had. The local Hillel, staffed by a rabbi, was a branch of the national organization that supported Jewish students, offered Shabbat and holiday meals, along with weekly prayer services. It wasn't exactly flourishing.

"I don't know. It's hard to get students motivated about anything besides their own classes and partying. You know that."

The small local Jewish community along with the even smaller Jewish students' group was typically busy dealing with anti-Semitic graffiti on campus, and protesting right-wing Jew-hating speakers when someone invited them. They also were involved in fighting the international boycott on Israel which SUM had thankfully not joined, so trying to salvage one course didn't seem likely to generate much interest or excitement. And though I didn't bring it up, I wondered if Stefan's conversion would muddy anything we tried to organize or encourage others to organize.

Stefan had never truly felt at home as a Jew, partly because his Holocaust survivor parents had hidden his true identity from him for years. Though I myself couldn't identify with Jesus or anything connected to the Catholic Church, here in Michigan Stefan had for the first time in his life felt spiritually grounded, at a Catholic Mass. It all spoke to him deeply and he'd ended up writing a best-selling memoir about his midlife upheaval. He received some of the best reviews of his life for that book, perhaps because it was such a surprise, and because it was so controversial. He had even been compared by many reviewers to one of his favorite authors, Joan Didion. For a while he had to hire someone to field all the invitations for speaking engagements, there were just so many of them.

Both his conversion and subsequent memoir had been completely unexpected for me, and Stefan worried that I wouldn't be able to accept him adopting a new faith, but how could I do anything else when it made him so happy? No, that wasn't the right word: it soothed some deep anguish in him that nothing else ever touched. But that was in our own little world. Stepping out of it, taking up a specifically Jewish cause now risked making the cause itself controversial if he were involved. Stefan's conversion memoir may have sold almost a million copies in hardcover, but despite his publisher's frantic demands for him to do talk shows, he had kept a low profile. "The book is selling itself," he kept saying, and he was right.

Again, as if he'd been following my thoughts or thinking them in parallel, Stefan brought out slowly, "I'm not the best person to take this on, even if we could figure out a plan."

Jewish media had for the most part ignored his book, but he and his publisher had received hate mail when the book came out. He was persona non grata in most Jewish venues, likely to be insulted and possibly even attacked as a traitor to his people—another reason to avoid public appearances. I understood that, given all the forced conversions in Jewish history, and of course the Catholic Church had played its own historic role in persecuting Jews as well as fostering anti-Semitism, but I also understood that a quarter of all Americans change their religious affiliation at some point in their lives.

So I would have to proceed alone, at least publicly, if I did try to reverse Napoléon's decision—but wouldn't it look like self-interest more than anything else? There was no one else Jewish besides me in the department who could conceivably join my protest. Even if there had been other Jewish professors, there was so much endemic turf war, the future of the course just wouldn't matter.

I reached over and squeezed Stefan's hand, which of course got Marco's notice, and he now wanted me to pay him attention, too, and I did, slipping off the counter stool to sit cross-legged in front of him. He rolled onto his back for a belly rub. Having him in our lives was a blessing: he reduced things to elementals. Playing with him, feeding him, walking him, watching his dreams with full-on twitching legs and nose and an occasional soft *whoop-whoop* took me completely out of myself. Most of the time.

Stefan said gently, "I know you had your heart set on teaching Jewish-American Literature again. It would make you really happy to teach it after everything that happened."

Marco had fallen asleep on his back, legs sprawled, and it was so quiet in the room that I could hear a slight rasp as he breathed in and out. I sat back down at the counter, tried my coffee and got up to reheat it in the microwave.

Everything that happened. Such bland words.

We hadn't really figured out a way to talk about the events that had driven us from our home, that had made both of us terrified we were going to die. Twice. Did we call it the Siege? The Shootings? The Arrest? The Trouble? Maybe the Troubles, plural, because it had felt so enormous and endless.

Not being able to fix a label on that terrible time made it worse. I hadn't said this yet, but I felt as if back in the spring we had been hit by a meteor, and were left with a gigantic crater in our lives whose depth and size we might never truly fathom, no matter how long we kept walking its perimeter. Ironically, we were both more popular with students than ever, some of them clamoring to work with us individually, and the media hadn't let us go either. We were still getting emails and calls from journalists and bloggers to see if we had "reflections to share" and wanting to know if we had "found closure." I always hung up on calls like that and deleted the emails because the word itself, *closure*, made me feel dirty. Charlie Chaplin supposedly said that "Life is a tragedy when seen in close-up, but a comedy in long-shot." If only Stefan and I could see it from a distance and hold on to that long view Chaplin had mentioned. Maybe then we could at least laugh sometimes about it…even if only in a sick joke that wouldn't make anyone but us laugh.

"Napoléon reminds me of that *Vanity Fair* article, you know the one I mean," Stefan said. I did. It was recent and unforgettable. The author, in exploring French anti-Semitism, reported that attacks on Jewish schools, on synagogues, assaults on Jews in the Métro and parks, and even rapes had doubled in the past year. We'd both read it more than once, disbelieving that the country we had visited with so much pleasure so many times now seemed possessed by demons. The day before this past year's Bastille Day, crowds had attacked a synagogue in Paris and it took hours for everyone inside to be safely evacuated. Shouts of "Death to the Jews!" were commonplace in mob violence and street demonstrations—and it all culminated with the massacre at the kosher market after staff at the satirical magazine *Charlie Hebdo* were slaughtered by Islamist militants. France's glorious art, culture, literature, philosophy, cuisine were nothing but playthings to be crushed by maniacs with giant boots.

Not surprisingly, thousands of French Jews were emigrating every year now.

The article had horrified me. I'd kept the issue, but under a pile of other magazines. Throwing it out had somehow felt disloyal, but I didn't want to ever come across it accidentally. Stefan having mentioned *Vanity Fair* brought that tide of ugliness into our gleaming kitchen, spreading it at our feet like toxic sludge.

"Do you think Napoléon is like that? A crazy Jew-hater?"

"*Au fond*, maybe." Down deep. "There's no way of knowing for sure. But we'll have to be really careful around him from now on."

"How? How exactly do we do that?" My tone must have agitated Marco, since he whimpered in his sleep.

Stefan shrugged. "We could get lucky and he might move on or SUM could get rid of him. There's no such thing as loyalty here."

"Too true."

Stefan went on as if he hadn't heard me: "He could get run down on campus by some student biking and texting at the same time. Or hit by one of those drivers in town who don't signal their turns." He paused and shut his eyes as if picturing one of those fates. "I can pray for it."

I had read somewhere that in Stefan's new faith, converts were considered to have special grace for a time and their prayers were viewed as very powerful. I didn't know if there was an expiration date, or if prayers that harsh were even appropriate, but it was as good a bet as any.

I told him, "Go right ahead. What have we got to lose?"

Part II

9

A FRIEND IN ACADEMIA who loves teaching as much as I do and has been at a university even longer than I have calls our world "crapademia." That's because we have to put up with so much bureaucratic and administrative crap which distracts us from our teaching, our writing, our research. It's a malign hot-house world that can make you sweat the way Humphrey Bogart does in *The Big Sleep* when he's hired by General Sternwood. That desiccated, cold-blooded old man could have stood in for any number of administrators at SUM.

And certainly for Napoléon, who was creepily (crappily?) treating us like servants or worse. I was appalled to get an email from him after our meeting, thanking me for my "cooperation." That choice of words meant that he felt certain I would pick the guest author for the Nick Hoffman Fellowship he was pushing on me. Didn't it?

Stefan wasn't so sure. "The email's really vague."

"But I *wasn't* cooperating. Not at all. It's either a warning, like telling me he *expects* me to cooperate—or he just ignored what I was saying."

Stefan cocked his head at me the way Marco did when we used a word he didn't know.

"It's not like I said a whole lot anyway." Despite the kind of person I had been hearing Napoléon was and despite how he had treated me in our meeting, I hated thinking that the first time I'd met with the new department chair, I might have come across as difficult or even obstructionist. I know I can sometimes be quip-happy or easily angered, but for the most part I think of myself as easygoing. It clearly wasn't going to be easy working with Napoléon. To me, the email was a clear, firm reminder that he was the one running the department, even if I had my own tiny bailiwick within it. And unfortunately, I didn't have figurative pots of boiling oil to dump on the heads of enemies if they tried to scale the castle walls.

Napoléon's next move was even more startling. He announced via yet another departmental email that there would be a mandatory day-long team-building "retreat experience" this coming Sunday, at a retreat center just south of campus. He urged faculty with plans for Sunday to cancel them "to do the work we need to do to move SUM forward." The subject heading of his email was "Urgent Empathy."

"Is that like Urgent Care?" I asked.

Stefan grinned.

"And 'mandatory'? Can he do that?" I asked. "Isn't that against university by-laws or a violation of the code of teaching responsibility? Nobody's ever told us to meet on a weekend. He has no right to demand we show up."

Stefan stopped smiling, then shrugged like someone in an authoritarian state submitting to one more invasion of privacy, one more loss of rights, one more erosion of freedom. That shrug said that Napoléon could do anything. "I've been there for a spiritual retreat, remember?"

I did. Stefan had done that after all the craziness we'd experienced at SUM, but the effect wasn't lasting. It had helped just a bit, because he was only "so happy for a time," as Mary says in *Long Day's Journey into Night*, a play seared into my memory because we had seen it twice at the Stratford Festival in Ontario. It starred one of Canada's great actresses, Martha Henry, and her performance had left us stunned and unable to leave our seats at the end. Thinking of O'Neill's dark and beautiful play, and remembering its impact, I had drifted off, but came back at Stefan's prompting.

"I know I described the setting to you," Stefan said. "It's really beautiful, you feel far from civilization. Sheltered. There's a small lake and really gorgeous blue spruce and oaks and hemlocks, gravel walks, wildflowers, a shrubbery maze. Though I'm not sure what it would be like in the fall...."

"You seriously want to go?" I asked. "The department doesn't need team building or Walden's Pond, it needs respect, it needs self-respect, it needs—" Words failed me, and that doesn't happen very often.

"Nick. It's not like the retreat center is in another town or anything, and we didn't have plans for Sunday."

"I can make plans!"

"If we don't go, we're on his shit list."

I sighed, because Stefan was right, and I knew it. But *team building*? Was Napoléon for real? What universe was he living in? He was heading up an English department, not a FedEx Office store. And why call it a "retreat experience"? Wasn't a retreat an experience already? Pairing the words made it all sound kind of bogus. I suspected we would not truly have time for reflection and insight, but that this was just going to be a glorified department meeting, with some godawful agenda he was preparing to surprise us with. The last thing I would have called Napoléon was someone who cared about team spirit, or empathy of any kind.

And I'm sure I felt like many other members of the department, old and new. We worked together during the week or worked in the same place and our paths crossed in the mail room and elsewhere enough to make it feel like we were colleagues who saw each other a lot. So why would we want to spend a block of time getting in touch with our feelings?

Maybe other departments at SUM had different dynamics, but I'd never felt that ours was especially convivial. Yes, there were the inevitable parties at someone's home to kick off the start of the academic year and bless its end, but people chatted with one or two friends and there wasn't much change in the groupings until someone left the university for another job, retired, or passed on to the next world. I had tried to make more friends in the department when we first came to SUM, but becoming involved in recurring crime solving and being a mere bibliographer were both giant strikes against me. I was bad luck, apparently, and also tainted as a scholar. Years ago at one of the first department parties we attended, a tweedy, pipe-smoking, shambling Milton professor who had since retired told me without preamble, "I can't imagine you're going to have a distinguished career." And he wasn't even drunk.

SUM had started as an agricultural college, something I usually forgot until I drove to the southern edge of campus and passed enormous university-owned farms, marveling at how close the crops, barns, cows, and horses were to our subdivision. It was a radical shift from the heavily built-up northern side of campus, heightened this time by the perfect Michigan fall day with clear, light blue sky and trees everywhere just starting to turn, smaller maples leading the way. The ride was a short one, but I felt we were going much further away.

To get there, we had to pass the big, fancy gun range where I had practiced with a Ruger .22 back in the spring and done much better than my instructor or I would've guessed for a first-timer. I tried pushing all that from my mind as we pulled up to the St. Thomas Retreat Center whose stone-pillared gates were planted with colorful annuals at their base. An ugly statue of the saint, I supposed, stood guard among the blooms.

"Saint Thomas," I said, "is he the one who doubted?"

Stefan slowed down as we rode in his Lexus RX 350 along a gravel drive lined with weeping willows. "That's him. He doubted the Resurrection."

"Is this a statement? Does Napoléon want the department to be reborn? Does he think we need a conversion experience?"

"That's Saint Paul."

"Sorry."

"You know, Nick, sometimes there's no hidden meaning to things, no irony."

"You're a writer, how can you say that?"

Stefan shrugged and we pulled up into a fairly empty parking lot ringed by a handful of gleaming log cabin–style buildings.

"Great place for a Paul Bunyan conference," I said as we got out of the car.

"Stop. That's the bookstore," Stefan said pointing to one cabin, "and that's Administration, and the other small ones are dorms."

"Are we supposed to check in?"

"I don't know."

The lawns around us were perfectly groomed and the air was heavy with the sweet, earthy tang of freshly cut grass. Concrete vases of white, purple, and red mums flanked the doors of each cabin, somewhat softening the rustic feel.

Stefan headed to the main building, which had large picture windows flanking the carved door.

I hesitated for a moment. We were early and I was mildly annoyed. That was one of the small continuing conflicts in our relationship: Stefan preferred being early, while I was happy to be ten minutes late since that was what I considered good enough. Sadly, I knew this mini-struggle had played out between my parents when I was growing up and it was firmly imprinted on me and colored how Stefan and I dealt with time.

My skepticism about our venue faded, though, as I caught up with him and we entered together. A vast room spread out before us, with the feel of a hunting lodge though there weren't any trophies. The massive cathedral ceiling had skylights which allowed warm-feeling light to filter down onto the huge slate-trimmed fireplace, while a bevy of fat, cozy-looking red plaid chairs and sofas that invited conversation and relaxation spread across the black, red, and yellow terrazzo floor. The walls were gleaming oiled pine, and reddish-brown stoneware vases with white roses and pink-and-white Peruvian lilies were perched on various tables and shelves.

It was surprisingly classy, spoiled by a white plastic banner with red-and-black letters reading URGENT EMPATHY that hung on the mantelpiece like a silly Christmas garland.

I tried to ignore it and surveyed the rest of the space. There were doorways on each side with signs overhead; the one on the right led to the dining hall and kitchen, the one on the left to restrooms and some kind of lounge.

Off to one side was a large refectory table piled high with croissants on trays in front of a phalanx of labeled coffee urns, which were flanked by cups and mugs as well as Badoit bottled water. It all felt very welcoming and relaxed—though I had my doubts about the cross hanging high over the fireplace's black-and-gold granite mantel. The French are so unreligious, "secularity" being one of their guiding ideals, so why had Napoléon picked this particular retreat center?

I went off to the men's room and was even more impressed because it looked very contemporary, with "jet air" hand-dryers, subdued lighting over the mirrors, walls of small white quartz bricks, glistening red-and-white granite flooring, and a long matching counter with large white bowls instead of recessed sinks. A jar of potpourri on the counter filled the room with something soothing yet spicy.

"Wait till you see the men's room," I told Stefan when I rejoined him. "It's not rustic at all—it's like something in a pricey restaurant."

"I know. I've been here before, remember?"

"Nick! Stefan! How nice to see you!" Napoléon swept forward from wherever he'd been lurking and I was afraid he was going to hug us, but instead he sort of ushered us to the table as if we were the first customers of a newly opened bistro. "You must try the croissants, I had them flown in from a wonderful bakery in New York whose chef is, of course, French. The coffee is Carte Noire and certainly you appreciate French coffee, why shouldn't you? Though there's also Dallmayr which you know is from Munich and quite lovely. Oh, the butter is Belgian. Nick, *je sais bien que toi, t'aimes la cuisine belge.*"

I almost replied that yes, I did like Belgian food, and were we going to have waffles, too, but restrained myself.

Everything was clearly labeled, down to the Bonne Maman preserves in a dozen flavors and I was impressed.

Stefan was very quiet in the way that only introverts can be—like a turtle pulling back into its shell. I could tell he was not affected by Napoléon's charm barrage as he got himself a plate, knife, and croissant, spread some butter on the side of the plate, set that down to pour coffee into a cup with SUM's logo on it, picked up his food and headed to one of the sofas. I followed suit, and the sofa was well-cushioned without being quicksand.

I was surprised by Napoléon's attire. Stefan and I had decided to wear blazers, buttoned-down Oxford shirts, and dress slacks because the new chair was always so impeccably dressed. But today, Napoléon was in what I guessed was Parisian Casual: a white cashmere T-shirt under a black shirt jacket, black chinos, and black brogues without socks. He looked like a fashion model and I felt overdressed. Was that his intent, to surprise the faculty and throw people off balance?

Now, I was used to the typical dismal refreshments of an SUM event, so that made the coffee taste even more delicious, and the croissants were to die for. They couldn't have been more buttery or flaky. But when Napoléon sat opposite us and crossed his stylishly clad legs I felt we were bizarrely being treated as the most fascinating guests at a chic cocktail party—anywhere but Michiganapolis. That sensation blossomed even more when he genially asked us, "How are your classes going?" and gave the impression of being utterly devoted to finding out how we felt. It wasn't small talk or filler either—Napoléon *appeared* to be sincere.

We both mumbled something, Napoléon nodding his approval and encouragement.

After a silence, Stefan went on, "I've got some really good writers. In fiction and especially creative nonfiction."

"That must be encouraging," Napoléon brought out as if imagining himself teaching a class like that. "Tell me, as a memoirist, where do you stand on the issue of memory and truth in a memoir?"

Stefan put his coffee down and I could read his surprise that Napoléon would ask something so informed: it was the big debate in the creative nonfiction community, with rival journals and conferences, and controversy as bitter as the fight between political parties. Stefan's signs were subtle: he leaned forward, clasping his hands, elbows on his thighs. That was his "tell." He was taking the question with utter seriousness.

"The mind isn't a DVR and memoir isn't journalism," Stefan said. "I advise my students to strive for *emotional* truth."

"A noble aim. But wouldn't different truths emerge from the same event, because they are ipso facto emotional? What does one do with competing memories?"

Before I could figure out if that was sarcastic or not, I heard cars pulling up outside.

"By the way," Napoléon said as he stood, "I've been thinking of having the department honor you with a conference of some kind, seeing that your work has made such a valuable contribution to Literature. I've been canvassing the other creative writing faculty for ideas. We'll talk soon."

Stefan turned to me, eyes wide, and mouthed, "What the hell?"

I turned to see that the next person to walk into the hall was swarthy Carson Karageorgevich, the towering, fiftyish head of Film Studies, who had never been pleasant to me except when he wanted something. He looked glum, signaled to me and stage whispered, "Let's talk!"

I thought, *Great*. He was followed by other faculty in twos and threes, the heavy scent of cut grass wafting in after them, and soon the room was buzzing with over two dozen of us, not quite the full departmental roster yet. Faculty seemed anywhere from annoyed to vexed that we were doing this—whatever *this* was. And when people caught sight of the URGENT EMPATHY banner, they all grimaced in one way or another.

Napoléon left us to greet the new arrivals, threw his arms wide like a Sunday preacher filled with the Holy Spirit, and cried "Welcome, *friends!*" in a voice and manner worthy of a stage actor. I couldn't help picturing him as the Chorus opening Shakespeare's *Henry V*.

"Please help yourself to a continental breakfast before we begin." They didn't get the same little spiel we had, but then it wasn't necessary since the labels were clear and everyone would recognize at once that this wasn't a typical lining up at the trough.

Free food and good coffee were quickly occupying more than half of the crowd, others were inspecting the large, open room or inspecting their peers suspiciously. But my colleagues seemed as surly as teenagers grounded for breaking their curfew, and the door kept opening and admitting more faculty arriving against their will.

Carson surged towards me as I walked over to pour myself more coffee, grabbed hold of my arm, almost dragging me away from everyone else. The rumor in the department was that he gambled heavily in casinos all across Michigan, though nobody had ever claimed to see him in one.

I'd always found him weird and furtive, and how he was acting right now wasn't making me like him more. His specialty was Grade-B horror films from the 1940s and 1950s like *Cat People* and *The Beast with Five Fingers,* which was ironic, since he was a large, shambling, tormented-looking man who could have been the brother of Lon Chaney, Jr. in 1941's *The Wolfman.* He even wore the same kind of loose, boxy, ill-fitting suits. But surprisingly, despite his louche appearance and his perpetual salt-and-pepper stubble that gave him the air of a vagrant, he had some kind of remote claim to the defunct Serbian throne. There was apparently a Karageorgevich royal dynasty, but if it was ever restored to power, I doubted he'd make much of an impression on people hungry for a leader—or even a figurehead.

We were in a corner of the room in front of a colorful period poster of the Mackinac Bridge, one of the world's longest suspension bridges, connecting Michigan's Upper and Lower Peninsulas.

"Nicholas," Carson said, ignoring as always that my given name was actually Nick—because my parents had both been reading Hemingway's Nick Adams stories before I was born. "I have a marvelous idea for your fellowship. Why not invite David Ebershoff?"

"Because of *The Danish Girl*?"

I was intrigued. That book was one of my favorite novels of the past ten years and Stefan used it in fiction writing classes because the characterization and setting were so deftly done.

"Yes! The movie's getting rave reviews, and I think I could swing it for Eddie Redmayne to come to campus, too. He's a friend of a stage director I know in London. Think of the publicity, think of the sponsors across the university."

He was right, especially about all the different SUM departments and programs that would want to put money into creating and promoting such a unique program that would be quite expensive. Having any kind of movie star or best-selling author on campus was sure to generate publicity and bring students flocking to the various events. But Carson came off as more frantic than enthusiastic, and why the hell did he have to literally corner me to push his idea? His green eyes were a bit crazed, his forehead beaded with sweat, and there was a slight tremor in his large dark hands. I felt as cornered as if he was going to throttle me.

My silence must have betrayed suspicion because he lowered his voice and said, "I need something big like this. I'm coming up for promotion to full professor and I'm getting nowhere with my new book, I can't find a publisher. And even if I could, Napoléon despises me for some reason. He said he's read all my scholarly articles and he thought they were pedestrian and undistinguished.

That someone like me didn't deserve to be promoted or even head Film Studies, and while he was chair, he would oppose my promotion and look for someone else to head the program. Jesus, Nick, I felt like Bob Cratchit being dressed down by Scrooge. I need to get promoted, Nick, *I need your help.*"

He sounded desperate, almost tearful, which put me off even more. The *Danish Girl* project might be a great idea, but even if it could be arranged, how would that be enough to guarantee Carson a promotion when he was reviewed if Napoléon was so implacable? Besides, publications were what the university worshipped. That, and bringing in grant money. And why should I do Carson any kind of favor? How did I know he wouldn't try to take all the credit in some way, given his desperation?

"Don't fuck my chances," he said, looming over me, looking taller than ever. "Don't treat me like Napoléon does or you'll regret it." And he lumbered off like a wounded bear.

10

I STOOD THERE for a while taking it all in, wondering, too, what Napoléon had in mind about "honoring" Stefan's success. Was that for real? Why hadn't we heard anything about it until now? Had he asked the other creative writing faculty not to say anything? I didn't feel comfortable raising it with anyone.

Napoléon wasn't making the rounds as I would have expected, and he wasn't even in the room just then.

While not everyone in the department had obeyed Napoléon's summons, everyone who was present at the retreat center looked surprised by the good food and equally good coffee. I kept hearing comments about both waft my way. It might have been somehow connected to the acoustics of a room with such a high peaked ceiling.

But that was just an overlay, because the general mood was still sullen, even hostile. In all the years that Stefan and I had taught in the department, no chair had ever called any kind of meeting "mandatory."

And despite the unexpected, superior quality of the refreshments, faculty had quickly reverted to form after arriving, clustering in the same groups they would be in if this were a department gathering anywhere off campus. Carson Karageorgevich had joined the hipster-looking Film Studies dudes who looked both half his age and like they worked at a Brooklyn start-up. The whole group could have made a cool United Colors of Benetton ad since everyone but Carson was Hispanic, Asian, or Black. They had brought diversity to the department, but not a huge spike in enrollments, which was the real intention as opposed to anything altruistic.

Ciska Balanchine was part of a low-voiced group of nearly ten younger and older women faculty who'd been glancing over at Napoléon before with hooded eyes. She looked very dramatic in a red pants suit with a Chinese collar, and a large gold chain around her neck, just this side of hip hop bling. I wondered if she was telling them about Napoléon having sexually harassed her, and in vivid detail. Or if they were sharing stories of harassment here and at other universities where they had taught. They tended to be somewhat separatist, understandably. But I'd heard one of them, Jasmine Alinejad, say to someone on her phone, "Men aren't very intelligent in *any* sense of the word, everyone knows that," when I passed her on a campus bridge one day.

When Jasmine first arrived at SUM, Stefan had left an auto-graphed copy of his memoir in her mailbox as a welcoming gesture, but she'd never thanked him or even acknowledged it. Weeks later, she did publish a review on her popular blog in which she attacked all religions as hateful, oppressive garbage and called Stefan both "deluded" and "sublimely ignorant." She went even further and called his conversion "cultural appropriation."

Her comments were so over-the-top that Stefan had actually chuckled when he read them. "It's like I personally insulted her by writing the book and giving her a copy!" Then he added darkly, "I could always ask her for the book back since she didn't like it. It's not inscribed, just signed. I attached a typed note because you know how bad my handwriting is."

"Are you serious?"

He laughed. "Of course not! But it's fun to imagine...."

"Yeah, but the blog she'd write wouldn't be much fun and she'd probably start a Twitter campaign to diss you or maybe even launch a Facebook group of Stefan haters."

Whenever Jasmine saw him on campus or in town, she scowled. I thought she might be homophobic without daring to admit it; Stefan believed she was jealous of how much he had published. Alinejad had only published a memoir, which was just a chapbook, one of those small paperback pamphlets with tiny print runs that many academic authors use to try building a career. Stefan's books had almost all been brought out by major New York publishers like Knopf, Scribner's, and Doubleday. That, of course, made him a tool of the patriarchy.

Forlorn again, Atticus Doyle was skulking with a morose group of adjuncts who might have been the farmhands rubbing elbows with the gentry in an old-fashioned rural English Christmas. He was, I thought, immensely photogenic despite his mood, but they looked like dejected high school losers: stressed out and browbeaten. Why had they even bothered to come? Did they think Napoléon was going to be their liberator just because he was opening up course assignments?

Viktor Dahlberg was off by himself, biting a fingernail and brooding in a chair by the window, wearing a funereal-looking black suit. My cousin Sharon had dated a Swedish-American engineer once and said, "Don't be fooled by the talk about how sensible Swedes are and how they value *lagom*, just having enough. You mix those genes, that culture, with something like American anyone-can-be-president jive and you get loony tunes, trust me. Too much inner torment." I felt sorry for Viktor and briefly considered going over to say hello, but his silence was too Gothic.

Over by the door, Roberto Robustelli was regaling half a dozen people with some apparently hilarious anecdote, as exuberant as an emcee at a comedy club. His story must have been pretty risqué because a few of them covered their mouths when they laughed as if in shock or embarrassment, and one or two were blushing.

Robustelli was dressed unusually for him in a royal blue suit, blue shirt, and purple tie—he looked like a TV news anchor at a very small local station.

After grabbing another coffee, I rejoined Stefan, feeling drained by Carson's peculiar plea. No one had sat by Stefan while I was talking to Carson, probably since Stefan was known as unlikely to be stirred into small talk. He was a good listener, though. When I sat down, the conversational volume in the room had risen enough for me to tell Stefan sotto voce about Carson's asking me to help him bring David Ebershoff to campus and not be overheard.

"It's a great idea," he said, "but wow, Carson sounds weirder than ever."

"We don't need this retreat, we need group therapy."

Stefan frowned. "You'd want to be sharing your inner life with this crowd?"

"No, I mean most everyone here needs the attention of a *group* of therapists."

He chuckled.

But I shook my head. "Why don't I like these people more?"

Stefan put an arm around my shoulders and gave me a squeeze. "Who says you have to? They're colleagues, they're a motley group, they don't have to be your buddies." That was easy for him to say. He could be happy not talking to anyone but me (or Marco) for days on end. He lived inside himself so much of the time that he reminded me of Katharine Hepburn saying in an interview that she didn't drink, because cold sober, she found herself absolutely fascinating.

"Do you think Napoléon was bullshitting us with that conference idea to honor you?" I asked Stefan.

He looked dubious. "I'm selling plenty of books, getting fan mail, I don't need to have more than that."

"But how could you say no?"

He shook his head. "Easy. I don't need more publicity. I don't want it. My books speak for themselves."

The door opened behind us and Heino and Jonas Bratfisch, brand-new hires in Digital Humanities, hurried in. They surged right past the coffee and croissants and half a dozen people without seeming to notice anything. They instantly huddled together on a settee near Stefan and me and started furiously working away on their phones and tablets at the same time. Slim, blond, blue-eyed, they were German-born wunderkinds—and identical twins—right out of graduate school. Napoléon had been the driving force in hiring them, though he had no background in Digital Humanities and had never said anything in favor of it—not in public, anyway. Watching the twins' thumbs whiz across screens, I wondered what kind of crowd-sourcing, 24/7 project they were involved in right now, and how large and far-flung their network of scholars was?

And I wondered why, as adults, they dressed alike: both of them were wearing red sneakers, red skinny jeans, and black turtlenecks. I could rarely tell them apart and if I wrote fiction, I would definitely want to work them into a short story. They were handsome, enigmatic, and curiously asexual. I'd never seen them talk to anyone else and as far as I could tell, they barely talked to one another, which gave me the creeps. Was their aloofness something cultural? Was it their unwillingness to put down any sort of roots because they saw SUM as a launching pad for better positions at a more prestigious university?

Maybe something more sinister was going on with them.... Up until recently, I had never succumbed to conspiratorial thinking, but guys like that could easily be spies for the administration, ready to root out anything or anyone unsavory. What if they were part of that secret campus committee I'd heard rumors about and they had already hacked everyone in the department...or were going to?

Like many professors of my generation, I did not have a high opinion of Digital Humanities (DH), which had been the hot new thing in academia for several years now, and was getting major grant money across the country. DH boosters compared its impact to the invention of the printing press, Europe's discovery of the New World, The Industrial Revolution, the coming of the iPhone, you name it. One of the professors hyping it had actually said in print that Digital Humanities could abolish student essays: "Why must writing, especially writing that captures critical thinking, be composed of words? Why not images? Why not sound? Why not objects?"

Those were questions too ridiculous for me *not* to have memorized them. And if pushed, I could sling some of the buzzwords in the field like "literary text mining," "geolocation extraction," and "network analysis"—but none of it touched me.

The projects I'd looked at from "digital humanists" basically aggregated "data" in literature and found patterns that weren't very interesting or surprising—like one study I'd read that showed the absence of positive images of Jews in German literature during the Nazi years. That one really put the "Duh!" in dud. But embattled humanities departments were snatching up these DH scholars to stave off collapse, look relevant, and angle for grant money. If they could give studying literature the sheen of science, surely it would have more clout and be more respected.

"You know," I said to Stefan, "for guys who supposedly believe in the democratization of knowledge, Jonas and Heino sure act like they're better than everyone else."

"Maybe their English is spotty?"

"Are you kidding? They're worse than Napoléon—they speak a dozen languages between them. Plus Digiteze."

"Why not give them a break, Nick? They're new here and probably shy. They're just different, and you know they say that lots of twins have a special relationship."

"They're spooky is what they are. And arrogant. They look at the rest of us as if we were lesser beings, I just feel that. Hell, I know it. They think they're the future and we're the past."

"Well, they're probably tired of having to explain what they do to people who think the Humanities don't need to be digital." He shrugged. "They don't bother me. I'm used to critics acting as if I'm nobody because I write books instead of writing books *about* books."

"I'm tired of them calling scholars like me 'sleepwalkers' and 'superannuated.' I read that in some DH manifesto those guys have on their joint web site. It says everybody in the Humanities should be parsing code, building software, creating databases. I am not a programmer, and Literature," I continued emphatically, "Literature is *not* data."

Stefan crossed his arms and considered that. "Everything is data now. Maybe you should encourage them to work on Edith Wharton and see what boring discoveries they could make." He winked at me.

I know he said that to cheer me out of my sudden bad mood, but before I could respond, I realized that Napoléon had returned to us and now was standing in front of the fireplace, serenely going over notes at a lectern that had just been brought in by what I guessed was a retreat staffer as nondescript as one of those black-suited scenery movers in a Kabuki drama.

Napoléon clapped his hands theatrically. "Friends! Let us begin!"

There was a lot of clattering of plates and mugs as people gradually drifted to the chairs and sofas scattered about the room.

But before he could welcome us or say anything at all, Roberto Robustelli rushed to the lectern, threw his arms around Napoléon and kissed him on both cheeks. Eyes wide, Napoléon tried to pull away, but Robustelli held on tight and rocked him back and forth as if they were long-lost relatives meeting at an airport.

"Maestro! We all have to thank you for the opportunity and the blessing to serve you and, of course, the university." Keeping one arm firmly around the chair, he waved the other to the room, and said, "Is this man amazing or what? I think we should all take a moment to acknowledge what a great idea this retreat is and how fortunate we are having Napoléon as our new chair. We are truly blessed."

I met Stefan's incredulous glance with my own. The room around us was as silent as outer space.

"Come on, people! Give it up for our terrific new department chair! Give him some love—come on and make some noise!"

Behind me, I heard someone mutter, "Is he angling to oust Ciska as associate chair?"

Applause started somewhat timidly, spread, and then became our version of thunderous. After a few awkward moments, some people even whooped or yelled like they were at a football game. The noise shamed me into compliance, and I felt myself sucked into some alternate universe where Napoléon was our Dear Leader and we were his devoted and dutiful followers.

And then the unimaginable happened: faculty started to rise for a standing ovation. I couldn't resist because there was no place to hide. Stefan joined me after hesitating.

Apparently pleased with having stolen the show before it had begun, Robustelli let Napoléon go, stepped back and applauded him almost prayerfully—he even bowed his head. But just before he did so, I saw a flash of something cunning and spiteful in his eyes. Was he mocking all of us with his flamboyance?

Napoléon's composure returned and now he started applauding Robustelli and then all of us, sweeping the room with his potent movie-star gaze. And he smiled, though I couldn't imagine what he was thinking. Me, I would have been pissed as hell.

Napoléon waved his hands as if scattering a flock of chickens, Robustelli left the lectern to sit down near me, enveloping me with his cologne nimbus, and the room went still, probably in a combination of relief and embarrassment.

"*Friends,*" he said. "My friends, my dear friends, it's so good to see you all here today. You know how much I value your contributions to the department, and I have marvelous news to share. You might be curious as to why we're meeting here, of all places, well, I shall tell you. SUM has just purchased this facility at my recommendation and we are the very first group to take advantage of its delights. Now, it is not Courchevel in the Alps which excels at hosting such gatherings and where we would

have magnificent scenery, more than one Michelin-star restaurant
to dine in, and myriad activities. However, one does what one
can, eh?" And he shrugged in a very Gallic way.

Why was he telling us about something that we weren't able
to experience? How did that help with team building? Stefan
muttered something, but I didn't bother asking what it was.

Viktor Dahlberg called out angrily, "This is a secular institution. Why are we meeting in a room with a cross?"

Anger swept across Napoléon's face like light snow on an
open windy field, but he was quickly his gracious self again.
"That is all being arranged. Once we have a donor who would
like this retreat center to bear his name—or her name—the
statue out front will be removed along with the cross and no
one will have grounds to complain." The last few words came
out clipped and sounded severe despite Napoléon's dramatically
big smile.

There was some murmuring among the faculty and I couldn't
tell if people were annoyed or in agreement.

"Now, then! I'm sure you will all agree that after recent dif-
ficulties and dramatic changes in staffing, our department could
profit from more esprit de corps. I believe that SUM should
begin to stand for Simpatico University of Michigan, a place
where we care for one another and respect each other. It is time
to build a community of trust, caring, and integrity. We can be a
beacon of hope to our college and the entire university."

The silence was profound, and the room crackled with dread.
I'm sure I wasn't the only one thinking we were going to be
compelled to do trust exercises and God knows what else in an
effort to force closeness and community on us.

"And so I've convened you here with that noble goal in
mind. We shall start off with an activity—I believe that's how
you'd phrase it—that will help to break the ice and I promise you
an unforgettable day. We will have time to deeply reflect on the
dynamics of power that undergird this noble institution—and so
much more. I think this is the perfect opportunity for us all to

enter into candid and loving dialogues about how we engage in the process of self-reflection as proud and committed members of the SUM community. Let's also look forward to the ways in which we can effect beautiful and lasting change in our hearts, our classrooms, and the campus at large."

The room was so quiet you might have thought we were a herd of Thomson's gazelles in Africa that was suddenly aware of the presence of a cheetah about to chase us and pounce on the weakest among us.

Napoléon may have been sincere, but he was sounding like a charlatan, a kind of self-help shyster. If we were going to do all this reflection and dialoguing, why wasn't the retreat being led by someone from SUM's counseling center? What qualified Napoléon to be in charge? And what exactly was he after?

"I would like to ask you now to close your eyes."

I heard Ciska behind me stage-whisper, "I'm not doing any bloody guided meditation if that's what he's planning." There was scornful laughter in the room and Napoléon said with what sounded like genuine warmth, "Let me assure you, I have nothing like that in mind. Please, simply close your eyes for one little minute."

I did, and assumed everyone else did, too.

"Now…Think about the most stellar events in your life. Things that happened to you all alone or with others. Personal, professional…something transcendent.…" His voice had softened and I started to wonder if he had misled us and really *was* going to do some sort of guided imagery trip. I could feel my shoulders stiffen at the thought.

Around me there was silence and rustling and the sound of a mug being set down on a table.

Suddenly I started to breathe faster because what was coming to mind wasn't stellar but horrible: *Watching Stefan being falsely arrested and carted away by a SWAT team.*

I felt Stefan's hand on my shoulder. I shook my head as if the images were flies swarming around me, but I kept my eyes shut—and then I gave up when lines of Byron came to me: "In my heart there is a vigil, and these eyes but close to look within." I didn't look up, though.

"Now, then," Napoléon continued. "Is there one of those moments you'd love to have return?"

Stefan surprised me when he said, "Reading my first *New York Times* review."

People applauded, though I wasn't entirely sure why.

"Yes…?" Napoléon prompted.

Stefan was grinning as if he were actually experiencing it all over again. "It was a rave, and even though the book didn't sell well, I cut the review out and had it framed. It was a dream come true and that's when I felt I was a real writer."

"A memorable moment, to be sure," Napoléon said and I studied him for any signs of sarcasm, but he seemed sincere. "Who else has something to share?"

Around the room we went, in a haphazard way, people piping up without being called on to speak, and I was amazed at the openness. My colleagues mentioned meeting their significant other, the birth of a child or adopting one, peak moments in some sport, launching into or finishing a book. Everyone took it seriously and the whole tone of the room shifted: we all seemed more relaxed, happy to be there—or at least less resentful or suspicious.

"Nick, what about you?" Napoléon asked mid-way.

I hesitated and then unaccountably found myself describing the first time Stefan and I drove across the Mackinac Bridge to the Upper Peninsula. "There was snow and ice everywhere, a world of white, and the sun started to set and everything went orange, then red. It was spectacular, and I felt like I was falling in love."

There were murmurs of approval and appreciation from other faculty, especially from native Michiganders so used to anyone from the East Coast being snotty about anything Michiganian. Stefan was nodding in reminiscence of that trip we'd taken to

STATE UNIVERSITY OF MURDER   115

explore the Upper Peninsula for our first spring break at SUM, and I felt surprisingly warm and contented.

Carson unexpectedly apologized: "Everything I can think of is an example of my white privilege, and I'm sorry for that." Head down, he said nothing more. Jasmine and a smattering of other faculty applauded, but stopped when Napoléon said, "Thank you for your honesty, Carson," in a way that sent the message: *"We're not going there."*

The last to speak were the German twins. Jonas said something surprisingly anodyne, even kitschy, about seeing the Statue of Liberty for the first time. Heino surprised everyone: "I have a question since we are all gathered here. Is there a department policy for office sharing?"

Napoléon frowned. "Excuse me?"

Heino spoke more slowly and emphatically: "I would like to know if there is a policy—in this department—for sharing an office?" He was glaring at Napoléon, which I found a little odd.

"I don't understand."

"Is there an official policy? In cases where two people like Jonas and I are forced to share an office?" Heino hadn't yet spoken up in department meetings and his voice was surprisingly deep, which made his questions sound ominous.

Eyes narrowed, Napoléon called out, "Ciska, is there such a thing?"

She said a wavering "No," sounding as puzzled as Napoléon looked, and you could feel tension filling the room like the aroma of an unpleasant candle. It was a truly bizarre moment.

Jonas had shifted away from Heino on their settee. He had turned red and was glaring at his brother. I'd never seen him express any emotion other than extreme concentration before.

Heino went on: "I do not approve of the way that Jonas is sharing the office with me."

Jonas snarled, "Shut your fucking mouth, asshole." And apparently for good measure added what I guessed was a German equivalent: *"Halt die Klappe, Arschloch."*

11

IMAGINE AN EARTHQUAKE out at sea sucking every drop of water from a crowded beach—that's how eerily hushed the room became, how stunned everyone was.

Then Heino delivered a personal, deadpan version of a tsunami, looking straight at Napoléon and ignoring his brother: "He claims I have more space, but this is not so. There are identical desks, chairs, bookcases, tables in the office, and yet I find that when I have been gone and return, my desk chair has been moved and the back re-adjusted, my desk lamp is not where I left it, sticky coffee stains cover my desk, and food wrappers from Burger King fill my trash receptacle even though there are two separate trash containers—one for each of us. And to make matters worse, yesterday I discovered what you Americans call French fries under my desk."

"Liar! *Drecksau!*"

Turning to his furious twin, Heino said, "Shall I produce them for you? I placed them in a plastic bag and wrote the date on a label." He pointed to the small messenger bag at his feet. "I also have photos of the discovery on my iPhone."

As transfixed by this drama as I was, Stefan whispered: "Oh my God, it's like he was collecting evidence at a crime scene."

Hands balled into fists now, Jonas attacked: "*Spinnst du?* Are you crazy? What would possess you to think that it is *your* desk and *your* chair? They belong to the department, not to you. So when you are not working there, I have an absolute right to use anything in the office in any way that I choose."

Heino shook his head sadly as if dealing with a spoiled little child. "I moved in first and chose my desk, and it is mine and mine alone. You are just jealous, I think, because I was there first and you imagine that is giving me an advantage. You have always been jealous of me."

Celine had told me that space was tight in our new building for faculty who had to share an office, and some desks were in fact a little bigger than others, but not dramatically so.

"You've always been a selfish pig!" Jonas shouted. *"Du Wichser! Scheiss die Wand an!"*

I had no idea what any of that German meant, but it all sounded nasty and there was now foam at the corners of Jonas's mouth.

Implacably, and as if his brother hadn't even raised his voice, Heino forged ahead in a monotone, but his eyes were still weirdly fixed on Napoléon though he was addressing his brother: "I use my own desk and my own chair when I am working there and I leave yours alone. Yet you are not showing me the same respect. You do not behave professionally. You want *two* desks and *two* chairs. This is irrational."

Without warning, Jonas lunged at his brother and started choking him. They fell to the floor in a whirl of punching, growling, and cursing in German. Everyone was frozen by the scene, but people shouted their surprise and dismay, clearly astonished as the two men rolled over a fallen tablet whose screen they cracked. It looked like each twin was trying to get the other in a head lock or twist an arm behind the other's back—as if they had gone to the same self-defense class. They were evenly matched—how long would it last?

The fury in their voices and on their faces was murderous. Ciska, Jasmine, and Viktor were all standing together looking horrified. A few people backed away, still transfixed, and slowly headed for the hallway to the left or the entrance, whether to escape or grab a cigarette or hide in a restroom, I couldn't tell. Everything seemed to be happening in slow motion now, and most of us were sitting or leaning forward as if this were some kind of bizarre exhibition.

These guys hate each other like Cain and Abel, I thought, fascinated and appalled at the same time.

Jonas and Heino had always appeared to be united in their restrained, withdrawn way, united against the world around them, living in some kind of bubble, so there was something obscene in witnessing their secret animosity suddenly break out this violently in front of us all. Obscene, and thrilling, I confess, like a backstage pass to a wildly controversial, disturbing play. It was unreal to watch them snarl and snap at each other like hyenas fighting over the same piece of carrion.

I couldn't believe the ferocity I was witnessing even though it was happening just a few feet away, perhaps because all my years of watching TV and movie thrillers filled with mano-a-mano struggles had inured me to the real thing. And honestly, if one of the twins had suddenly leaped into the air in slow motion, run up the wall, flipped upside down, and landed a devastating mid-air martial arts kick on the other, I don't think I would have been the least bit surprised. Crouching Tiger, Hidden Hatred.

The fight stopped as quickly as it had erupted. Heino pulled himself away, face flushed, hair mashed with sweat. There was blood on his turtleneck. Jonas lay on the floor panting, blood trickling from one corner of his mouth. Given the whirlwind of their struggle, I was surprised neither one was moaning in pain or looked seriously injured—at least as far as I could tell. Heino stood, spat copiously at his brother, just missing his face, and stalked out of the room, in search of a restroom, I suppose, kicking the broken iPad out of his way. He was limping slightly.

I understood now how violence could break out anywhere and witnesses wouldn't intervene. It wasn't callousness, it was shock. And even though the fight was over, I felt the unbelievable images flashing through my mind like the after-effects of a strobe light.

Ciska rushed up to Jonas, knelt by him and asked, "Are you okay?" She put an arm under his back and helped him sit up. He blinked furiously as if he was momentarily uncertain where he was and what had happened.

"Shouldn't we call 911?" Ciska asked Napoléon, sounding very official, but also alarmed.

Napoléon drew himself up and shook his head imperiously. "We are not going to have a scandal in my department. Can you imagine the consequences?" And then he shouted at the room, "Everyone put your phones down!"

I turned and half a dozen people had been ready either to call 911 or post something on Facebook, Twitter, or Instagram. Possibly all of the above. None of them looked abashed, but everyone complied. For the moment.

I don't think any of us had ever seen Napoléon this angry. His eyes narrowed and he was glaring, his body as tense and coiled as if he were ready to round up all the phones in the room and smash them.

Napoléon might not want to have a scandal in his first semester as chair, but it was too late. Faculty present would be eagerly talking about this fracas and word would spread across the university like embers from one of those raging wildfires that hit California on a regular basis these days. News of the altercation would spread beyond SUM even if nobody went on the Internet (which seemed highly unlikely), and it would probably be picked up by enemies of academia as proof that we were all out-of-control loons. I remembered an old saying from my early days of teaching, passed on by a much older colleague: "Telegraph, Telephone, and Tell-a-Professor." Academics were

notorious gossips and this was a wild and juicy story that didn't
even need hyperbole to be impressive, but would just get better
and better each time it was repeated.

And now, as if some invisible cordon had been removed,
everyone still in the room pushed forward to gawk and comment
and ask what the hell had just happened. But they stood back
from Jonas, who had started the assault, as if he might strike out
at one of them or was himself toxic, even though he was calmly
seated on the couch, Ciska by his side, holding a bottle of water
for him to drink. He looked shell-shocked but otherwise not
seriously hurt.

Ciska asked if he wanted to go to the ER. "You could have
a concussion," she said, taking a handkerchief from her pocket
and tenderly wiping the blood from his face.

"No." He shook his head. "I'll be okay."

That would be one of the last words I'd ever use if Stefan
and I had gotten into a similar crazy brawl, but Jonas appeared to
mean it. And now I watched him take in the fact that he was the
center of attention. He smiled sheepishly at all of us, weirdly calm
and unembarrassed. "Really, I am fine. This was just a little family drama." His attitude was astonishing—I would have expected
him to be mortified.

Napoléon walked over and patted Jonas on the shoulder as
if approving of his stiff upper lip, and then clapped his hands for
all of us. "Friends, let's take a break. The croissants are still fresh
and the coffee is still hot." Then he sat down on Jonas's other side
and started to speak to him softly, but emphatically. Ciska rose
abruptly and stalked from the room, head down.

Stefan tapped my leg. "Caffeine," he said, and we got up,
walked around the couch to get fresh mugs of coffee. There was
a bizarre party atmosphere around us—almost everyone seemed
jazzed, as if they'd absorbed the energy of the fight but not its
anger. We could have been spectators with ringside seats watching a thrilling boxing match.

Not everyone was ebullient, though. Viktor Dahlberg joined us looking shaken. We all filled up on coffee and moved out of the way so other faculty could do the same.

"I'm not used to such emotionalism. You know," he said, "I grew up in Minnesota, and we're Swedes or Norwegians in my extended family. If you felt the way one of those two men did just now, you either ran away from home or went into the barn and shot yourself."

I waited to see if he was joking, but he nodded solemnly as if recalling instances of both.

Viktor wasn't done: "On the other hand, when Germans feel something, they write music or poetry—or they go to war. As you saw just now. Do you think this will help us get rid of Napoléon?"

Stefan and I exchanged a puzzled glance at the sudden shift. "What do you mean?" I asked, sipping my coffee.

Viktor frowned, apparently startled that I wasn't following his meaning. "Napoléon is the chair. He let violence break out at a retreat that is supposed to foster cooperation. Could it be any worse?"

Around us everyone was munching on croissants while talking heatedly about the fight and reliving it, saying, "I can't believe it!" and "What the hell is wrong with those guys?" and "Office sharing *policy*?" and "You'd never see two women acting like that—men just know one answer to every problem: violence. Men are so stupid, and even worse when they have advanced degrees because they think they're the opposite."

That last comment was Jasmine Alinejad's and she stiffened briefly when she realized I'd heard it, then raised her mug to me in mocking salute. Or was it a curse? Her richly embroidered paisley dress and heavy amber necklace and bracelets gave her the look of a wannabe sorceress. She was one of the professors my students complained about the most because she liked to belittle them in class, mocking them when they were wrong or unprepared. Based on complaints from his own students, Stefan had summed her up once as a nasty piece of work. And now I guess she was sexist, too.

Three adjuncts walked past and one said, "Too bad *Napoléon* didn't get attacked. Now *that* would have been some serious fun. I would have paid to see it." And they all laughed like they'd had a few too many beers. But why did they dislike him so much when he was helping to raise their status in the department?

Stefan asked Viktor, "What could Napoléon have done?"

Looking as serious as if he were testifying in court, Viktor replied, "If Napoléon were setting the right example, something like this would never have happened. But he's arrogant, divisive, antagonistic, and he's stirred things up. He obviously thrives on controversy when he's in charge. Who knows what's next? I am so hungry," he said and moved off to the table.

I suddenly felt a bit lightheaded and told Stefan I needed to sit down. I think the fight had retriggered the traumatic events from last spring.

We found the farthest corner, a sort of alcove by one of the picture windows where three chairs formed a little grouping.

"That really happened," I said.

Stefan nodded, watching my face intently.

Roberto Robustelli steamed over to us and fell into the empty chair, gleefully ignoring the signs that we wanted to be alone.

"Gentlemen!" He clapped his hands together in delight. "That was some fucking circus, am I right? Who would have thought those little pricks had it in them? Maybe Digital Humanities isn't just for nerds, maybe it actually has some balls!"

He said that last remark loud enough to make a few people laugh, and others cringe. With a sudden flash of insight, I saw him as an archetype: the clown, the trickster, the devil of discord. He was as flushed and ebullient as if he had just scored some sort of personal triumph—and all because two of his colleagues had behaved so very badly.

"You're a vampire," Stefan said decisively. He had obviously been thinking along the same lines as I had.

"Excuse me?" Robustelli frowned. "I'm a *what?*"

"You're a vampire. You feed on trouble and chaos."

Now Robustelli laughed appreciatively. "Well, to tell ya the truth, I do have one big fucking appetite when it comes to people acting like jerk-offs, if that's what you mean. And this department is turning into an all-you-can-eat buffet." He smacked his knees, grinning, and then sauntered off, to charm other faculty, no doubt, head high and shoulders back as if he had bested us in a debate.

Stefan shuddered. "How do people like that get to where they are?"

"It's *because* they're like that."

Stefan looked dubious.

I asked, "Do you think the remainder of the retreat's been canceled?"

Stefan groaned. "Are you kidding? We'll probably have to process our feelings about what happened with the twins for the rest of the day. You know what that means: sharing circles or something just as horrible."

"Why don't we leave? Say you have a migraine."

He nodded. "I could do that, but what about you?"

"I'll say I have to drive you home because you can't see straight. Who's going to know it's not true?"

Stefan considered that.

I looked up to see what had become of Jonas. He was still sitting with Napoléon, but they both looked angry and were speaking very fast in hushed voices. Napoléon was shaking his head furiously and then something Jonas said apparently set Napoléon off because he rose abruptly and crossed the noisy room, heading for the men's restroom, I assumed. Jonas walked to the glass door opening onto a patio. People got out of his way as if he had the plague. He went outside and lit up a cigarette. Shoulders slumped, Jonas looked miserable.

Carson Karageorgevich lumbered over to where we were sitting, asked if he could join us but didn't wait for an answer. He looked fired up, eyes glowing, cheeks flushed. He'd caught the fever, too.

"It's too bad those little fuckers didn't do *more* damage," he said.

I asked Carson what he had against the twins.

He practically snarled at me. "Haven't you heard? They want to take over Film Studies. They keep talking about the need for new blood as if we were all ready to retire, which isn't even remotely true. How the hell Digital Humanities could help boost enrollments is anyone's guess."

All this must have been going on while we were away traveling during the summer. I wished right then we had never come back.

"Listen, Nick, Stefan, I don't know what they're planning, Jonas and Heino, or if they even have a plan, but I don't trust them, they're nasty little creeps. They act like Digital Humanities is going to save the world or at least save all of us. They brag about how it's scientific and objective, but it's just one big fucking scam and they're the worst con artists in this department. It's just too damned bad they didn't finish each other off."

"Hey!" Stefan said. "That's not something to joke about."

Carson actually looked offended, as if the shootings at Parker Hall had never happened. "Do you think I'm joking?"

This was all too much for me and I headed to the men's room, not sure if I wanted to douse my head in cold water, puke, or just hide out in one of the stalls.

As soon as I pushed the men's room door inward, I saw someone in a far corner lying under the hand dryers as if he'd been dropped from a great height, slack-jawed and staring, his head lolling on his left shoulder, right arm across his belly, the other sprawled outward as if reaching for something. It was Napoléon.

I stopped, suddenly feeling very cold. The dim lights and

potpourri aroma filling the room now felt oppressive, even menacing. I couldn't breathe.

Had he been assaulted, was he delirious from a heart attack or stroke?

I rushed over and just as I was bending down to feel his neck for a pulse, I heard the door open and Roberto Robustelli said, "Holy Mother of God!"

I whirled around.

Wide-eyed and pale, he bellowed, "Is he dead?"

12

I TURNED BACK TO Napoléon, who I now realized did not look just dazed or ill. He was void and emptied out, a shell of himself. Those stylish clothes of his could have been painted on, they looked so unreal now.

I had seen death before and had hoped it would never happen again, yet here it was, as Henry James called it: "the distinguished thing."

I could hear my pulse beating in my ears and though I knew I should have been checking for *his* pulse in case I was wrong, I backed away from Napoléon's body as far as I could and leaned against the wall to keep from falling. I had never passed out before, but thought I might be on the verge of doing so now. My breathing was rapid and shallow.

The doorway was filling with people and I heard cries of "Call 911! Call 911!"

Ciska Balanchine shoved past the throng, moved to Napoléon's body, bent over and calmly held her index and middle fingers to his throat. It looked weirdly like a kind of benediction. After a moment, she shook her head perfunctorily, not showing any signs of surprise. She might even have been suppressing a smile, but I couldn't swear to it. Maybe it was a grimace of contempt on her face, and my own weakened state made me misread her.

"Is he dead? Is he dead?" The clamor at the doorway was unbearable and I wanted to shout at everyone to shut up. I didn't have to. With icy steadiness, Ciska shouted, "Be quiet!" Standing erect in her red suit, she was majestic and fierce. "Everyone go back to the meeting room, sit down, and wait for the campus police to arrive."

"Campus police?" I managed to ask, feeling dizzy. "Why?"

"Why? Because there's a knife sticking out of his belly, that's why, and it looks like murder, you dolt."

I heard gasps from the doorway and then the words "knife" and "murder" echoed down the hall with feverish strength.

Ciska was shaking her head. "Do you think he took a bathroom break to off himself? Not bloody likely, is it?" Ciska pointed to Napoléon's right hand which I now could see was almost covering what I was pretty sure was the carved silver handle of that antique stiletto from his office desk. "And because 911 calls from SUM are answered by our campus cops—how did you not know that, Nick?"

I tried answering but couldn't.

The hero of the historical series I'd fallen in love with was always quoting an Old English saying: *Wyrd bið ful aræd*. Fate is inexorable. And mine seemed perpetually tangled with death, even though I lived in a world, academia, where reputations might be savaged and even destroyed, but people still tended to flourish no matter how miserably unkind and ungenerous they were. In fact, the villains usually triumphed, to earn enormous salaries and escape the public scorn and shame they deserved.

"Bugger off, Nick," Ciska advised, "this is a crime scene." She shooed me into the hall where Stefan grabbed my arms.

"Are you okay?"

"I'm not dead, he is."

Stefan led me back to our corner and made me sit down, saying sotto voce, "Do you know how callous that sounds?"

I shrugged. Isn't that what anyone would think at a time like this? I remembered Dr. Frankenstein in the original Thirties movie shouting about his monster, "It's alive—it's alive—it's alive!" as thunder boomed in the background, and thought I might start laughing because the scene in my head was so bizarre. Was I becoming hysterical?

It's a truism that animals smell fear, but that has to apply to humans, too, because I swear something rank and stifling hit my nose that couldn't have been anything else *but* fear. That stench filled the large, comfortable meeting room and was transforming it into something very different: a refuge threatened by some unknown enemy. Or maybe it was now a prison.

If the fight between the twins had been unreal, discovering Napoléon in the men's room went way beyond the surreal.

They got him, I thought, calming down a little. *They got Napoléon.*

He had just been talking to us moments ago…and now he never would again. My hands felt clammy and I rubbed them on my pants to dry them, and then together to generate some heat. But whatever my body was up to, I felt unnaturally calm as I surveyed the room. Standing or sitting, people were in the same groups as before, but huddled closer together as if for warmth or protection. Everyone was speaking in hushed voices and was keeping as still as if their own lives depended on not moving. Even boisterous Roberto Robustelli was subdued.

It seemed certain that someone in this room, one of the three dozen people here, was a *murderer*, and we all knew it. It was somehow easier for me to believe that than to believe—or accept—that Napoléon was dead.

Ciska strode to the deserted lectern and her very presence instantly stifled the murmuring and speculation. I had never noticed before how resolute and square her jaw was or how her dark eyes were filled with ruthless determination.

"Now I know we're all gutted by what's happened to Napoléon," she said firmly, with a steely glint in her eyes, "but this is a time for us to stick together and defend the reputation of the department, which has suffered so much in recent years."

"Gutted" struck me as a really unfortunate choice of words, but that was another one of her British expressions.

"I'm sure we'll all be interviewed by the police about what's transpired, and I urge you all to tell the truth. All the same, remember who you are and what you represent."

There was a surprising note of condescension in her voice. She sounded like a high school principal lecturing unruly students before a guest speaker was set to appear. And despite her adamantine stance, there was a strange edge of buoyancy to everything she said.

Napoléon was dead, and she didn't look shocked. Was she glad he'd been killed, glad to be in charge of the department now, as I assumed she would be—or both?

Ciska studied us, nodding her head as if we'd all just been introduced and she was trying to memorize our faces and names. Then she joined Jasmine Alinejad and that coterie of women who were seated as far away from the rest of us as possible.

"She loves this," I said to Stefan. "A crisis, being in command—or at least telling people what to do."

"You sound surprised."

I was. I had never seen this side of her—had anyone?

Stefan took my hand. "So what was it like? Was it horrible to find Napoléon?"

I had to think about it. "Horrible, yes. Even though at first he just looked like he'd had a stroke or heart attack or brain aneurysm. I mean that's what I thought. I didn't know for sure he was dead until Ciska told me. That's when I saw the knife, the stiletto. In his stomach. Remember how it was in his office and he was playing with it?" I felt detached from my words, as if I were reading somebody else's postcard from a place I'd never been to.

"We're not very lucky, are we?" Stefan muttered.

"Hey! No matter what's happened, we have each other. Some people never find a soul mate, or even a partner of any kind. And look at your career—you've never been this successful or sold so many books...."

Abashed, Stefan smiled at his own pessimism.

Me, I was surprised to have said anything so upbeat in this moment of chaos. However, that was about all the cheerleading I had the energy for. I'd been wide awake and snarky when we had arrived, but all that focus became blurred by discovering Napoléon's body. I came out of the fog, though, with a simple chilling question: *Who killed him?*

Ciska Balanchine, Viktor Dahlberg, Carson Karageorgevich, Roberto Robustelli, and Atticus Doyle all had reasons to be angry at him, but was any one of them filled with enough rage to take his life?

This was a university, after all, replete with back-stabbers, but usually not literal ones. At SUM, faculty and administrators were very much like the nineteenth-century upper-crust New Yorkers in Edith Wharton's novel *The Age of Innocence*, adept at taking life "without effusion of blood." That was the modus operandi of people on our Midwestern campus "who dreaded scandal more than disease and who considered that nothing was more ill-bred than 'scenes,' except the behavior of those who gave rise to them."

Ciska walked over to us now, sat down, leaned forward and took my hands with what felt like the sincerity of a daytime talk show host fishing for outrage and tears. "How are you doing, Nick? Do you need anything?"

I pulled my hands away with difficulty, and sat as far back in my chair as possible, folding my arms. "I'll be okay. Really."

"If you want some time off, I'll get someone to cover your classes."

"I said I'm fine. I'll be back in class tomorrow."

"There's no shame in being gobsmacked by what happened."

All I could think of right then was a line from Samuel But-
ler's *The Way of All Flesh*: "If it was not such an awful thing to say
of anyone, I should say that she meant well."

Ciska probably thought she was being helpful, yet I felt put
upon. She seemed intent on turning me into a victim, into someone traumatized. I didn't know how I was, but I didn't want her
or anyone else managing me.

And as if I were incapacitated, she asked Stefan for his phone
and if it was locked. It wasn't, and when he handed it over she
entered her number. "Call me anytime," she said. "I'll always
be happy to talk to you." Something felt very weird about this
moment, but I couldn't identify what.

Ciska returned Stefan's phone. "Murder is very stressful,
please take care of yourself, Nick," she said, like your grand-
mother gently encouraging you to stay hydrated when you were
ill. With that, she left us and went to stand outside, to await the
campus police, I supposed.

"Shit," I muttered. "The only thing missing was her talking
about me in third person like I wasn't there."

Sirens announced the arrival of an ambulance and two of the
new all-black SUM police cars we could see through the large
window near us. The flashing red-and-blue lights were so daz-
zling I had to look away. An EMT in long-sleeved black shirt and
black pants rushed in, his huge red bag with a white star on the
side bouncing on his hip as Ciska followed to show him where
Napoléon's body was.

They were followed by four cops who were also sheathed
in black from heavy boots to caps and wearing aviator-style
Ray-Bans. Though they weren't heavily armed like a SWAT
team, they were still menacing to me and their stances—as three
of them slowly spread out across the room and the fourth button-
holed Ciska—made them look almost like bodyguards. Each of
them was over six feet tall and as big and broad as a TV wrestler.

The EMT emerged from the men's room slowly, a grim expression on his bland face, his bag like a ball and chain. He reported in a low voice to the cop standing by Ciska, who then spoke into his shoulder microphone: "Dispatch, this is Joe Valentine and we have a man with a knife in his gut." He went on to give the location of the center while the EMT left, head down. After the EMT whispered to him, he had added, "Looks like a homicide."

Everything from that point on seemed to happen with nightmarish clarity, perhaps because the room was so still, and the events were triggering my panic and despair from last spring.

Before I knew it, my campus nemesis entered: Detective Valley, a graying, pasty-faced beanpole who believed that professors were worse than binge-drinking, dorm-room-trashing students. Everyone present rose as if to greet some visiting foreign dignitary. Everyone except me and Stefan. But Valley seemed oblivious, and they regained their seats.

Somewhere in his fifties, Valley had a rolling, challenging walk and a quietly aggressive stance. He and I had never gotten along, given my apparent magnetic attraction for murder and his undisguised contempt for the people like all of us here that he was tasked to protect. Whenever he looked at me with his critical, demeaning gaze, he could have been a moralizing old-time sheriff in Gold Rush country scowling at the lecherous town drunk.

Valley was accompanied by a younger detective, and both of them wore dark gray suits, white shirts, and red ties. Valley told him, "Take the photos with your phone and have the area sealed off." He called over one of the officers by the door and said, "Make sure everyone's quiet," and that cop moved closer to the faculty in their chairs and on the sofas, his dark, intimidating presence enforcing silence. I waited for Valley to show everyone his badge and ID, but he apparently thought we all knew who he was—or *should* know.

There was soon yellow tape that read CRIME SCENE—DO NOT CROSS marking the entrance to the hallway leading to the restrooms: a giant X that I could see from where I sat. I felt as if the tape had somehow been plastered on me, too, and wondered if other faculty felt the same.

That's when Valley seemed to notice me. He glared, but I was a full professor now and had a fellowship named after me, so I wasn't the same frightened, tenure-crazed man he'd intimidated and harassed in my earlier years at SUM.

"Detective Valley," I said, trying not to sound spiteful.

"I knew *you'd* be involved," he spat out as if he'd just lost a big hand at poker.

Valley turned to one of his minions and said imperiously, "Nobody leaves until I say so." He approached the clearly apprehensive crowd, flashing his badge now, and announced in his crisp, no-bullshit voice, "I'm Detective Valley of the campus police. We're going to talk to all of you briefly, but that's going to take some time, so get comfortable. Nobody's leaving." I understood he couldn't force people to stay, legally, but who would have the nerve to leave, and why would they? His advice about getting comfortable was surely counter-intuitive—how could you relax at the scene of a murder when you were going to be grilled by the police?

"Who discovered the body?" Valley asked Ciska.

"Professor Hoffman," she said, and Valley breathed in deeply and held it as if counting to ten before exhaling.

"Who else is in the building?" Valley asked.

Ciska thought a moment and said, "Two people assigned to the retreat: a staffer who does set-up and someone who prepares the food and lays it out." She hesitated.

"They're probably both preparing lunch. I'll go get them," she offered, but Valley kyboshed that with a wave of his hand and sent one of the cops to the kitchen. He returned with a middle-aged, tough-looking woman with grizzled salt-and-pepper hair who had a serious air of being put upon, and the reedy, elderly man who had set up the lectern before and struck me now as someone who could have been a Walmart greeter. He gave us all a vague smile.

"Hey, I just work here," the woman complained, as belligerent as Thelma Ritter in *Rear Window*, but Valley stared her into submission and she found a seat on the arm of one of the couches. She surveyed all of us and crossed herself as if we were ominous and evil. Then she jumped up, apparently having noticed the mess on the table of urns and mugs, and started cleaning up and re-arranging, putting paper plates and ripped-open sweetener packets in a trash bin at one end of the table. Her gangly, elderly co-worker joined her and their efficiency lent an air of stagey normality to the scene—as if they were student actors doing a scene together.

Valley turned to me now and said, "Don't move until I get back." He headed to the men's room to inspect the body, I assumed, but his command was so peremptory it got everyone looking at me and I could feel my face turning red.

I'm sure some of them were thinking I was responsible for Napoléon's death, or why else would Valley be singling me out? I just shut my eyes to make it all go away. When Stefan tried to ease my mind with some whispered bromides, I said, "Please don't." He fell silent, but there was no chance of reverie, because Stefan nudged me before I knew it to tell me that Valley was back.

He was standing halfway between me and Ciska and asked her if there was a private room in this building. She shrugged and Thelma Ritter piped up, "Small office. Near the kitchen. Can't miss it." She jerked her head at the kitchen hallway on the far right, not even bothering to point with a finger. I wondered if she'd had dealings with the police before.

Valley again pointed a finger at me, then at the kitchen hallway, and I rose sheepishly to follow him. The "office" was more like a remodeled closet where somebody had crammed in a standard gray metal filing cabinet and a matching desk. There was just room enough for a desk chair and a stool on the other side. Valley shook his head in disgust and called out, "Somebody bring me a real goddamned chair!"

One of the cops instantly appeared with a low yellow molded chair that must have come from the dining hall and switched it out for the stool.

"Sit."

I did, but he didn't, and we were uncomfortably close in that cell of a room. I could make out that his eyes were bloodshot and he'd recently cut his chin shaving. Valley slipped a mini tablet from a jacket pocket, opened what looked like a recording app, and briefly typed something with his thumbs, then set the tablet on the desk.

He stopped and glared down at me. "I want to record your statement."

"Okay."

"Can I see some ID?"

"What? You know who I am."

He repeated his demand and I slipped my wallet from my inside jacket pocket and showed him my driver's license.

"How do you know the deceased?"

"He's— He was our department chair."

"I understand you found the body. Tell me what happened and when."

I looked down at my watch to estimate when I had found Napoléon, but the numerals blurred. "I don't know, it was half an hour ago or maybe more, I went into the men's room, and he was lying there dead."

"You could tell just by looking at him? Did you try CPR? Did you check to see if he was breathing? Did you call 911? No? How do you know he wasn't alive when you found him? Maybe you let him die?"

The barrage of questions left me confused. "It all happened really fast. Someone found me there and then there was a crowd, and—"

Valley cocked his head at me. "Right. And if Stefan were lying there, you'd do nothing, too."

"That's different. I love Stefan."

"And you hated this Napoléon guy." Valley looked as smug as a hardboiled detective in a film noir confronting a very bad liar.

"No!" I knew my denial wasn't one hundred percent convincing because while I didn't loathe Napoléon, I had quickly grown to dislike him in the last few days and I'm sure my face betrayed that.

"Take me through your story again."

It wasn't much of a narrative, but I did what Valley asked. This time he wanted to know who had been in the men's room before me. "Did you see anyone coming out of the men's room before you went in?"

I didn't know and couldn't remember, and the more he badgered me, the cloudier things became.

Valley scowled at my confused answers, and finally ushered me out of the room like a party crasher.

But I knew he wasn't done with me, not even remotely.

Part III

13

STEFAN HAD EVEN LESS to say to Valley, so he and I were the first to leave after Ciska announced the obvious: the retreat was cancelled.

Our drive home felt longer because we were both silenced by the enormity of Napoléon's death. And what had seemed bucolic and pleasant in the landscape now struck me as menacing. At one point Stefan just muttered, "Robustelli," and I assumed he was thinking of the extravagant way Roberto had praised Napoléon. He chuckled a bit, but the image didn't amuse me.

I had to smile, though, when we got home because Marco was so happy to see us, running around in ecstatic circles. Remembering a line Edith Wharton had written in her diary, that her dog was "a heartbeat at my feet," I scooped Marco up into my arms. He licked my nose while I ruffled his fur. I loved the unique way he smelled—like fresh popcorn. And I envied him. I was constantly aware that life was so simple for Marco: food, walks, playing with toys, naps, barking at the TV when it dared to parade a dog across the screen.

"I'll order pizza for lunch," Stefan said, and he went to the counter iPad to go online.

"With extra pepperoni," I said. "And extra cheese. And extra Valium."

He grunted at my meager joke. We both felt the weight of the day's events.

I set Marco down and he trotted over to his water dish, slurped some and then took himself off to the kitchen door and turned around, telling us he needed to go potty, so I let him out into the yard. The fence was high enough to keep deer out, which meant that we didn't have to worry about him rolling in anything foul. Flowers were a lost cause: He'd already dug up all the bulbs that were there when we moved in—he was a terrier, after all.

I went to the half bath off the kitchen and when I came back in, I closed my eyes and breathed in the aromas of that room: three shelves of cookbooks; a pumpkin spice candle that we'd lit the night before and left open after blowing it out; Marco's dog bed; and the roasted warmth coming from the oven Stefan had turned on to keep the pizza warm when it arrived.

Stefan brought out two Köstritzer Schwarzbiers from the fridge. He had recently become a beer aficionado and insisted on having the "official glasses" for each brand so that we drank it as it was meant to be savored. That required clearing out a whole cabinet as he bought more and more glassware for Duvel, Hoegaarden, Leffe, Blanche de Bruxelles, Stella Artois, and others I couldn't recall.

We sat and toasted silently in heavy, thick-stemmed glasses embossed with the Köstritzer label. The earthy, toasty, chocolate flavors were just what I needed right then. I looked around the red-and-white kitchen and felt even more at home, perhaps because of the tragedy at the retreat.

Stefan got up to let Marco back in when we heard him scratching at the door, and we watched him settle onto his round fluffy dog bed and fall asleep.

"I didn't do it," I said.

Stefan set his beer down hard. "What?"

"I didn't kill him." I tried to shake the image of Napoléon's body lying on the floor of that men's room but couldn't.

He frowned. "Of course you didn't."

"But Valley thinks I killed Napoléon—because I didn't try to help. That it was deliberate."

"That's his job. He's a detective. He probably suspects everyone for the murder."

"You don't know that. And what's worse, I'm the one who found him. I'm a prime suspect."

"Bullshit. Anybody could have gone in there before you did and stabbed him."

I considered that, and wished I had been truly paying attention to the faculty around me at the retreat. I asked Stefan if he had noticed anyone going to the men's room right before I found Napoléon.

He closed his eyes for a few moments, then opened them. "Maybe one of the twins. Or both of them? But I couldn't swear to it. And what would they have against Napoléon? He recruited them, right?"

I wasn't listening with full attention because I was picturing Napoléon's body.

Stefan read my mind. "You can't beat yourself up for not trying to help him. We've both read enough crime fiction to know that if that knife nicked or severed his abdominal aorta, he would have died within minutes."

"But what if it didn't? Stabbing someone in the gut doesn't always kill them—it's not like in TV shows and movies. There are all those organs in there and muscle and even layers of fat. *Napoléon could have been alive when I found him.*"

Stefan clearly didn't know how to respond.

"Do you believe in fate?" I asked. "You know that series I'm reading, set in Anglo-Saxon England? The hero is always saying that fate is everything, that it's inexorable. Are you and I *fated* to wind up in situations like this? Or did we make a wrong turn somewhere—would we be living different lives in New York or Massachusetts or—"

"—or Bulgaria?" Stefan shrugged. "Who knows? But this is the life we're living. For better or for worse. It's a *fait accompli.*"

"I like your pun. But better keeps turning into worse way too often. Why do I keep running into Valley? He gives me the creeps."

Now seemed the right time, so we decided to share what we'd each told our estimable detective and it all sounded suspiciously threadbare—to me. Stefan was unruffled.

"Why wasn't I more observant?" I griped after the pizza came. Stefan put some slices on a baking sheet and stuck it in the oven while Marco watched every movement, licking his chops.

"Shock."

"But I didn't notice anything *beforehand,* I mean right before I found Napoléon."

"You needed to pee, right? That narrows anyone's focus."

I had to laugh because he was right. I never did take a leak at the retreat center, as if finding Napoléon's body had shut *my* body down.

"So how are you feeling now—really?" Stefan asked softly.

I hesitated, unsure what to say. "Weird...kind of spaced out..."

The timer rang for the pizza and we ate most of it with Marco watching us hopefully. I tried getting him interested in chasing a ball, but even looking at and sniffing food beat playtime for him.

The pizza was very New York: thin crust, lots of cheese, not too much sauce. It was great comfort food and I could feel the tension across my back and neck diminishing. It reminded me of happy afternoons in junior high or high school, stopping for "a slice" with friends after school, enjoying the time between being supervised by our teachers and being supervised by our parents. The simple freedom. I'd never been especially rebellious, but I hadn't been comfortable with the restrictions of my teachers or the way my parents hovered over me. I wasn't into drugs, dangerous sports, or sleeping around back then, but I never liked being told what to do, even if it was good for me—especially if it was good for me.

While we cleaned up, Stefan made me look into his eyes and said, "You're just not the murdering type."

I think that was meant to cheer me up or at least make me smile, but it had the opposite effect. "Isn't that what people always say when they find out a serial killer was living next door?"

Stefan put up a pot of coffee and we soon drifted out to the living room with steaming mugs and sat at either end of the couch. Marco followed us, jumped up, and snuggled against Stefan who started to scratch his chest. Neither of us had any more prep for our classes the next day because we had thought the retreat would occupy us all of Sunday—the retreat and complaining about it afterward.

I felt suddenly giddy. "It's like we've been given a reprieve, or a vacation!"

Stefan's eyes widened, but then he seemed to dismiss what I'd said, and asked, "What did you think of Ciska?"

"How do you mean?"

"The way she took charge, like she was planning to, like she was *ready.*" Stefan put his mug down on the coffee table.

"Seriously?" I asked. "You think she could kill Napoléon?"

"Why not? Somebody did. Napoléon was usurping her authority and sexually harassed her, right? And we don't know how bad that was. Plus, it sounded like he was also a symbol for her."

"Or a symptom. Were you surprised when she stepped up and started telling us all what to do?"

Stefan thought about it. "She did seem pretty commanding. For her."

"For anyone."

"But maybe she's just good in a crisis. When has there been a situation like this where the department was all together in one place, in all the years we've been here?"

"Why are you defending her?"

Stefan reared back a little as if I'd insulted him. "How am I defending her?"

I set my mug down on the table, hard, trying to find the words, but I felt too weary.

"Nick, come on, *relax.*"

"Don't fucking tell me to relax! Not after what I've been through." It wasn't logical, but it made sense in the moment. I could feel my face becoming hot and red, and that somehow made me angrier. I really did need to relax, but I hated him telling me to. Does that ever work, telling people to chill out when they're angry or upset?

Stefan's eyes narrowed, his face hardened, and he started to speak, but then he shook his head and said nothing. He moved closer and took both my hands, held them while I tried to pull away. "Look at me," he urged. "I'm sorry I offended you. Okay? Can we move on?"

I got my hands back, crossed my arms, and finally said, "Okay."

Stefan closed his eyes for a moment and when he opened them, said, "I think we should call Vanessa."

I knew exactly what he meant before he continued.

"If you're worried about being a suspect," he said, "let's consult with her."

I had just been thinking that. Our former neighbor Vanessa Liberati was one of the best defense lawyers in Michiganapolis and had helped us enormously in practical and emotional ways, last spring when our world was coming apart. One surprise: She'd advised us to get a gun and learn how to use it when we'd been besieged and threatened, and that ended up saving our lives.

Born in Brooklyn, Vanessa had unexpectedly found herself in mid-Michigan where she began to flourish. Her strong Brooklyn accent was almost a flag borne into battle. She could sound brash when she said "tawk" for talk and "cawfee" for coffee, and I think that made some Michiganders take her less seriously, which was a real mistake.

Her dismal views of cops and the justice system had surprised us. According to her, too many cops tampered with evidence, lied on police reports, were corrupt and violent, and were eager to destroy property in SWAT team raids. In Vanessa's experience, most of the local judges sided with the police: for them, defendants were guilty until proven innocent and defense lawyers were despicable scum for challenging that.

"I see what all of them really are," she told us more than once, "not what they pretend to be, and that gives me a leg up. That's why I win. I don't buy their bullshit for one second." It was a strange revelation hearing this kind of unflinching language from a tall, model-slim, striking redhead with dramatic green eyes who favored Louboutin shoes, Lanvin suits, and Hermès handbags right out of designer ads in *Vanity Fair*.

I didn't hesitate getting out my phone and calling her, and when I started to explain, she said, "Not over the phone. I can come by after dinner, okay? Is that soon enough?"

Vanessa showed up around nine that evening decked out in a gold-and-black brocade blazer, black leggings, a cream-colored blouse, and gold-and-black pumps.

"Wow," I said.

She grinned. "I had a dinner date."

I pointed to the bottle of Vieux Télégraphe Châteauneuf-du-Pape she had in one hand. "What's the occasion?"

"You need to ask? If you're calling me for advice, you probably need some really good wine."

"Thanks!" She was right, of course. Stefan took the wine and went to the kitchen to uncork it while I found us three glasses.

Marco doted on Vanessa and jumped onto the couch to keep her company when she sat down. "Hey, pooch," she said, scratching him behind the ears. He was in heaven. And then she glanced around the living room. "Interesting house. Not what I would have figured for you guys, but I know you had to move. I woulda done it, too."

I thought then that we should really have a housewarming when things calmed down, but when would that be?

After the wine was poured, she toasted us and the new house.

After clinking glasses, Stefan and I sat in the chairs opposite her and she started: "It's about the death at the retreat, right?"

"How did you know about the murder?"

"This is a really small town, how else? But it's not murder until the medical examiner says that it's murder."

"He had a knife in his gut," I said. "And I'm sure that the EMT guy said it looked like murder."

Vanessa shook her head. "Cause of death is determined by the medical examiner, not by anyone on the scene. Anything's possible. He could have been stabbed after he was dead."

Despite all the crime fiction I'd read, that somehow hadn't occurred to me.

Vanessa held her glass up to her nose and breathed in contentedly. "So tell me, does either one of you have exposure?" We must have looked blank because she went on, "Could the police make a solid case against either of you? Tell me exactly what happened."

I sipped some of the peppery wine first, then took her through a quick summary of the retreat up to finding Napoléon's body. I filled her in about how he had been starting to shake up the department, and that he had been pissing people off.

"And he directly threatened a handful of people, threatened their future at SUM, their advancement, their status. And he enjoyed it."

"Sounds like he was a real piece of work, but who isn't over there at SUM?" With her accent, it came out as "ovuh theah." She nodded a few times as if filing facts away somewhere. "All right. Did you touch him? Did you touch the knife?"

"No!" Stefan and I had seen far too many TV crime movies where innocent people stupidly pick up or touch the murder weapon.

"Did you have any reason you would want him dead?"

"I wanted him gone, yes. Dead, no."

"Whoa! Don't ever say that to anyone. It's too easy to ignore the second part and fixate on the first. Got it?"

"Yes. Got it."

"What was your beef with him?"

I told Vanessa I thought he was being anti–Semitic when I met with him in his office, but the real issue was trying to influence who I chose for the Nick Hoffman Fellowship.

She closed her eyes for a moment and then smiled as she opened them. "I don't hear anything that's problematic. Those aren't powerful motives, so I don't see a problem here, exactly. I mean, yeah, you found the body, but that's no proof of anything. Now, that detective whatshisname, he doesn't like you, but..."

"But what? And his name is Valley."

She frowned and somehow her freckles seemed more noticeable at that moment.

"I wouldn't think he'd manufacture evidence unless he *seriously* hated you. It's rare, but it happens."

I shrugged. "He doesn't like any professors."

"Can you blame him? No offense intended, but SUM is crazy from top to bottom, present company excepted. I hear horror stories all the time." Vanessa drank some more of the Vieux Télégraphe as if it could help her focus. "So listen to me, Nick, and this goes for you, too, Stefan: if that detective wants to question you, don't say anything, just call me. You don't know what other people told him this morning and if there are any conflicts in their statements."

That alarmed me. "Why would there be conflicts?"

She shrugged. "Witnesses remember things differently. It always happens." She finished her wine and Stefan got up to refill her glass.

"But I'm not a witness."

"Yes you are, unfortunately, to the extent that you found the body. So don't let Valley or anyone else bully you into talking. You don't have to say anything here in your home or even let him past the front door, or go to the campus police department. Unless they arrest you, which I don't see happening. And even then, you don't have to answer questions. He will try to trick you into

talking, but you don't have to say anything. Remember that! If
for some *farkakteh* reason they *do* arrest you, call me immediately."

Stefan and I exchanged wary glances.

"Hey! I didn't mean to bum you out, guys, but it's hard to
make this stuff peppy, and you need to be prepared. Trust me, I'm
on this. It won't be as heavy as the last time I represented you."
She smiled encouragingly. "Tell me about that knife."

I described his stiletto and how Napoléon had toyed with it
during our meeting in his office. Vanessa just listened.

"Is his office locked?"

"I wouldn't think so. At night maybe. The door from his secretary's office is open even when he has meetings. And her door's
open all day even when she's in the copy room or someplace else.
She'll leave a Post-it on the door saying where she is and when
she'll be back."

"Hmmm. What's his secretary like?"

"Grim," I said.

Stefan asked Vanessa, "Do you think she killed him? That he
was an abusive boss?"

"Just wondering. Let's talk about something else. Are you
watching *Game of Thrones*?"

Well, that changed the mood entirely because Stefan and
I had both read all five of the George R.R. Martin books the
series was drawn from and we were devoted to the show. But we
weren't fanatics and didn't gripe when it took liberties with the
source material. The three of us happily launched into a deep
discussion of politics in Westeros, Vanessa confessing at one point
that she wanted a dragon. "Doesn't have to be a big one. A starter
dragon would be fine."

14

I AVOIDED SOCIAL MEDIA and the news the next morning, Monday, but the students in both of my classes, which met back-to-back in the afternoon, had apparently read everything available online about Napoléon's death. They regarded me with awe, as if I were some minor celebrity, someone who'd gotten into a Twitter war with their favorite hip hop singer, perhaps. They wanted details, but I said it was a police matter and I didn't feel comfortable talking about it. That impressed them even more, as if we were on an episode of *Law and Order: LA* or some other cop show. One of the multiply-pierced students with tattooed arms in my first class called out, "You are such a bad-ass!" and the rest of the students whooped and applauded.

I took the compliment even though there was no way I deserved it.

My assistant, Celine, had a hot cup of Constant Comment tea waiting for me when I was done for the day. Her office was rich with steam and the orange, spicy aroma of that tea.

"You didn't have to do that."

"Oh, yes I did." I took the tea and she briskly followed me into my office, looking younger than usual in a purple-and-black top and black slacks. She was wearing her hair in a short Afro now and it haloed her warm, open face. She had some new perfume on, something cinnamon-y, and I asked what it was.

"Don't laugh. Paul Sebastian For Men. My husband uses it and I love the way he smells."

I sat at my desk, put down my shoulder bag beside me on the floor, and tried the tea. It was very good, and I felt as always more relaxed around her. She was one of the few kind and sensible people in our snake pit of a department, not remotely given to drama.

"How were your classes?" she asked. Surviving the attack in May on Parker Hall and on our offices there had turned us into something different than boss and employee. We weren't friends, didn't socialize, but we'd been through a trauma together and that gave us a very deep connection. It was as if we belonged to a secret society that was never mentioned or even hinted at.

"Both classes were great. You want to hear about the retreat, though? Like my students did?"

"Of course I do, but only if you want to talk about it."

I hesitated, then waved her to the chair at the side of my desk and she sat down, hands folded attentively in her lap.

I guess I *did* want to talk about it with someone who hadn't been there, someone sympathetic and insightful who would pick up what I might have missed. So I described the previous day at the retreat center from the moment Stefan and I had driven up. Celine looked intrigued when she heard how cheerful and friendly Napoléon had been to me and Stefan. The fight between Heino and Jonas shocked her.

"What was *that* mess all about?" she asked.

"I have no idea. None. It was truly bizarre."

"I tell you, in the real world they would be fired for acting like hooligans."

Celine had worked in state government, in real estate, and in accounting before she was hired at SUM. She was even more outraged to learn that Napoléon had been pressuring me to pick his own candidate for the Nick Hoffman Fellowship—I had to weave that into my story since I hadn't seen her since my meeting with Napoléon.

"Never! Élodie le Bon? Good Lord! That woman is poison. Her Twitter feed is so vicious it reads like someone hacked it and was trying to make her look like a stone-cold bitch. She's won all these awards but she's still a miserable excuse for a human being. Anyone who says anything remotely critical of her or her books gets trashed. Anyone like that is *nulle*, useless, a moron, a *connard* or *connasse*. And that's just on one of her good days."

"She sounds awful. Wait—you read French?"

She nodded. "And Spanish. I'm part-Creole, remember?"

"I never put that together, sorry. But I wasn't going to do it, you know, I wasn't even going to consider Napoléon's choice."

"Good!"

I switched gears. "Do you talk much to Napoléon's secretary?"

"Only when I have to. She's weird."

"Did she ever mention any planning for a conference or something like that to honor Stefan's career?"

Celine looked blank.

I explained that Napoléon had briefly shared the idea with us before more people arrived at the retreat center.

"I bet Stefan said no," Celine said firmly.

"Well, only to me. There wasn't time to tell Napoléon he wasn't interested. I guess that's not going to happen now, which is a relief." Stefan's memoir was intensely personal and he didn't want to feel more revealed to public scrutiny than he already was. If Napoléon was serious, I'm sure it had nothing to do with celebrating Stefan's success and everything to do with boosting Napoléon himself.

Celine prompted me: "So what happened next?"

I went on with my story and she laughed when I got to Roberto Robustelli's wild cheerleading and how he'd startled Napoléon with a hug, but her face went grim when I described finding the body, and she crossed herself.

"Lord, what a way to go." Celine shook her head disapprovingly.

"Stabbed, you mean?"

"No, in a toilet. And now we have a killer on the loose in the department."

"It wouldn't be the first time."

She sighed. "You've got that right."

"And once again, I'm mixed up in it."

"No wonder that skinny detective hates your ass."

I had to laugh since I'd never heard Celine talk quite like that.

"Well it's true, isn't it?" she said.

But she started laughing, too, and in that companionable moment I suddenly had the uncanny feeling that everything was going to work out just fine. Even though I couldn't have said how or why. Look at where we were! It was as if the sterile setting of our new building didn't just defy chaos and confusion, it could probably purge them from anyone who made a home there. It had been the physics building; it was a place of scientific clarity, not cruelty.

Then I caught myself. I was thinking thoughts as nutty as Eleanor's in *The Haunting of Hill House* when she keeps remembering the line "journeys end in lovers meeting" from a song in *Twelfth Night*. Whatever journey I was now on, it had nothing to do with lovers.

Wait, how did I know that? I came out of my fog to find Celine calmly expecting a reply to her question, but I had something else on my mind.

"Have you heard any rumors on campus about Napoléon, like who he might be sleeping with, or trying to? Has he broken up with anyone? Have you heard anything like that?"

"No I haven't. You think it was an ex-lover who killed him, someone he kicked to the curb?"

"Maybe. Or a jealous husband or somebody's boyfriend… Napoléon was a lady's man."

She frowned. "That's one way to put it."

"You know what I mean."

"You mean he was a player. 'Lady's man' sounds too refined."

"Well he was French, after all. They would call him a *tombeur*,

I think." Then I added, "*Would have* called him. But anyway, someone with his wild past probably had a wild present, too."

"No doubt."

I trusted Celine, so I told her about Ciska Balanchine's anger about being undermined in her role as associate chair, and how she'd been sexually harassed somehow, and about Viktor's fury over the Sweden program being stolen from him, and Carson Karageorgevich and Atticus Doyle both feeling deeply disrespected in different ways. As I laid it out for her, I realized that Napoléon was a thief. He wanted what other people had, for self-aggrandizement.

Celine considered what I'd shared with her, then shrugged. "Not to minimize what all of them told you—and by the way, why aren't you charging all these people for consultations?—but SUM excels at making people miserable and every department has unhappy faculty for one reason or another. And maybe they dream about killing a colleague or their chair, but to actually go ahead and *do* it?" She shook her head. "That's a gigantic step."

"It's happened at SUM before."

"True. But what if the killer isn't anyone in the department?" Celine asked, cocking her head and squinting as if trying to make out music from another room. "What if we're dealing with some feud that Napoléon had going on over there in France that followed him to Michigan? Someone that famous would have racked up plenty of rivals and enemies along the way."

I asked, "Why kill him at SUM?"

"Maybe they thought with the high rate of murders in the U.S., it would be easier to get away with. Too many crimes, not enough cops."

"But I didn't see anyone at the retreat who wasn't faculty—except for two staffers from the retreat center."

"Was that place airtight? No? Well, then. And it's on Lincoln Road, right? Easy to sneak into, easy to get away from. If you're planning a murder, someplace out of the way, but not inaccessible, that's where to do it."

I had in fact noticed a door at the end of the hallway where the restrooms were. It was unmarked. Could it have been connected to another room with an exit? Why wouldn't there have been a sign? I closed my eyes and realized I hadn't taken stock of any way in or out of the main building except for the one we'd used, but the kitchen had to have an exterior door for deliveries, and safety.

But whatever the building's layout, if Napoléon had been killed by someone from France, then how would anyone, no matter how intrepid, find the killer?

"Our lawyer says it's not a murder until the medical examiner says so."

"You're telling me that Napoléon stuck a knife in his own gut? What, he was trying harakiri? Professor, *please*."

There was a knock on Celine's open office door that startled both of us. Viktor Dahlberg came through and stood at the doorway of my office, looking furtive.

"Nick, could I have a word?"

I steeled myself for more misery and said, "Of course!"

Celine leaned toward me. "We have some info about possibilities for the fellowship to go over—but that can wait."

She rose and went back into her office. Viktor walked in and closed the door between my office and Celine's behind him. He stood there, fingers twitching, eyes not meeting mine.

"What's going on? Take a seat, please."

He sat down. He had gray stubble on his chin and cheeks that wasn't there the day before and was wearing the same clothes he'd had on at the retreat. Where had he been overnight?

"That was very strange yesterday," Viktor began stiffly, almost as if he had memorized the words. "Horrible." His head was down and I couldn't see his eyes, but his handsome face was tense. "I caught a glimpse of Napoléon from the open doorway when we were all crowding around. I've— I've never seen a corpse before except in movies."

Viktor wildly scratched his right ear, looking like someone

who'd been bitten by some of Michigan's infamous blackflies. Then he stopped abruptly as if realizing how strange that must appear.

I waited to see where he was going.

"I know that it's wrong, Nick, but my first thought wasn't about Napoléon or the department or anything else. It was about Sweden." And now he looked right at me, eyes glowing and a cruel smile on his face. "He can't take the program from me now."

"That's true." I didn't add anything because he didn't seem to want me to.

"But I think you should know that people are saying *you* did it."

"*What?*"

Now Viktor seemed to calm down a little, as if he'd delivered a difficult message from a demanding employer and his job was done.

"What are you talking about?" I asked. Suddenly my heart was racing.

He held out his hands in a what-can-I-tell-you? gesture. "It was known that he was pressuring you about the Nick Hoffman Fellowship."

"How was it known?"

"He talked about it openly, I think, to Ciska at least, probably to other faculty, too."

It was irrational, but I felt humiliated that Napoléon had brought up his choice for the fellowship with anyone else but me before we had discussed it. Why had that bastard been talking up Élodie le Bon to other people in the first place? To get their support? To make it seem like a done deal? Nothing added up....

"Listen. I don't care what he said, Viktor, because it was *just an idea*. There's no way in hell I was going to take his recommendation."

Viktor seemed remarkably relaxed now that I had become more emotional. He sat back in the chair and crossed his legs, the anxiety completely drained from his face, and I began to suspect that he had an ulterior motive for being in my office, though I had no idea what it could be.

"Nonetheless, there is talk," he said, "that you're the one who killed Napoléon."

"Bullshit!"

He glanced away, then nodded mechanically, almost stupidly, like a bobblehead dog on a car dashboard. "You were found with the body, no? And Ciska said that you were behaving very oddly."

"I discovered his body, I wasn't 'found' with it. And I was *shocked*." My chest was tight and I felt very exposed right then, the subject of gossip and dangerous speculation. "Why would I kill him?"

"Because he was working with the Board of Trustees and the university lawyers to have SUM take control of the Nick Hoffman Fellowship and give it to him."

"That's nuts! That can't be true."

Viktor peered at me, eyebrows raised. "You didn't know? You must have known."

"No...I...didn't." I didn't know and I didn't believe it. But then hadn't Napoléon mentioned something about the board when we had met? That they would be in favor of bringing in Élodie le Bon?

Viktor wasn't done. "I'm sure Ciska told the police what she saw at the retreat center, when she was interviewed."

"Told them what? There's nothing to tell. He was stabbed, I found his body, end of story." But the words sounded unconvincing even to me.

Viktor stood and rubbed his hands together as if he had just had a very satisfying meal. "That's certainly one way of looking at it," he said, and he opened the door and left my office, smiling.

Despite all his "information," I was very much aware that he hadn't mentioned the wild slugfest between the twins. Did that mean Napoléon's death was going to overwhelm everyone's memory, or was there some specific reason Viktor hadn't brought it up?

"Are you okay?" Celine asked at the doorway as soon as he was gone. "You sounded angry just now." She hovered there as if I might shout at her, too, though that had never happened.

"Viktor told me that people in the department think I killed Napoléon." And at the back of my mind, I was puzzled: why had he seemed so quietly combative? And delighted by telling me?

"Whoa," Celine brought out. "What people? And why?"

"Well, Ciska Balanchine, for one. And because Napoléon was supposedly scheming with the board to have SUM take over the fellowship. Which is crazy. They couldn't get away with it."

She rolled her eyes. "These folks gossiping about you need to get real and mind their own business. But that's not ever going to happen." She paused. "Do you want me to ask around and see if there's some truth to that nonsense?"

I assumed she meant checking in with some of her peers across the university, and I said yes. "I know Napoléon's secretary is weird, but maybe you can find out who's been in his office lately, or if anyone's been in and out a lot."

"Why?"

"Because of that stiletto he was using as a letter opener. I know it's not much, but somebody stole it, and his secretary might have an idea who it was, or when it disappeared."

"Oh, right. I'll try. She's not the easiest person to talk to." Then Celine clapped her hands together and said, "Shall we do some work before you go home?"

"Absolutely."

"I'll gather the folders and send you some links from my laptop that we can look at together."

Talking to Celine even this much about work began to diffuse my anger and my dread and make me feel like life could be normal again.

That, of course, was a fantasy.

15

THOUGH CELINE AND I made some progress working towards who I'd offer the fellowship to that academic year, and the selection process had my full attention, by the time I was driving home, I'd gotten riled up again. I was pissed off by what Viktor had said in my office and by his strange attitude. Even the quiet of our cul-de-sac irritated me.

I was livid and wanted to shout at someone, anyone. Marco instantly picked up my boiling frustration when I walked into the kitchen. He didn't come over for a greeting, just stood a ways off, watching me, wagging his tail tentatively, alert. He followed me at a careful distance to the fridge when I took out the Bloody Mary mix, and a bottle of Grey Goose vodka from the freezer, but then he backed off and chose his dog bed as the best vantage point—to wait it out, I guess.

My own seething anger made me think of the German twins who had erupted so mysteriously at the retreat center. They proved what I'd heard a sociologist say at a conference: "Academics don't have good means of conflict resolution. That's why so many of them end up writing murder mysteries." The audience laughed, but he was deadly serious. I wondered briefly if I needed some time at the firing range with my Ruger, but then realized I'd be close to the retreat center and that image brought a terrible taste to my mouth. It also didn't seem wise to have a gun in my hand anywhere when I was this angry. I was also too frazzled right then to pack up and head to our health club to swim off my rage.

When Stefan came downstairs barefoot, wearing ripped jeans and a plain black T-shirt, he applauded the vodka and mixer. He said, "Hey! Why not one for both of us?" He tried to hug me hello, but I pulled back. I wasn't in the mood for being comforted just then.

Stefan backed off with a quiet "Okay."

My reply was "Sorry." I sat at the table with my drink, downed half of it and would probably have plunged into a vat of Bloody Marys if one were available—that's how crazed I felt. Could Ciska really tell the campus police anything damaging about me? And was the Board of Trustees really trying to shaft me?

Stefan made himself a drink and joined me without saying anything more—seeming as serene as if we were happily back in the Loire Valley on one of our earliest vacations together, having an apéritif at a château hotel whose terrace gave us a gleaming, seductive view of wooded hills, the winding river, and an even older château miles off in the distance. Sit, chill, enjoy.

The drink was definitely relaxing me, and boy, was I glad to be married to an introvert. Whenever I was in a really foul mood like now, Stefan didn't pester me with questions, because he was sublimely comfortable with silence. I knew that when I was troubled, he could silently let me get over or through whatever I was dealing with, for as long as necessary. But after a sip of his drink, and some time on the floor massaging Marco's neck, he got busy. He set the table, took out a container of frozen pumpkin sirloin chili, defrosted it in the microwave, and then heated up a bowl for each of us. That was clearly a message to come down off the ledge he sensed I was on—but only if I was ready.

I heard it, felt it. I ate slowly and gratefully, the meaty aroma, the warmth, and the flavorings of cocoa and cumin settling me down, as effective as a deep shoulder massage. Marco abandoned his dog bed for the elusive promise of table scraps, and sat there carefully eyeing our bowls.

"We've never had Bloody Marys with dinner before," I said after a while.

Stefan smiled, looking very boyish for a middle-aged man. Then he added soberly, "But then we've never *both* been at a murder scene before. Not like that one. And *together.*" With a crooked smile, he said, "It seems appropriate."

Our dinner continued with intermittent chat about our classes while I calmed way, way down. I loved teaching, had loved it from my very first class years ago, and it meant more to me than any scholarly writing I'd done. Being able to mentor students was especially important given how badly some professors in the department behaved in the classroom.

Relaxing in the kitchen over some mocha java coffee from Coffee Magic, a local roaster, I finally was ready to talk about Viktor's infuriating comments in my office. We fed Marco his dinner and watched him chill out as much as I had, until he was curled up in my lap, snoozing while I gently stroked his back. Then I told Stefan everything.

When I was done, and before he could comment, I tried to look at the situation dispassionately, as if it had entangled someone else. "Okay, was he for real? Could the Board of Trustees really want to grab the fellowship? How would they even try? Would it make sense for me to talk to Vanessa and find out what options I have if they do?"

Stefan breathed in deeply. "Napoléon was greedy, that's really clear. That was his pattern, wanting to take things from others. He was probably like that as a kid. I know, I know, we don't have to psychoanalyze him," Stefan said to cut me off from objecting. "And if the trustees were big fans of his, then why *not* try a hostile takeover of the fellowship? I don't understand how they would go about it, but SUM's lawyers are like zombies in suits—they're relentless, especially when they're wrong." He paused. "That's what I've heard, anyway."

"So it's *World War Z*?"

"They're not that fast. More like *The Walking Dead*."

"Wonderful."

Stefan sat up sharply. "You know what? Maybe Napoléon made it all up, or maybe he *did* talk to the board but he knew there was no chance of messing with the fellowship, or they weren't interested and he just raised it with whomever to cause trouble."

"So he was trying to intimidate me by spreading rumors? And Viktor didn't know that?"

"Could be."

I had trouble believing that Napoléon had invented the story because I had no faith in the Board of Trustees doing anything honest, especially since they were routinely reappointed to their five-year terms and seemed to care more about their little fiefdom than about the university. I'd gone to one of their meetings years ago where the head of SUM's adjuncts' union had presented a solid case for higher pay and better working conditions for the "contingent" faculty.

The air in that lavishly appointed room had reeked of privilege and disconnection from reality. The meeting itself opened with fulsome, cringe-worthy praise from one member to another for their service and dedication and who knows what else. Whether they were in business or politics, they came across as grandees from some faded aristocracy exchanging flowery, meaningless, pro forma compliments at a masked ball. They even bowed their heads to each other—in thanks? In fake humility?

I heard buzzwords like "communality" and "openness" and "team spirit" at the meeting, yet it all felt hollow. I zoned out, which was easy to do in that stuffy dark-paneled room with dim recessed lighting and obscenely comfortable leather chairs. When the meeting was over I swore never to attend another one. It was just administrative theater. They would do whatever they pleased whenever they wanted to, and feedback from faculty and students meant nothing. They weren't quite evil, but they were pernicious, a cancer on the body of the university.

"But what would be in it for them, for the board?" I asked, trying to think clearly. "Napoléon could have been pushing some kind of hostile takeover of the fellowship, but why would they approve that? Maybe they agreed with him about bringing in that French writer, but honestly, one more high-profile speaker isn't going to make much of a difference in terms of PR, is it?"

"You pissed them off by getting the bequest—you're basically a nobody as they see it, looking down from Mount Olympus. So the board might have wanted to put you in your place. And I'm sure the Development Office would love nothing better than controlling the cash. Can't you just see their grasping, greedy little hands? They're quite territorial about gifts to the university, at least that's what I've heard. Someone in that office is probably pissed as hell that the fellowship money came with so many stipulations."

Those were sobering possibilities. Had my face betrayed disgust for the board when I was at the meeting years ago? And if so, had I been added to an Enemies List because of that? It wasn't unlikely. These were people who in another country and another era would have expected salutes and adulation.

Marco stirred in his sleep, stretched out all four legs and then curled back up. I thought how lucky he was to be spared the chaos and confusion of human life.

Stefan loaded the dishwasher and took out the garbage. I carried Marco out to the living room and set him down on the hearth rug where he started to snore lightly. I sprawled on the couch, trying to let go even more, and idly wishing there was something physically wrong with me so that I could register for medical marijuana, which had inexplicably been legalized in our otherwise conservative state. Stefan put on a CD of Saint-Saëns piano trios and sat opposite with his head back and eyes closed, enjoying the glittering post-prandial concert.

"What if somebody killed Napoléon because they needed

to silence him?" he asked thoughtfully. "What if he uncovered somebody's secret? Isn't that what most people are afraid of, being exposed?"

"Then killing him would be too risky. It might lead the police right *to* the secret."

"True."

But then I found myself warming to Stefan's idea. Why couldn't Napoléon somehow have discovered a secret about someone important, something that could damage or even destroy a career? It could be an affair by a Bible-thumping member of the Board of Trustees, or maybe a dean of one of the colleges was sleeping with a student? A celebrity like Napoléon would have been hobnobbing with SUM's elite, so who knew what he might have observed or uncovered—or what someone might have confessed to him while drunk? Or even in bed?

I shared those thoughts with Stefan, and he reminded me of a recent scandal at another university in Michigan where a student's murder by a roommate had been covered up by the administration—with help from campus police—out of fear that the story would create panic and tarnish the university's reputation. Of course once the cover-up fell apart, the story exploded onto the national stage and there were mass protests, firings, obstruction of justice indictments, and more than one lawsuit.

"How would we ever find out, though, if Napoléon knew more than he should have?" I mused aloud. "We're not hackers or anything, so we can't access his laptop or phone, and we're not burglars, either, so it's not like we could easily break into his house and look for clues."

"I know," Stefan said ruefully. "It's too bad we have such a limited skill set."

I sat up sharply as if I'd been injected with adrenaline. "Why did Ciska come here to talk to us that night before the retreat? Just because she lives nearby? That doesn't make sense now. She was up to something."

"Like what?"

"Viktor implied Ciska saw something in the men's room that would implicate me in Napoléon's murder. There's nothing, but what if she's trying to frame me? What if she killed him and I'm going to be blamed for it?" I had a horrifying vision of being dragged off to jail for something I hadn't done, of the police storming our new house the way they'd invaded our old one. And this time they might shoot Marco, since according to Vanessa, local cops were notorious for doing senseless things like that in a raid.

Stefan sat up, too, frowning, body tense, face tight. "She said the university didn't need another pig like Napoléon, or words to that effect, right here in this room. What if he never stopped harassing her sexually?"

I followed his thought: "She was incensed when she talked to us about Napoléon."

"But there's no evidence against you," he said firmly. "None. How can there be?"

Stefan answered his own question before I could formulate a reply: "Ciska could have gotten a fingerprint of yours when she was here and then planted it on the knife. I've seen it done in movies, it can't be all that hard. Which would explain why she came over—she was planning to kill him and implicate you." Then he shook his head. "That doesn't make sense, though. How would she know you'd be in the men's room at the right moment?"

I couldn't answer that because I was trying to remember the details of that evening and picture when Ciska could have lifted a print from my glass—if that's what she intended to do. But the details were blurry—it was her dark mood that dominated my recollection.

Marco started growling in his sleep. That's when I remembered something odd I had sensed when Ciska was here, and I had to bring it up. "When Ciska dropped in, I had a feeling like—"

"Like what?"

"I don't know for sure. Like the two of you knew something I didn't, I guess." It sounded lame, but there it was.

Stefan nodded vigorously. "It's no biggie. She's writing a memoir and she's been asking me for advice."

"You've been helping her?"

"Well, yeah. In a general way. She's associate chair, I didn't think blowing her off was a good idea."

"What's the memoir about?"

"She hasn't told me. She hasn't said much about herself— we've mostly talked about technical things, like what was the legality of revealing information about someone else's life, and then practical stuff like finding an agent. She also asked me for reading recommendations."

"When was all this?"

"Last month. We exchanged emails. I didn't mention it because it wasn't important and I was focused on getting my semester underway."

"Huh." Stefan having any contact with someone who might not just be a murderer, but a murderer covering her tracks by implicating *me*, well, that made me feel like I was in my car and suddenly driving on black ice.

Stefan clearly picked up my unease. "Nick, it was just a few exchanges, and right now, I don't think she'd be asking me for help with anything."

I saw his point. "But if she does contact you, I want you to let me know immediately."

"Of course!" He added, "She might just be writing a memoir about what it's like being a woman academic and getting harassed, or worse."

Then he sat forward, eyes wide as if he'd suddenly discovered something. "You know, this whole situation could be more complicated than we think. What if someone on the Board of Trustees wanted to get rid of Napoléon *and* get rid of you, too? Just because we heard the board loves him doesn't mean it has to be one hundred percent true, or true anymore. We've seen how he's treated his subordinates—what if he hasn't acted any better with the trustees? It's possible that he's been making enemies all across campus."

But as if my ears had been plugged on a plane and we'd unexpectedly changed altitude, I suddenly felt very clearheaded, and everything we'd been theorizing about now seemed extremely dubious, despite my own speculation before about the board being out to get me.

"Aren't we being paranoid?" I asked. "I mean, all that sounds almost like a conspiracy."

Stefan sat back in his chair, his face clouded. He was angry, but not at me. "After what happened to us in May," he said, "nothing is impossible. Nothing."

That was the stone cold truth, and I flip-flopped: paranoid or not, of course we were chewing over all the possibilities, no matter how improbable. Stefan and I had always been like the couple in Henry James's *The Ambassadors*: "The circle in which they stood was warm with life, and every question between them would live as nowhere else."

That was even truer when there was death outside of that circle.

16

CISKA MAY HAVE BEEN calm at the retreat center when she took charge, but by Tuesday morning, perhaps because of local press coverage of the aborted retreat and what was being called the "suspicious death" of our chair, she was in a state of panic, judging by the bizarre email she sent out:

> *To the Department:*
> *As the interim chair of the department I confess I feel a terrible urgency to reach out to all of you. Napoléon's death is an enormous shock. I can assure you I myself was gobsmacked. Appealing to the better angels of your nature, I strongly urge you to cancel your classes tomorrow and join me in a day of deep reflection and mourning in Shattenkirk Hall. We have a small auditorium on the first floor which is perfect for that purpose. Lunch will be provided. All are welcome: faculty, graduate assistants, and students—anyone whose life has been touched by this exceptional man.*
> *Ciska Balanchine*

I was up before Stefan and read that extraordinary message on the laptop in my study with Marco snoozing companionably in the other club chair. None of us in the department had known Napoléon all that well, and yet Ciska was writing about him as

if he'd been an integral part of the department and the university
for years—and as if he'd had an enormous impact, too, on many
people. It sounded awfully fake. She could have been a minis-
ter doing a eulogy about someone she had never met and was
working from notes gathered after a brief talk with the grieving
family. And I found it even more ridiculous that by appealing to
our "better angels" Ciska was referencing Abraham Lincoln's first
inaugural address. I guess it could've been worse, but snarky lines
from *The Boys in the Band* popped into my head: "Who *is* she?
Who *was* she? Who does she *hope* to be?"

Though I'd gone to the retreat despite reservations, I'd be
damned if I'd participate in this gathering Ciska was pushing on
us with her hyperbolic rhetoric. Marco stirred when I groaned
my dismay.

Relax, I thought. Re-lax.

I was certainly in the right location to let go, because
my study with its glossy emerald green walls was my favorite
room in the new house. It was filled with all my books dating back through graduate school and college to childhood in
antique-looking cherry wood bookcases with Gothic-style fini-
als. The green-and-blue Persian rug was a gift from my parents
and the combination of those two colors reminded me of one of
my favorite novels, *Women in Love*, where they're worn by one of
the main characters in the opening scene.

The room was decidedly old-fashioned and not remotely
Art Moderne, but it was comforting. I felt as walled off there
from Ciska's alarming state of mind as if I were on the Starship
Enterprise and the shields had just gone up. Though honestly,
I wouldn't have minded something more earthbound like the
concrete-roofed bunker Winston Churchill worked from in London during World War II.

Before I could finish my first cup of coffee, my campus mail
Inbox started filling up with a flurry of aggravated and irate
replies to Ciska from my colleagues. It was clear they'd been
simmering about having felt obligated to attend a retreat they

wanted to skip, next having been involved even tangentially in what was likely a murder, and finally having submitted to chilling interviews by our campus police. Now someone *else* was making ludicrous demands on their time? Insupportable. The game was on and she was the quarry.

Carson Karageorgevich got in the first hit in an email sent to everyone in the department. He accused Ciska of violating department by-laws, and since he chaired the Policy Committee that governed how the department was organized and run, I assumed that he was right. I skimmed his verbose email and gathered that he was obsessed with "due process."

Jasmine Alinejad attacked Ciska from a different angle and surprised me by chiding her for "sentimentalism" and "grief-mongering," whatever that meant. I would have expected Jasmine to be more supportive of any woman helming the department right now, but with Napoléon gone, there was evidently a power vacuum, and she might have gone after anyone trying to assume his role even temporarily.

Atticus Doyle and the other adjuncts complained as a group that Napoléon's death wasn't a sufficient cause for anyone losing a day in the classroom. After all, they argued, it wasn't as if the country, the state, or the university had suffered some kind of natural disaster or terrorist attack. Their manifesto actually called for canceling Ciska's plans and instead organizing "A Day of Awareness" focused on the systematic mistreatment of adjunct faculty.

Good luck with that, I thought.

Viktor Dahlberg made it very clear in a short email that he had no interest in a "breast-beating feelings festival." He in turn received some emails from Alinejad and other female professors attacking him for being a misogynist and an advocate of violence against women, thanks to his use of "breast-beating." He fired back that she was disgustingly literal, which generated ever more cyber-carnage.

The rest of the proliferating emails were a chaotic mix: people either supported or disagreed with the latest eruption—or said they would stay neutral about "official mourning" until they had more time to process Sunday's events. It was a hot mess.

Ciska stayed out of it but that last thread seemed to outrage her, because her response was: "The day is exactly *about* bloody processing!" I know she used the word "bloody" because it was one of her Anglicisms, but it seemed wildly inappropriate. And blowing up at people who criticized her was not going to earn Ciska any points whatsoever. I was tempted to suggest, privately, that she see a therapist.

Stefan had apparently checked his email on his iPhone upstairs or in the kitchen before bringing a cup of coffee into my study, so he was pretty much up to speed.

"Ciska's falling apart," he observed. Barefoot, he himself seemed very calm in his blue tank top and Nordstrom's blue-checked lounge pants, and he smelled freshly showered.

"Tell me about it. My students would say she was seriously losing her shit."

"Much more poetic," he joked.

Marco had woken up at the sound of Stefan's voice, jumped off the chair to greet him, and leapt back into his lap when Stefan took that chair and settled in with his coffee and his phone. I envied his composure and the general way he had always seemed so confident and poised in his masculinity. I guess good looks and good posture always help.

Stefan muttered something as he read through the proliferating department emails. Then he said aloud, "Nick—check out what Roberto Robustelli just sent."

I did, and it had upped the morning's craziness factor. Roberto's email was short and could have passed for satire: *"We all have to commend the associate chair for her courage, commitment, and team spirit in a dangerous time. Leadership like that is a blessing."*

"What's courageous about freaking out and wanting everyone else to support you when you implode?"

"Not much," Stefan said. "If he's not needling her somehow, then this could be a kind of Mafia kiss of death."

I frowned. "Meaning?"

Stefan explained: "Signaling that she's finished." He thought that over. "Or he could be trying to egg her on to something even more outrageous so that she gets canned." He looked down. "Get this! Ciska just sent out an apology. Whoa, that was fast…."

> *To the Department:*
>
> *I most sincerely regret if I have offended anyone in acting swiftly to try showing my admiration and regard for a fallen comrade. Cancel your classes only if you would feel comfortable and humane demonstrating respect for the dead, only if a culture of compassion at SUM matters to you. Join us in what will be a more than memorable time in which we can re-consecrate ourselves to the mission of being our best selves and offering a model to our colleagues across the College of Humanities and the campus at large, a model of sensitivity, enlightened thinking, responsibility, and compassion. And of course, how else will we find closure if we do not seek it together?*
>
> *Ciska Balanchine*

I read it again, slowly, in a state of disbelief. "That's not an apology, it's a passive-aggressive Fuck You. Even if she used the word 'compassion' twice."

"You're right about that." He grimaced like someone with a sore tooth.

"Ciska despised Napoléon—what the hell is this bullshit?"

Stefan sipped some coffee and put his phone down on the chair arm. "Could be she feels she *has* to do something as associate chair. Maybe she's being pressured by somebody higher up."

"The mournathon she wants us to attend makes as much sense as the whole department going bowling. After Sunday's disaster, she should just let us all alone and not try to bring people together."

Stefan nodded.

"And *closure?*" I asked. "Napoléon hasn't been dead seventy-two hours, for God's sake. Besides, this kind of shindig should be run by someone from SUM's Counseling and Personal Growth Center, somebody trained to get people opening up about how they feel. Why would anyone share how they felt about anything with Ciska leading the group? Napoléon at least had some charm. Ciska has counter-charm."

"That's harsh."

"No it isn't," I said. "If she's telling people I killed Napoléon, then she's truly malign. And I need to find out why she's doing that."

"Agreed. But there's that 'if.' Viktor could have made the whole story up—and don't ask me why right now, because I'm starving. Let's get some breakfast."

We removed to the kitchen where Marco got his bowl of kibble and organic fat-free yogurt first. Then Stefan started scrambled eggs with cream, *fines herbes*, and fresh snipped chives, and I handled the rye toast and set up thick-cut bacon to microwave. Neither task demanded my full attention, so every now and then I checked in to the continuing stream of department emails, and then there was unexpectedly one from Dean Bullerschmidt.

"Stefan, get this, the dean is saying that Ciska has, I quote, 'grossly exceeded her authority and acted in violation of university protocols.' Somebody must have griped to him about her plans."

I pictured cruel-eyed Dean Bullerschmidt typing with his blunt, beautifully manicured, perfumed fingers. He was a bizarre combination of the Fat Man and Joel Cairo in *The Maltese Falcon*, unctuous and threatening, a bully who had always longed to rise higher in the university than dean and hated every witness to his failure to do so. He was the kind of man you could easily picture as a Byzantine emperor sentencing his rivals and enemies to be tied up in a sack and dropped from a cliff into the sea—after they had been blinded. I'm sure that would have been my fate with him in charge. But as much as I found him disagreeable, I was happy that he had stepped into the fray the way he had.

Stefan brought out Irish butter and Bonne Maman orange marmalade after the table was set and we sat down to a little feast. I couldn't help thinking that part of our enjoyment of food was the simple thrill of being alive. Maybe that was morbid, but it seemed a relief.

"You know," Stefan said, "we're lucky none of the news reports say anything about who found Napoléon's body, because otherwise we'd be besieged by phone calls. It didn't even leak onto Twitter."

Both of us had dealt with intrusive reporters of all kinds before, and I crunched on a slice of bacon while appreciating our reprieve from media scrutiny.

"Too big a crowd there at the retreat," I said, looking for an explanation. "And Napoléon *was* famous."

Stefan put down his knife and fork and bowed his head.

"Are you praying?" I asked, a little embarrassed.

"No. Just imagining if it had been you, if something had happened to you—but I was also thinking that Napoléon didn't deserve to die like that."

"How *did* he deserve to die?"

"It was a figure of speech."

"Yeah, well, whatever. He did deserve to be bounced, but that was never going to happen. Not for a while, anyway. A new chair always gets three years before a review, right?"

"Ciska wants to be chair now that Napoléon's dead," Stefan said decisively, rising to pour himself some more coffee. Leaning back against a counter, he said as if plotting a course on a map, "That first email she sent was all about positioning herself as proactive, as a leader."

"Well, it was an epic failure and the dean smacked her down. Hard."

"But you know how unpredictable this place is. She could still end up as chair, interim chair, I mean. Look how President Yubero installed Napoléon, with the blessing of the trustees. Nothing is normal around here anymore."

"Was it ever? This place is totally fugazi."

"Fugazi?"

"You know, fucked up."

"I know what it means, but I think you better stop watching so many cop shows. It doesn't fit you."

"Neither does being a murder suspect." I finished my delicious eggs. "Let's say Viktor was telling me the truth, and Ciska has been spreading it around that I killed Napoléon, what would be her motivation? There's only one thing I can think of: *she* killed him. He assaulted her, or worse, and she thought the only way to get justice was to take care of the situation herself. And she chose the perfect place. There were so many people at the retreat, how would anyone have noticed her slipping into the men's room after him?"

Stefan nodded. "Anything is possible. But Ciska is kind of noticeable. Don't you think someone would have seen her?"

"Forget that for now. Why blame me?"

"Maybe she would have blamed anyone who found his body—"

"—because like I said, *she did it*. She murdered Napoléon. There's no other reason she would be pointing the finger at someone else."

17

THE CRAZINESS ESCALATED the next morning with another email from Dean Bullerschmidt, this one curtly summoning the entire department to his office for an emergency meeting at the end of the day.

SUM was known across academia in the Midwest for being top-heavy with overpaid administrators, and Bullerschmidt was Exhibit A for anyone wanting to make a case about bureaucratic bloat and abuse. He was not respected in his field of Religious Studies (he thought Judaism was solely religious, not cultural as well), and on campus his reputation was abysmal among faculty because of his preference for early morning breakfast meetings which he presided over rudely and arrogantly. Anyone working with him—no matter what the project—was also barraged by emails and toxic attitude: he seemed to believe that nobody else on campus worked as hard as he did. Acting martyred when they were obscenely privileged was far too typical of SUM's administrators.

Bullerschmidt reigned appropriately enough in a nineteenth-century granite and sandstone Gothic Revival building bristling with turrets.

"It could have been worse," Stefan pointed out. "He could have asked us to see him first thing in the morning, right? We'll be tired at five P.M. but at least the meeting won't spoil the whole day."

"*Any* time we spend with Bullerschmidt is hateful."

The dean had once pressured Stefan not to publish a book about a student suicide on campus, because it would be bad for SUM's image. After the violence of last spring, he'd wanted us both gone from campus for a year even though neither one of us had a sabbatical coming up. He would have bent the rules to make that happen, but only because it was all about PR. That attack, in which we'd been the targets, was an incident the university would've liked to pretend had never happened. Changing the name of our department and moving it to another building wasn't enough. If SUM had a witness protection program I'm sure Bullerschmidt would have tried to hustle us off to another state.

Of course, not one administrator ever asked us if we needed counseling after our trauma. We were an embarrassment, not colleagues who might need support and consolation.

"What do you think the meeting's about?" Stefan's narrowed eyes and eager tone convinced me he was making mental notes for a book, or a short story at the very least. I hoped it was in the school of Edgar Allan Poe or Stephen King.

I shrugged. "Maybe Bullerschmidt wants everyone in the department to sign promises that we won't talk to the press—like some kind of non-disclosure agreement or something ridiculous like that—which he can't do...well, he can try, I guess, but that's bullshit. Nobody would agree to it."

Out of morbid curiosity, Stefan and I arrived early and the dean's office wasn't exactly as I remembered it, which made me think it had been remodeled yet again over the summer while we were in Europe. Summertime was SUM's favorite season for any changes of whatever kind they wanted to keep on the down low. But where was all this money coming from at a time when ever-increasing numbers of adjunct faculty continued to be paid so poorly?

The whole suite still looked more like a high-tech kitchen

than anything else: everything was white marble or brushed stainless steel. But the place seemed noisier, and filled with more of his myrmidons, one of whom asked if we were there for the meeting and led us deeper into his lair. It was all as weirdly contemporary as before, but I thought it took longer to get to his office, and that we passed more desks and small offices on the way, as if progressing through antechambers on the way to a royal audience in the throne room.

"Ah," the dean said with no sign of enthusiasm from behind a lavish semicircular desk carved from a hunk of white-and-gold marble. If parents only knew how much administrators were paid at SUM, and how they lived—

"Professors Hoffman and Borowski." Fat, imposing, and saurian, he exuded a peculiar mix of boredom and exasperation, as if he were a mob boss and we were some lowlife punks who had once again failed to carry out an easy hit.

He was snazzily dressed as usual, this time in a chalk-striped deep blue suit, sky-blue shirt with a white collar, wide burgundy-and-blue patterned tie with a matching burgundy pocket square that flowered in his jacket pocket. His gold tie clip was encrusted with what I assumed were real diamonds. Set in a round, babyish face, Bullerschmidt's blue eyes looked more intimidating than usual as he lumbered out from behind his desk to usher us into his private conference room next door.

This was windowless and blank-walled and could easily seat two dozen people around an oval ebony table and another two dozen in uncomfortable-looking chairs arranged along three walls. The dark carpeting and dark wood paneling made the room feel gloomy and claustrophobic. But the reddish-brown chair at the head of the table was unlike anything I'd ever seen before on campus: the wooden arms and back were so elaborately carved that Stefan took a photo of it on his phone and found it almost immediately on the Internet for sale at $5,000. A perfect choice for a typical grandiose SUM bully who left us waiting there while he returned to his office for more charming greetings, I supposed. It seemed odd to me that he didn't have an assistant handle this part, but almost everything at SUM seemed odd right now.

Except my classes.

I headed for the back of the room, to sit as far as possible away from where Bullerschmidt would be seated, though I realized as I took my seat it would have been smarter to sit by the door. That way I could vamoose if whatever this meeting was about suddenly went sideways, but it was too late to make a change. Stefan sat next to me, glumly asking under his breath why I hadn't picked a spot near the exit. Why indeed?

As if a tour bus had pulled up outside a famous monument and disgorged its passengers, the room began filling up with the same crew that had been at the retreat, and everyone paused briefly, looking up from their phones, deciding whether to sit at the table or in the chairs along the walls. Was the table more prestigious or more exposed, would taking a wall seat make you feel safer or one of the *hoi polloi*?

Once seats were chosen, they all turned back to their phones, silent, heads bent in veneration of always being available—or perhaps they were all playing video games. There was no murmuring, there were no conversations at all. My colleagues were as grim and silent as if they'd been taken hostage and were afraid of being beaten if they spoke even a single word.

Ciska Balanchine had claimed a seat to the right of what was clearly the Dean's chair at the table, given its higher back, as if she were the guest of honor at some Edwardian dinner. She didn't make eye contact with anyone in the room, and was resplendent again in red and gold. Like everyone else, she was held captive by her smart phone. I stared at her, still struggling with what I'd been told by Viktor, tempted to confront her right then, but there were too many people around.

As the room filled to capacity, the silence reminded me of a Latin phrase my European-educated mother liked to quote when I was growing up: *Cum tacent, clamant.* Translated, it meant something like "We scream with silence."

I was sure that if the room's occupants revealed what they were really thinking right then, the chaos would make the walls shudder. That's how tense the room was, and I could feel my throat tightening. Why hadn't I stayed away and waited for someone to tell me what happened at the meeting? And why hadn't I brought a bottle of water?

The German twins Heino and Jonas took seats near us, also against the wall, and they were speaking to each other in German as equably as if there had never been conflict between them, let alone that crazy imbroglio at the retreat center.

"Look at them," I whispered to Stefan, and he knew what I meant.

"Bizarre," he said softly.

The room was already feeling overcrowded and too warm when the dean entered with a round wicker basket in one hand.

"I would like everyone to turn off their phones," he ordered, "and put them in this basket so that we can all stay focused."

As if those words were a signal, the conference room door was shut by someone from the outside and all I could think of was a corny movie from the Fifties, *Land of the Pharaohs*, where Joan Collins was sealed up in a tomb with her husband's massive gold coffin, and the sand came rushing in from all directions to seal the tomb and suffocate her along with all the royal servants who would attend the pharaoh in the Afterlife. I could see her as if I'd just watched the movie the night before, lying on the floor of the tomb and weeping, "I don't want to die."

Why hadn't I brought my Xanax with me? Stefan often reminded me, but I kept forgetting to have it on me. Stefan quietly took my hand.

The dean passed the basket to Ciska. Looking alarmed, as if somehow she was complicit in this move, she hesitantly complied, and so did everyone else in the room, some spitefully, some graciously, some as carelessly as if they were tossing away a burner phone. The basket zig-zagged its way around the room, from someone sitting against the wall to someone at the table, back and forth, growing heavier and more symbolic of our incarceration. The dean seemed to be glowing with satisfaction that he would ostensibly have our full attention for whatever was coming.

While the basket lurched our way, I studied the room.

Viktor Dahlberg sat at the table next to Roberto Robustelli and Carson Karageorgevich, which surprised me because I didn't think they liked one another. Atticus Doyle and the other adjunct faculty were seated at the end of the table where they could face the dean. Jasmine Alinejad and the women professors I was beginning to think might be her coterie—or power base?—were defiantly lined up against the wall opposite the door, glowering.

Among the large number of faculty I barely knew, there were other combinations that might have been random but somehow felt purposeful, unlike a typical gathering of our faculty which always felt haphazard and disconnected. It was almost as if the dean had caught everyone in the middle of various conspiracies and rounded them all up. I had the creepy sensation that there were new power dynamics and alliances in the room that I was totally locked out of. Perhaps because we were the department's only out gay couple. Perhaps because Stefan, the department's writer-in-residence, was my spouse. Even the people who taught Queer Theory typically kept away from him (and me by extension) because he was a living author within reach, and therefore unworthy of respect in their myopic worldview.

Perhaps because something else was brewing in the wake of Napoléon's death.

Or had even preceded it. What was the phrase I had read in a P.G. Wodehouse novel? "Wheels within wheels." Remembering that line for some reason made me realize there were no refreshments, not even water on the huge table. Either this was going to be a short meeting, or else the dean wanted us to remain uncomfortable, maybe even to suffer. My money was on the second possibility.

When the basket reached us, Stefan put in his phone reluctantly since he did all his business as an author via email or texts. Me, I didn't mind as much.

When the basket returned to him, Bullerschmidt sat there, his nose wrinkling with disgust as if we were foul-smelling supplicants and he was our liege lord. Without any kind of phony preamble thanking us for showing up and acknowledging that we were very busy people, he said, "SUM prizes...Safety...Security...Civility." Then he looked slowly around the room before continuing. "That is the new motto of our college. In that vein I can assure you all that the College of Humanities is cooperating fully and completely with the investigation into the death of your former chair."

I wondered what civility had to do with anything right now but didn't have time to worry that particular bone because the dean rolled onward in a rich baritone that seemed wasted on a university administrator. He should have been an anchorman on local TV: a very large fish in a very small pond.

"Know that you have our deepest sympathy," he intoned like an unctuous mortician. "But be aware that you must not impede the investigation in any way, shape, or form."

Stefan and I exchanged curious looks, and Carson Karageorgevich spoke up to say what I imagined most of us were thinking: "Why would you assume anyone would get in the way of campus police?"

"I assume nothing," the dean said without even looking at Carson. "I'm merely reminding you of your responsibilities."

"That's why we're here?"

Now the dean *did* look at Carson, and smiled. "I've brought you here to talk about continuity in your department. I understand that Professor Balanchine has temporarily assumed the chair and I want to thank her for stepping up in the way she has."

Ciska nodded her head and looked like she was about to issue the academic version of "Aw, shucks," but she didn't get a chance.

"I have decided, however, to appoint someone else as interim chair. Professor Robustelli."

Carson went pale, Viktor closed his eyes as if wishing he could teleport himself out of this mess, and Ciska burst out with "What? Are you joking?" The room stirred with a swirl of puzzled comments and questions, but the only person who didn't look surprised was Robustelli himself. A grin flickered on and off his face, and I wondered how many people caught it.

"He knew," Stefan whispered to me, and I nodded.

Jasmine Alinejad said to the dean, "You're violating the department's by-laws."

Bullerschmidt smiled as silkily as if he'd sprung a trap on her. "In fact, you will find that the university's by-laws supersede the by-laws of any individual department. Under exigent circumstances, a dean may make interim appointments. I would say that the death…and possible murder…of a department chair would fit that description."

The word *murder* sent a visible chill rippling throughout the room.

Bullerschmidt added, "I have the support and confidence of the Board of Trustees in this decision." And there it was once again: faculty were rendered powerless.

"I'm not working with that bastard!" Ciska announced, arms crossed like a furious superhero about to unleash one of her powers.

Robustelli smiled like a stage villain, and said, "No worries, I've already selected someone else."

"This is fucking outrageous and sexist," Jasmine spat out. "Ciska is the first female chair we've ever had and you're ousting her!"

The room erupted in shouting, and some of my colleagues

must have thought they were in Parliament because they cried, *"Shame!"* Face as flushed as if she'd been slapped hard, Ciska jerked herself out of her chair, snarling, *"This is a bloody coup!"* She grabbed a red leather shoulder bag from the floor and circled around Bullerschmidt to the door, stopping there to face Robustelli. "And you—! You're a fucking lowlife traitor." Then she jerked open the door and stormed off.

Applause broke out across the room, leaving the dean stony-faced. And our new chair yawned ostentatiously as if to show that he was unfazed by Ciska's exit and by how her peers seemed to support her.

I didn't applaud, but my heart was with Ciska—even though she might be working against me—not for what she said, but for her dramatic defiance. If only more faculty followed her example by confronting the powerful instead of bowing their heads to avoid conflict.

The conference room door was open now, and from where I was seated, I could see Detective Valley lurking just across the threshold, like a vampire waiting for an invitation to enter a home he meant to despoil.

18

DEAN BULLERSCHMIDT NODDED magisterially, which somehow worked to silence the room. "I believe we're done here," he said ominously.

My colleagues exited as swiftly as if they'd heard the siren for a tornado warning, and I waited till the dean himself had left the room before Stefan and I stood up to go. Bullerschmidt was not at his opulent desk or anywhere in sight, and I walked right past Valley even though he called my name as we made our way out of the busy suite. The detective caught up with me and Stefan at the elevator.

"Professor Hoffman, I'd like to talk to you about your former chair." His words were clipped, unemotional, and he had his usual look of a scavenger.

Stefan grabbed my arm to keep me quiet, but I turned to face Valley after punching the elevator's Down button again. "Is it a murder? Am I a person of interest?"

Valley said nothing, which was clearly a ploy to keep me talking until I revealed something incriminating. But I didn't fall into his trap. "My lawyer is Vanessa Liberati."

Stefan slapped my back in support.

Valley smiled, suddenly more genial: "I understand your rights, Professor. But why wouldn't you want to talk to me? Is it because you have something to hide? Don't you want to tell me your story since everyone else is telling theirs?" He paused as if that fact had significance, as if it could scare me somehow, as if I were merely an uneducated felon who knew nothing about police tricks. "It won't take much time, my office is five minutes across campus."

The elevator arrived and Stefan pulled me into it. We stared Detective Valley down until the doors closed.

"That was creepy," Stefan said as we headed to his SUV, which was parked in a nearby faculty lot.

"Valley is always creepy."

Campus had mostly emptied out and it was already past our college town's version of rush hour, so we were home in a few minutes, following a route that never took us past our old house.

After tending to Marco's needs, we got down to the serious business of dinner while our pup enjoyed a post-prandial nap. Stefan opened a bottle of Peninsula Ridge Estates Equinox, a smoky, fruity white blend we'd bought a case of on a wine tour through Canada's Niagara region. I took a long slow drink from my glass and it brought back the sunshine and great food of that distant time. I'd only been back at the university for over a month and already I was longing to get away. How was that healthy?

Something about all the current chaos made me crave pasta again, which meant I would have to swim more laps the next time I was at our health club. I set some fresh tagliatelli to boil and grated some imported Parmesan, the rich aroma and the rhythmic scrape of cheese on metal relaxing me as much as the wine had. I chopped two cups of fresh basil leaves in the Cuisinart and blended in a cup of crème fraîche, pouring the finished sauce into a large bowl. When the pasta was done, I added it to the bowl, stirred in a cup of the grated Parmesan, and brought it to the table, which Stefan had set with the gold-and-white French linens my parents had given us as a housewarming gift.

"This is fantastic," he said after a first bite. Then, talking with his mouth half-full, he said, "I can't believe Roberto's going to be our new chair. He's a thug, a goon."

I laughed and Stefan asked what was going on.

"I just realized that if he's chair, he only teaches one course per semester, right? And you can be damned sure it's not going to be freshman composition. That's what Napoléon wanted him to teach, so *his* problem is solved. Nobody's going to tell him what to teach anymore. And all those poor students will get a break."

"True. But is he going to be any less power-hungry than Napoléon was? I don't think so. He'll just be louder, brasher, more offensive."

I poured myself more wine while that sunk in.

Then he said, "I have to admit that I admired what Ciska did at the meeting."

I nodded. Meetings at SUM were too often like quicksand. Nobody ever left despite what was going on and every moment dragged you further down till you felt like you were suffocating.

"It was crazy," I said, "but kind of brave to just freak out like she did. I'm still going to have to find out if it's true, though, what Viktor said about her, I mean—that she's trying to implicate me in Napoléon's death."

He nodded, swallowed, and said, "I'm coming with you. You'll need a witness."

As we continued dinner, I tried not to think about how bizarre our life had become now that we were contemplating a confrontation with someone who might have accused me of murder. They say everyone is the hero of their own story, but couldn't I just switch genres?

Given her fondness for Anglicisms and for all things British, it wasn't surprising that Ciska lived in a house that looked as if it had been transplanted from England. The smallest home on her street a few blocks away from us, it was a charming red brick cottage with two leaded-glass windows upstairs and downstairs, and ivy-covered trellises flanking the front door with its elaborate lion's-head door knocker. The tiny, well-trimmed lawn was walled off from the street by a yew hedge and I felt I was stepping completely out of my own world when we walked up the gravel path lined with pink hydrangeas leading to her front door.

Answering my knock, Ciska was all smiles. "Oh, bless you for coming! That meeting was horrendous." She made it sound as if she had invited us, or at any rate had expected us, which was weird in itself. Unless she thought we were making a sympathy call.

She ushered us into a low-ceilinged, chintz-filled living room made smaller and more confining by exposed wooden ceiling beams and the oppressive pattern of tiny pink roses on the drapes, sofa, and overstuffed armchairs. Side tables and the wooden mantel teemed with china figurines of shepherds and their friends. Everything was as pink and white and cream-colored as an over-decorated birthday cake, and the room was filled with the cloying aroma of pink-and-white lilies standing in a huge pink vase set inside the fireplace. Luckily neither of us was allergic. To the flowers or her color scheme.

"Please sit down! Will you join me in a sherry?" Still wearing red, Ciska sounded a bit manic, unless she was putting on an act for some reason. But I said yes to sherry and so did Stefan. He was frowning and must have been wondering—like me—why Ciska was so glad to see us if she had been spreading lies about me. It didn't add up.

We settled on the well-padded couch. There was a bottle of some kind of Amontillado on the very low oaken coffee table with curved-in legs that reminded me of a turtle, and Ciska rushed to get us sherry glasses. I don't know much about sherry, but it was smooth and nutty, with a pleasant hint of molasses and salt.

Ciska watched us sip as happily as if she had bottled it herself, and she beamed when we told her how good it was.

"Lovely! And again, I can't tell you how very grateful I am that you stopped by after I was sabotaged once again, by someone I trusted, someone I was working with."

I didn't hesitate: "What are you talking about? You mean the dean?"

She knocked back her sherry but still held the glass, tightly, and crossed her legs, looking as mournful as a kid whose puppy had just been run over.

"I *trusted* him," she repeated, eyes down.

"Who?" Stefan asked.

"Roberto."

"*Him?*" My voice had shot up an octave with surprise. "Roberto? You trusted him how, to do what?"

"To help me get rid of Napoléon, or try to, anyway." And she was suddenly quiet, musing darkly, shut off from us as if we were creditors threatening to take this house away from her.

Now I was totally confused. Stefan's eyes had gone wide, and I suppose mine had, too. Was Ciska implying that she had wanted Roberto to *kill* Napoléon like some kind of hitman? I waited for her to come out of her funk. She did when Stefan coughed to get her attention and asked if he could have more sherry.

"So sorry! Of course! Help yourself!" Now Ciska was smiling again, but with a bitter edge.

"Tell me what you're talking about," I said sharply. "Because I'm not following."

"Neither am I," Stefan said more gently, and motioned for me to tone it down.

She sighed and it didn't seem to make her feel any better, but now she was meeting our eyes at least. "It was a sort of cabal, I guess you'd call it. I know those twats on the Board of Trustees thought Napoléon was a superb pick. But Roberto and I, and some other faculty, we went to the dean to personally inform him about everything that Napoléon was doing wrong. How he was trampling on our rights—"

She broke off because Stefan muttered something that I didn't quite catch but sounded like mild disapproval. "Okay, yes, that's a bit strong. But you have to admit that taking away Viktor's beloved summer program was a terrible thing to do."

"Viktor was involved, too?" I asked.

"Oh, yes, of course he was."

Stefan cleared his throat, and I guessed he was warning me not to mention what Viktor had told me about Ciska trying to implicate me in Napoléon's death—not yet, anyway. I nodded at him. It definitely wasn't the right time to bring that up because it might stop Ciska from telling the story she clearly wanted to tell us.

"Viktor and I have met at conferences here and there and I knew how much the Sweden program meant to him. Perhaps too much, but what's wrong with that kind of dedication? And Carson's been treated shabbily as well, worse than that. He's only an associate professor you know, and Napoléon told him to his face—*to his face*—that he would *never* be promoted to full professor. Napoléon said that he would move heaven and earth (my words, of course) to make sure it didn't happen."

"What did Napoléon have against Carson?"

Ciska shook her head. "You'll have to ask him."

"Where did Roberto figure into this?"

She almost snorted in anger. Leaning forward a little, eyes bright and angry, mouth tight, she said, "He was the ringleader. Roberto was the one who suggested that the four of us go to the dean to complain, once he found out how the rest of us were being sabotaged and attacked. You probably know he was furious about being made to teach freshmen—it's not like he kept that a secret. Well, he *said* he was furious. Maybe it was all some kind of ruse, because now it looks like he and the dean were in cahoots."

Curiouser and curiouser, I thought.

"Jasmine Alinejad wanted to join us," Ciska said, her tone changing and her face starting to flush.

"What did Napoléon do to piss *her* off?

"She wants the department to have more Middle Eastern and Asian guest speakers, which may be a valid point since we do tend to be Euro-centric, but it's hard to take her seriously. I mean, she writes about Iranian novelists in her scholarly work, but she doesn't speak or even read Farsi. Everyone on campus who's Iranian has tried reaching out to her, inviting her to dinners, parties, meetings—even out for coffee. She always refuses. I think she's afraid of being exposed as a phony, an imposter. And that so-called memoir of hers? Pure drivel."

I hadn't heard about Jasmine's lack of language skills. "How can you write about books you only read in translation?"

"Indeed," Ciska said, with her chin high, and once again I marveled at how the academic world could reward people who didn't deserve it.

"But wait—isn't Jasmine in the department because you pushed for her to be hired?"

"Rubbish! Jasmine is nothing more than a diversity hire, a bit of window dressing. She should be teaching at a community college, not SUM. Having her in our department is a joke." Ciska fiercely waved a hand in the air in front of her as if banishing Jasmine—or cutting her down.

Her anger about Jasmine surprised me.

Stefan said as if thinking aloud, "It sounds like entrapment when you all went to see the dean, like Roberto wanted to sabotage the rest of you. But why? What's the point? Why would he do it?"

Ciska actually wrung her hands like someone in a melodrama. "I don't know. Maybe to build a power base by pushing us out of the way?"

"It could have been pure spite," I said doubtfully.

"God, he's such a wanker!"

I couldn't disagree with that assessment.

"So we met with the dean and he seemed surprisingly

sympathetic," Ciska went on. "He agreed with us that Napoléon was abusing his authority—or I thought he agreed, anyway."

"But what did you think was going to happen when you all complained to Bullerschmidt?"

"That he would dismiss Napoléon. I know, I know. I was naïve...." A seasoned academic like Ciska, naïve about how power worked at our institution? I found that strange. Administrators at SUM were routinely arrogant, high-handed, biased, incompetent, and dishonest—if not worse. Why would they bother to take faculty complaints seriously? I knew of one department chair who had actually been mentally unstable, hiding under his desk when challenged, putting his hands over his ears and shouting, "I can't hear you!" Faculty complaints had no effect—it was only when he did that at a university luncheon with dozens of witnesses that he was quietly removed and given what was called a "special assignment" to the provost. That was code for keeping someone out of sight and out of trouble.

It had been at the back of my mind so I had to say it. "You could have told the dean what happened between you and Napoléon." Whatever that was.

She breathed in deeply. "Well, actually, you know I did. Right after it happened. He just wouldn't believe me."

"Seriously?"

"Oh, yes, I told the dean everything," she said dispassionately, her gaze shifting inward as if recalling the plot of a film. "I was flattered that Napoléon praised my book. You're authors, you know what it's like when a reader truly, deeply understands a book you spent years on, *gets it*, as if you'd written the book just for them. It's brilliant."

I knew she meant that in the British sense of "fantastic." Now, my books about Edith Wharton didn't get that kind of response from anyone, but I'd seen it happen plenty of times for Stefan and I always shared his delight.

Stefan said, "Yes. It's the best, almost as good as a great review."

He was sitting back, legs crossed comfortably, looking surprisingly relaxed. Me, I suddenly felt like a voyeur, because I wanted to hear Ciska's story and find out exactly what had taken place between her and Napoléon, but my own curiosity left me slightly nauseated. It was like suddenly discovering that an actor you admire is an addict and you're torn between ignoring the news completely and delving into all the grotesque details.

Ciska had withdrawn from us again. Her eyes were shut and her arms crossed, as if to fend off the memories that were all around us now, whether they'd been revealed or not. I could almost smell them, like a wet, smoking log in a fire that can't quite get going.

Stefan asked her, "What exactly happened with Bullerschmidt?" It seemed to work. She opened her eyes and shook her head as if coming out of an intense fog.

"I told him everything. How flattered and pleased I was that the new chair, and someone so famous, liked my new book. And when Napoléon invited me to his office to talk about it, why would I have suspected anything? He said he wanted to congratulate me and he brought out a bottle of twenty-year-old Armagnac he said was a gift from Catherine Deneuve. So I had a drink with him. I had several. It was five o'clock and his secretary was leaving. He went out to say good-bye to her, and then he closed his office door, which didn't seem strange until he came up behind me and started massaging my shoulders. I tried to pull away, but have you ever sat in one of those horrible chairs he had?"

I nodded.

"So you know you can't get out of them easily, that you're sort of lying back, almost. I'd had a few drinks, and then he came around the chair and suddenly was on top of me, grabbing my breasts and sticking his tongue in my mouth. I managed to knee him in the groin. He called me a bitch and tried to smack me but I was able to slide out of the chair under him, and finally got away.…"

I could see it all too vividly. Napoléon was strong and fit, she'd been disarmed by his flattery and his Armagnac, and felt vulnerable.

"That's probably why he decided to take over course assignments from me. Revenge, plain and simple."

I had no problem believing that.

"I never reported what happened to the campus police because I knew nobody would believe that I had been sexually assaulted. They'd ask me how many drinks I had, why did I stay when he closed the door, what was I wearing—and worse." She sat up a little taller as if facing someone posing those questions. "That's what's happened to students on campus who've been assaulted. *They* get blamed. And Bullerschmidt said that to him it sounded like a date gone amiss. Yes, he actually *said* that, he called it a date. SUM administrators are notorious for covering up any kind of scandal, especially sexual assault." Then she added grimly, "And when I spoke to a counselor at SUM, she said I should just work on myself and forget going public. I remember her words exactly: 'He's famous and powerful. You'll be turned inside out by the media. Is that what you want? Publicity? Shame? How can you find closure if you let that happen?' "

Stefan looked as horrified as I felt.

"But at the retreat, you didn't seem angry at Napoléon," Stefan observed.

"I was livid, but I had to suppress it. Can you afford to antagonize the chair of your own department?"

"Did *you* kill him?" I blurted out.

She flinched as if she'd quickly crossed a carpeted room and been shocked by static electricity. "Of course not. I loathed Napoléon, but I didn't want him dead. I wanted him disgraced and scorned. I wanted paparazzi to torment him non-stop. I wanted his life to turn into a stupid hashtag with millions of people reviling him on Twitter."

She was as fired up now as a Sunday TV preacher ranting about hellfire.

"Stabbing him in the gut like that would be too quick. I wanted to see Napoléon *suffer.* I wanted him to feel like Pharaoh's Egypt being hit by one plague after another. *That's* what I wanted."

Stefan must've looked skeptical, because she said to him, "Don't you get it? Killing Napoléon would have been too easy, it would have been like letting him off the hook when he deserved to hang from one like a butchered steer."

She closed her eyes as if daydreaming. "I wanted to crush him. That's not murder, that's pleasure."

19

CISKA SEEMED SO terrifyingly clearheaded and honest in her anger that I finally raised what Viktor Dahlberg had told me, because it seemed like the right time. But afterward, she looked even angrier if that were possible: red-faced, lips clamped shut, legs tightly crossed.

"Viktor said *what*? That I was accusing you of killing Napoléon? Bollocks!"

"But why would he lie?"

She shrugged scornfully. "I have absolutely no idea. Maybe he just wanted to cause trouble."

"Why would he do that to Nick?" Stefan chimed in. "It doesn't make sense. Viktor came to Nick to complain about Napoléon a few days ago, and then he turns around and slanders Nick, accuses Nick of murder? I just don't get it."

Now Ciska seemed to relax. And she sighed as if dealing with some dim-witted students asking questions whose obvious answer was on the syllabus they'd been given the first day of class.

"Viktor has never been right in the head since his wife died. And he's a Swede, anyway, isn't he? Or half-Swedish? They're all a bit off even though they're supposedly some of the most contented people in the world. For God's sake, look at all those gloomy Swedish thrillers, all that snow and misery and torture. It's their dark side coming out."

Just then my phone pinged and when I slipped it from my pocket I read a text message from Vanessa: "It was murder. Call me." In my head I heard her voice pronouncing the key words in her text as "muhrduh" and "kawl."

I quickly texted: "Home very soon" and told Ciska that we had to leave. Stefan thanked her for the sherry and she walked us the short distance to the door as if she were a chatelaine in a baronial manor. We all said good night quite amicably, but I didn't feel satisfied by her answer about Viktor.

It was a short walk home through thickly treed streets. All you could hear was the intermittent barking of dogs that sounded almost musical as they challenged and answered one another from neighboring houses. I texted Vanessa to ask if she wanted to come over. She did.

Vanessa showed up ten minutes after we had let Marco romp in the yard and fed him his night-time snack. He was thrilled to have company so late and she grinned as he danced around her feet. She wore an elegant black pants suit, low heels, and a sheer black-and-white Burberry scarf I'd seen on my cousin Sharon. All that black made Vanessa's luxurious waves of red hair and creamy freckled skin even more dramatic.

"I don't have much time," she explained, declining a drink. "But I wanted to see you. I have to plan a trip to France to interview a witness. High-profile case."

Tonight she sat in one of the black chairs, with Marco gazing up at her adoringly, and briefly told us what she'd heard from a source close to the county medical examiner: "It was for certain murder, and the killer either had some knowledge of anatomy or got lucky. Napoléon Padovani died quickly. There were no defensive wounds, so he either knew his killer or he was surprised."

"Or both," I suggested.

"And Nick, on the police side, I've heard that you are definitely *not* a suspect. Things can change, of course, but I don't see that happening."

I told her about Valley trying to get me to go to the station and how I had refused.

She clapped her hands together in satisfaction. "Excellent! I like working with clients who listen to me and take my warnings seriously. You have no idea how many start yapping as soon as they see a cop or a detective, or march off without an arrest warrant, and that makes my life harder. People are so easily intimidated."

Then she checked her black-and-gold Ferragamo watch and said, "I have more prep for tonight, but here's some more advice: I know your predilections, so stay out of the investigation. Let the campus police do their job. They almost never deal with murders and so they'll put all their resources into a case like this. They'll get it done. Without you."

When she was gone, Stefan asked, "Are you going to drop it?"

"Drop what?"

"Don't be cute. I know you. You're a Taurus, you're stubborn, you can't let things go."

"Well, I'm damned sure going to find out what's going on with Viktor."

The lights were turned down low, Stefan had put on some chill-out, dreamy instrumental music by Hennie Bekker, and we were having a nightcap of Angel's Envy bourbon side-by-side on the couch. Marco was snoozing in one of the black chairs, looking very contented.

"Either Ciska was lying or Viktor was, and I want to find out why."

Stefan frowned. "And if Viktor says Ciska invented the story because she's, I don't know, deranged somehow, what happens then?"

"I'll set up a cage match like that combat scene from *Mad Max*. Remember? 'Two men enter, one man leaves.'"

Stefan went with my dark joke. "Or one woman. My money's on Ciska."

"'Dying time is here,'" I quoted again from the movie.

"No doubt." He took a sip of the bourbon and shook his head. "I just can't see Viktor turning on you."

"Why? He's not a friend. The department is crazy, people do and say crazy things there, so why shouldn't he accuse me of murdering Napoléon? Maybe he was drunk when he said it."

"*If* he said it."

"Well, that's what I'm going to find out, and who knows what the hell he's already told Valley? Who knows what anyone present at the retreat saw, or heard, or just thinks they did?"

I wasn't teaching the next morning so I packed my gym bag and headed to our palatial health club, Michigan Muscle. We'd been going there for years and watching the haphazard agglomeration of brick, steel, and concrete grow and spread as it became more popular, renowned as the largest and most deluxe health club in the city. But its intimidating size was one of the reasons many people who started there ended up quitting and going to smaller clubs where they felt less exposed and overwhelmed. These were usually members who'd been sent there by doctors because of heart attacks, or being overweight, and the supermarket abundance of Michigan Muscle wasn't really right for them.

Since Stefan and I had joined twenty years ago, Michigan Muscle had expanded to half a million square feet seemingly without a rational plan. Elevators and stairs were never where you might expect them to be and despite all the signs, if you didn't know your way around you could feel trapped in a maze. It was a wilderness of racquetball and tennis courts, yoga and Pilates studios, cardio rooms, stationary bike rooms, massage rooms, meeting rooms, locker rooms, several pools, free weight areas—everything exposed to glaring LED lights reflecting off the countless mirrors and glass doors. The clientele was varied, ranging from students using their parents' ID cards to contestants training for weight lifting competitions to people in rehab, and on to SUM retirees.

Though I liked free weights and took occasional classes,

swimming was what I was now finding most beneficial physically and emotionally. I had beefed up since I started keeping to a routine—though I wasn't nearly as buff as Stefan—and I liked the pools because they were never as crowded as other parts of Michigan Muscle, at least not in the mid-morning. After spending an hour swimming laps, I'd feel liberated and calm, and the particular stroke didn't much matter: butterfly, backstroke, and crawl were all equally healing and invigorating for me.

I headed to one of the three men's locker rooms to change into my trunks. The locker rooms had been remodeled in the last few years with gorgeous wooden lockers, brown leather club chairs in each lounge, sixty-five-inch flat-screen TV, and retiled shower stalls, hot tub, and sauna. The carpeting, walls and tile work were Nile green and beige, which I'd been told by the manager was a soothing combination. I sometimes ran into members of my department at Michigan Muscle, but most of them seemed to prefer a gym closer to campus. I thought that today I could use my time to let my unconscious deal with Napoléon's death and everything that had happened since. I needed to let go. Badly.

I'd arrived between the gung-ho morning vanguard and the lunchtime crowd and there was hardly anyone changing in the three middle rows of lockers, and the lockers along the back and sides that formed a large U-shape were empty. The lounge area was at the open side of the U along with coat racks, counters for towels and two doors leading to the showers and on to the adjoining sauna, steam room, and whirlpool beyond. I showered in my flip-flops and mid-thigh swim shorts, then headed out through the shower area to the pool I liked best because the water tended to be warmer than in the others. Only one lane was being used, the one closest to the door, so I picked the far lane. I nodded at the lifeguard who looked as pretty and bored as an Abercrombie & Fitch model: long, lean, and blond.

I wetted my goggles and put them on while sitting on the pool's edge, then slid into the water. I liked having a lane to myself and not worrying about bumping into anyone, but also the silence under water felt deeper. I was soon finding my rhythm, not going for speed but steadiness, especially with my flip turns which could sometimes be ragged.

After the first twenty laps, I took a break, standing in the shallow end, and that's when I spotted Viktor in the other occupied lane. He swam with fierce intensity as if chasing someone or being chased and I admired his elegant flip turns, though the way he cut through the water so swiftly seemed menacing. Each of his brutally efficient, powerful breast strokes was like a shouted "Don't fuck with me!"

He pulled himself out of the pool, grabbed a big, beige, fluffy towel from a nearby cart, and draped it around his shoulders. I'd never seen him at the pool, locker rooms, or showers before and he was more muscular than I would have guessed, with quads like a cyclist and a gymnast's taut round glutes that were barely contained by his ultra-tight Speedo. There was a large purple-and-black bruise on his chest that made me wonder if he'd had some kind of injury.

Viktor didn't seem to notice me, which was fine, because I wasn't sure exactly how to approach him—and I wasn't going to curtail my time in the pool anyway. I needed it too badly. It was one of the few places in my life where I felt completely in control.

When I was done and showered with shampoo that supposedly got chlorine out of your hair, I found Viktor dressed, in jeans and a yellow Lacoste shirt, sitting alone in the lounge watching some CNN story about a new terrorist attack. Newspapers were scattered open on the various side tables.

"*Nick!* I've been waiting for you. We need to talk."

"Yes, we do. Give me a few minutes." While I dressed, I rehearsed what I wanted to say to Viktor, without wondering what was on *his* mind.

When I was done and had packed up my gear, I found him

sitting in the same chair, and he asked, "How about lunch upstairs, on me?"

I was startled, but swimming had left me ravenous and the club's little restaurant did a surprisingly good sirloin burger with crispy truffle fries (they also specialized in protein shakes but I found those either bland or revolting). We took the circuitous path upstairs to the black-and-chrome, industrial-looking bistro, which was starting to fill up in the hour before noon. Viktor headed for a booth far away from everyone else and also away from the TV situated over the bar and tuned to MSNBC, which was covering the same terrorist incident. I followed him, and didn't try to read the news crawl or chyron—Stefan would be sure to tell me all about it when I got home. I set my gym bag on the bench beside me; Viktor stowed his under the table.

The server who brought us water and menus could have been the twin of the lifeguard at the pool and when I raised the possibility, he laughed and said, "Good guess!"

I ordered my burger medium rare, and asked for a root beer. Viktor ordered a Cobb salad and a glass of the house Chardonnay. "It's not oaked," he told me.

"Yes, I've tried it before, but you didn't invite me to lunch to talk about wine."

He shook his head, and I decided to wait for him to open up first.

"Let's wait till our food comes, shall we?"

"Sure, why not?"

He paused as if trying to find a safe topic. "What do you think about Robustelli as the new chair?"

I had to correct him. "*Interim* chair. I don't know what to think. He's colorful, I guess." I was not going to commit myself to anything more than that. Not with Viktor, and not with anyone I couldn't be certain was trustworthy.

"He's a *Skitstövel.*"

"I don't know that one—what's it mean?"

Our waiter dropped off the drinks and said our orders would be out very soon.

"Literally, it's 'shit boot.' But in English it would be something like asshole, douchebag, you know.... Maybe worse, depending on who you're talking to." He smiled and I couldn't put together his current mild manner with the ferocious way he'd been swimming just before. Someone that determined and strong could have easily killed Napoléon or at least attacked him, but this man sitting opposite me didn't just seem harmless, he seemed almost pacific, one more university professor trying to stay fit.

"You have a very powerful, clean breast stroke," I said, and then wondered if it sounded fawning.

"Thanks. I won some medals when I was younger. I thought I might someday be an Olympic swimmer, but my parents pushed me to go to medical school." His handsome face grew very cold. "I did, for a while, but vomited the first time I saw an operation...." He switched gear dramatically: "You know, Robustelli can't be trusted. He's power mad and a grabber. Ask around and you'll find out that's why he left Columbia for SUM. Think about what a step down that is, from Manhattan to Michiganapolis! Nobody makes that kind of change unless he's been driven out—or was arrested for something. I did hear a rumor once about trouble with the police. Roberto was up to all sorts of shenanigans at Columbia."

The word sounded quaint, but the activities not so much.

"Like what?"

He snorted. "The usual. Suggestive texts to graduate assistants, dating his students, possible sexual harassment of other faculty."

"Was anything proven?"

"It was swept under the rug. That's what I've heard. Much easier that way."

"For the school, not for the victims."

Viktor nodded. "Of course. That's. how it goes. Nobody wants an ugly court case in the news, and you know what he's like—imagine the fireworks."

Our food came and I eagerly bit into the juicy burger whose crumbly texture was as perfect as the smoky aroma and taste.

"Roberto is vulgar and loud," Viktor continued, "but that doesn't mean he's all bluster. Look how he's managed to become chair so quickly. And depose Ciska."

"You told me in my office that Ciska thought I killed Napoléon." There—I'd finally said it.

Viktor actually looked blank, and it didn't seem like an act. "*I* said that? To *you*? *Really*?"

He looked down at his salad, took a sip of his wine, and shook his head again as if I'd shocked him in some way.

"I guess so.... Maybe she said it, maybe she didn't. I'm sorry. I wasn't thinking straight." He breathed in deeply and pushed away the salad he had all but ignored up to that point.

"Because of the Sweden program?"

"No, because of Ciska. We've been sleeping together for quite a while. It started at a conference in Dublin and— Well, you don't need to know the details."

"And so—? What happened?"

"She dumped me the night before the retreat. I was devastated."

"Why? I mean, why did she dump you?"

"We argued about her being stoned all the time."

"Pot?" Ciska didn't seem like a stoner, but now that medical marijuana was legal in Michigan, anyone who got registered for it could be.

"Pot, booze, anxiety medication, whatever she could find. I was starting to feel that she wasn't really there, even in bed." He blushed a little and looked away from me, the table, and away from everything else it seemed. He was holding his breath and I thought he might be about to cry.

I finished my burger while he composed himself.

"And she lied," Viktor said, looking me dead in the eyes. "Constantly. Little things, big things. It didn't stop there. She got physically violent with me." He unconsciously touched his chest, which I thought might explain the bruise I'd seen at the pool. "She's stronger than she looks, and I think she's dangerous."

I asked, "Do you think *she* killed Napoléon?" I wolfed down some fries even though they weren't hot anymore.

"Who else? He'd raped her and there was no chance she'd get justice anywhere."

"She told me and Stefan that it was an assault, not rape," I said. "Do you think she's telling the truth?"

"About that, yes, absolutely. The details were too graphic. It was rape."

He sounded utterly sincere, but now I didn't know whether to believe him or believe Ciska—unless neither one of them could be trusted. About anything.

20

THE NEXT MORNING, Stefan had gone running, and after he showered and changed for the day, he announced, "I deserve French toast. We both do."

I wasn't going to argue, since what was the point of exercise if you couldn't indulge yourself afterwards? And Stefan's challah French toast was always perfect. He used a bit of the aromatic, citrus-y Fiori di Sicilia in the batter instead of vanilla, heavy cream instead of milk, and plenty of fresh-ground cinnamon. Plus he never forgot to lightly toast the bread first so that it would absorb more batter, and he didn't let the bread become soggy before frying it.

I made a pot of Sumatra-blend coffee while he prepared everything and got the griddle hot. While it brewed, I kept talking about Ciska and Viktor, trying to sort truth from lies, speculation from reality. This was a rehash of our dinner conversation from the previous day, but this time Stefan had something new to offer when he interrupted my fourth go-round.

"Nick, maybe they *both* killed him, like a small-scale *Murder on the Orient Express*. What if they didn't really break up and that's just a story Viktor is putting out as a cover?"

I thought about it. "To cover what, exactly?" I sipped my coffee.

"To cover up that they were in it together, of course." He

waved his free hand. "Or who knows what else? Everyone has secrets."

Secrets were a continuing thread in Stefan's fiction, thanks to his parents having hidden their pasts as Holocaust survivors from him. "Do you remember the quote I told you I wanted to use as the epigraph for my next book? It was from Dorothy Dix."

"She was who, exactly?"

"This famous advice columnist back in the early-twentieth century. She had millions of readers. She once said, 'The grave soul keeps its own secrets and takes its own punishment in silence.'"

"Nice, but Ciska and Viktor don't seem very grave, do they? Look how much they already told us, and some of it is probably true."

"Some."

"Are you saying the murderer is someone who's suffering and quiet? Not sure? Well, it's a good line to start a book with anyway."

When the French toast was nicely browned, Stefan plated two pieces for each of us with sliced strawberries and caramelized pecans, then brought our breakfasts to the table. I poured on some Vermont maple syrup and dug in.

Eating calmed my mind and I was grateful for delicious food made with love, and then shared with the man of my dreams. Stefan also seemed content to eat in silence for a while.

"This is marvelous," I said.

Stefan grinned. Then, pouring some more syrup onto his plate, he said, "Can you believe what *anyone* in our department says? They all have agendas. So if my idea of a cover story is wrong, lots of other nefarious things are still possible. If they did break up, Viktor could have been trying to damage Ciska's credibility, which would mean that *he* killed Napoléon. Turn it around and Ciska could have been trying to make Viktor look bad because *she* killed Napoléon. Didn't she say he was deranged—or something like that? That's a really serious charge."

Lyrics from a Sixties song were going through my head: "We

gotta get out of this place/If it's the last thing we *ever* do." But we couldn't, and so we had to make the best of our situation no matter how abnormal our lives became.

"Now I think it's too obvious that *either* one of them did it," I said, spearing some slices of strawberry, soaking them in syrup, and forking them up.

"So who else?" Stefan asked.

I put down my knife and fork as if that would somehow make me think more clearly. "Look who's our new chair."

Stefan scowled. "Roberto's a buffoon, how can anyone take him seriously? He's just a braggart, he wouldn't kill anyone, he'd just bad-mouth them."

"I don't know, he sounded pretty angry when he told me Napoléon wanted him to teach composition classes, and he can be fiery. It could have started as an argument that escalated."

"But how did he get hold of the stiletto?"

"Like anyone else, he could have stolen it from Napoléon's office. It was just lying on his desk, it wasn't hidden. Not at all." Those were easy words to say, but for a moment I was staggered by the whole idea of someone waiting for Napoléon and his secretary to be gone, sneaking into his office to steal the stiletto, planning to kill him somewhere, and then actually going through with it. My sense of reality had become profoundly distorted since Stefan and I had been living in Michigan and teaching at SUM, and I didn't see how it would ever recover.

"Carson was angry, too, so he had motive," I went on. "Napoléon told Carson he was doomed and would never be promoted to full professor. That's not just humiliating, it's also a huge financial blow over time if he stays at SUM, and trying to get hired somewhere else would be difficult in the current climate."

"Okay, and?"

"What if it's true that Carson gambles, like people say? He could be in serious debt. Remember what he looked like at the retreat? Like someone on the edge. So killing the man who stood in the way of his getting ahead professionally and eventually getting out of debt, that's not hard to believe at all. Plus, he's kind of a gorilla. I saw him once working out at Michigan Muscle. That dude is huge. You just don't see it when he's wearing those ugly baggy suits."

"But Napoléon was killed by a stiletto that got him in just the right spot, so would you have to be strong to do that?"

I didn't know, but I was moving on anyway. "Then there's Atticus Doyle. Napoléon wouldn't give him any kind of support when he complained about some of his students, and then Napoléon actually mocked him. Even though he's just an adjunct, Atticus teaches more classes than I do and he's not making even half my salary. On top of that, he's a much better writer than Jasmine, but he's the wrong gender, plus he's white and also straight. No diversity cred to his name. He could have thought a new chair might give him a break, possibly even push for him to get a tenure-track position."

"Then why didn't Atticus kill Jasmine Alinejad instead of Napoléon? Wouldn't it make more sense for a murderer to target someone blocking your way up the ladder? Or someone you *thought* was in your way?"

"That does make sense." Something from my office conversation with Atticus came back to me right then. "Wait—what if Napoléon was having an affair with Atticus's wife? You know how beautiful Florice is and have you ever seen a photo of Napoléon with a woman who *wasn't* gorgeous?"

It was all suddenly coming together and I had to drink some coffee to clear my head. "Okay," I went on. "Atticus said his wife had become really distant, or something like that, and she was also getting strange phone calls, and staying out late. Well, maybe he wasn't troubled only because some of his students were harassing him, maybe it was because Florice was sleeping with Napoléon. Remember, she's from Quebec so they had a French connection." I paused. "I know that sounds dirty somehow, but you know what I mean."

"Where's your proof?"

"I really can't prove anything, but Atticus did say he suspected that his wife was having an affair. I didn't want to pry, and the whole subject made me uncomfortable. It's not like I know him well enough to ask anything so serious about his marriage."

Truth be told, I really didn't know Atticus at all, and suddenly I felt ashamed of that. I might have felt sorry for his second-class status in the department, but I had never reached out to him to show that I admired his work and thought he deserved to be treated better, and should have a tenure-track position. Stefan and I hadn't ever invited Atticus and his wife to dinner. That made us unconsciously complicit in a system of oppression, despite sympathizing with his plight as an over-qualified adjunct. Doing nothing to make his life in the department even remotely more pleasant was deplorable.

"But Atticus raised the affair first," Stefan noted. "Or possible affair, if I follow your drift."

I ate some more French toast, crunching on the pecans, mulling over why I hadn't picked up on what Atticus had shared with me. It's not like I was shy or prudish.

"He was in pain," I said, working it out slowly for myself. "He was clearly distressed. I guess I thought asking questions about his wife would make him feel worse."

"Even if you'd asked him, it might not have made sense to you. What's the Tolstoy quote I always get wrong, you know the one I mean…?"

I did. It was the famous opening line of *Anna Karenina*: "Happy families are all alike; every unhappy family is unhappy in its own way."

"That fits the department, too," Stefan said. "We've seen so many people come and go, but it's always dysfunctional."

Our department wasn't the only unhappy family at SUM. I heard similar stories all the time about craziness across campus. Think of it this way: university professors don't work nine-to-five jobs, aren't supervised or accountable in the same ways most working people are, and so they live in an environment where the worst aspects of their personalities can blossom and thrive. They have to do something egregious to even get reprimanded. As we moved dishes, mugs, and cutlery to the dishwasher, Stefan asked, "What about the twins?"

"Heino and Jonas? They were fighting with each other at the retreat, not with Napoléon."

Stefan demurred. "Didn't you notice how Heino was complaining about sharing his office while he kept his eyes fixed on Napoléon?"

"I did, but I thought he was doing that to shut his brother out. And Napoléon is, Napoléon *was* the chair, so why wouldn't Heino talk right to him?"

Stefan shrugged as he closed the dishwasher. "Maybe there was something more complex involved. I don't know what, but if the twins could go after each other like that, why couldn't either one of them have killed Napoléon? They were *enraged*, they were totally out of control."

"What motive would either one of them have to kill Napoléon? They're new. And so is he."

"But Napoléon really pushed for them to be hired. He got money from the dean for *two* new positions in Digital Humanities, remember? So he knew them well enough for that."

"Fine. But why would either one of the twins murder Napoléon if he's the one who got them hired here?"

That clearly stumped Stefan, and he scratched his right cheek the way he sometimes did when he was puzzled. "You're right. Forget the twins, they don't make any sense as suspects. But someone else in the department clearly had a gigantic grudge against Napoléon. If he could infuriate a handful of people that we know of in only a few months, who's to say he didn't have more enemies, for whatever twisted reasons?"

I had to agree. "He was definitely a genius at sadistic multi-tasking."

The house was still redolent with the aromas of our breakfast when the doorbell rang and I was surprised that Marco snarled, which was completely unlike him. I told him to be quiet and he actually snarled more aggressively, with his ears back and his teeth bared. Puzzled, surprised, Stefan and I looked at each other and at our peaceable, loving canine housemate. The doorbell rang again and Marco raced to the door barking as if his life—or ours—depended on it.

I followed quickly, picked him up, and handed him to Stefan who was able to restrain him despite his squirming and looking fierce. When I peered through the porthole window in the front door I felt like snarling myself.

"It's Detective Valley."

Marco had stopped struggling in Stefan's arms but had settled into a low-level growl. He had never reacted like that to anyone appearing unexpectedly at our door. I guess he'd been saving his puppy ire for someone who deserved it.

"How about letting him into the yard," I suggested, and Stefan returned to the kitchen and I could hear the back door open, then close. That's when I opened up the door for Valley, but I stood in the doorway so he couldn't just enter.

"Why are you here? I told you to talk to my lawyer."

"I don't need to contact your lawyer. You're not a suspect and neither is your spouse. That's official. I'm here to ask questions about one of your colleagues."

I was so startled by Valley's definitive assertion of my innocence—and by his acknowledging Stefan as my spouse, not "partner"—that I actually took a couple of steps backward, bumping into Stefan who'd rejoined me in the entryway. I turned to him and he nodded, so we let Valley into the house and ushered him into the living room. He was looking surprisingly dapper in a black, narrow-lapelled suit and narrow, dark gray tie. His shirt was pale gray, and his brown wingtip shoes looked very new. Then it hit me why he might be so much better groomed than in years past.

"You're married again. Or dating someone you really like."

His eyes narrowed. "How—?"

Stefan waved Valley to the couch and he sat down on the edge, looking watchful and alert, but that didn't faze me.

Smugly, I answered Valley's unfinished question: "Men tend to let things slide when they're divorced and then they shape up once a new woman is in their life. You've been working out and it shows, and you dress better than you used to." I didn't add that he also wasn't as surly as he'd been in the past.

"Nice guesswork," he said neutrally.

Stefan and I each took a chair facing Valley and it made me feel in control, as if we were *his* interrogators, even though he'd said he was there to ask about someone else in the department.

"When is the last time either of you saw Atticus Doyle?"

"At the department meeting," Stefan said. "Why?"

"He's missing. He didn't meet his classes yesterday, his wife hasn't seen him, his car is gone, and he's not answering his cell phone."

"Is he a suspect?" Stefan asked, but Valley's face didn't change, which I think we both took as some kind of "yes."

"Can't you track him by his phone?" I asked.

Valley shook his head. "Not when it's off."

"I thought that didn't matter."

Valley sighed. "People watch too much TV. Maybe the NSA can track a phone when it's not on, but this is just a local police matter. For now, anyway."

He was right about that. There'd been some coverage in French media, but it hadn't exploded yet, though the French Consul General in Detroit had expressed his "alarm." I'm sure we would soon see a flood of justly-deserved complaints about American violence, profiles of Napoléon as a martyr to our Second Amendment, and exposés of SUM's history of violence and crime.

Valley continued: "What can you tell me about Professor Doyle's relationship with Napoléon Padovani?"

I hesitated, but my eagerness to find out what was really

going on outweighed my concern that I might say something damaging to Atticus.

"You know he was only an adjunct, right? They get hired only on a year-by-year basis. Well, as I understand it, Napoléon sort of threatened him when Atticus went to him for help with one of his classes."

"What kind of help?"

I explained the Justice League students and their hostility to Atticus. As I did so, Valley's face expressed disbelief, then disdain.

"What is wrong with you people?" he snapped. "You're all nuts at SUM."

"Listen, I thought his students were way out of line, but that's not the point."

"So how exactly did Padovani threaten Doyle?"

"Well, Napoléon basically said Atticus should leave SUM if he couldn't cut it here. If that were me, I'd take that as a serious threat."

Stefan observed quietly, "And there's more. Atticus thought his wife, Florice, might be having an affair. It could have been with Padovani."

Valley smiled. It wasn't a good look on him. "A source told me she *was* having an affair. And Doyle knew it."

"His wife *told* Atticus?" I asked in disbelief.

"She didn't have to. He was an intimate part of their tryst. Doyle supposedly liked to watch his wife have sex with other men. And Napoléon Padovani was a real show-off, the same source said, so it was a match made in heaven." Valley was expressionless now, and I couldn't imagine what he was thinking.

"How would anyone know all that?" I asked.

Valley shrugged. "It's a small town."

The idea of Napoléon, Florice, and Atticus in a ménage-à-trois was truly mind-blowing, but cutting through all of the lubricious images suddenly swirling around in my head was one blazing thought: If it was true, then Atticus had lied about his wife when he opened up to me in my office. *Why?*

21

"YOU LOOK SURPRISED," Valley said.

"Well, of course," I said. "You never know what someone else's marriage is like."

Valley glanced from Stefan to me and back again.

"In case you're wondering," Stefan said sharply, "we're not freaks, we're not into scenes, we would never do anything like that."

"It wasn't even on my mind," Valley said, eyes gleaming sardonically. For some reason, he seemed delighted to have dropped this little bombshell on us.

Stefan asked, "Do you think Atticus snapped somehow?"

"It's a theory we're considering but don't mention this to anyone else."

"Why would he snap now?" Stefan asked.

Valley ignored the question, consulted his phone for what seemed to be notes. "Who were his friends in the department? Is there anyone else he might have confided in? Don't know? Okay. Any ideas about where he might be?"

I didn't want to admit it, but it had to be said. "The adjuncts and the tenure-track faculty don't tend to mix, even at parties. A lot of the adjuncts are transients, in a way."

"Doyle has been teaching at SUM for over five years. Doesn't sound very transient to me. How well do you two know him?"

"Not well at all," Stefan said.

"But he's some kind of writer and you're the, uh, the writer-in-residence. Didn't you have something in common? Didn't you have any interactions with him?" The question was very pointed.

"I haven't run into him much this semester. Except at department meetings," Stefan explained, "and chatting in the mail room. It was the same when we were in Parker Hall. Being a writer doesn't make you automatically connected to every other writer."

It sounded somehow lame and halfhearted.

Valley turned to me. "You were seen with him in Shattenkirk Hall two Tuesdays ago and he went to your office."

The statement chilled me since it seemed to be implying something.

"He was depressed and he needed to talk to somebody," I explained.

Valley nodded a few times. "So you weren't strangers."

"I never said that. I just happened to be there."

We heard a short yelp at the back door and Stefan went out to the kitchen to let Marco in. "Put him on his leash," I called, and Stefan said, "Got it."

He returned with Marco securely in control, but it wasn't enough. Marco was snapping at Valley, scrabbling and trying to free himself.

Valley rose slowly, almost tauntingly, as if daring Marco to attack him, and said, "I'll call you if I have more questions."

I walked him to the door. Without thanking us for our time, he left, and Marco seemed to calm down. When Stefan let him off his leash, though, he lunged towards the couch and sniffed it intensely as if planning revenge on this intruder.

"Marco is a good judge of character," Stefan said.

"Maybe we should bring him to campus and see if he can sniff out the murderer."

When I arrived at my office with my lunch later that day, Celine told me that Roberto Robustelli, our illustrious new chair, wanted "a word" with me.

"Did he say what about?"

"No."

I set down my messenger bag and Tupperware, and headed down the sterile hallway to the chair's office. His secretary said he'd be right back and he had nothing on his schedule at the moment so it was a good time. I tried not to stare at her nameplate, thinking that Grace Lovejoy would be a great name in a Dickens novel—or a porn movie. She looked even grimmer than usual today wearing a very unflattering beige coat-dress, and I debated saying something about Napoléon. Had she liked working with him? I had no idea. And even if she did, it hadn't been for that long, so wouldn't "Sorry for your loss" be presumptuous, or even silly?

Something else came out anyway: "When's the last time you saw Napoléon's antique letter opener?"

She stopped typing, gave me a baleful look, and snapped, "The police asked me that same question and I can't remember. It wasn't always on his desk. He liked taking it home because it had personal meaning for him, and sometimes he forgot it was there."

Then she went back to her work, cutting off any more communication between us. She would have made a good border guard along the old Berlin Wall.

Something else popped into my mind and I took out my phone and clicked my way into the faculty-restricted part of our department web site where the chair's schedule was always posted. I checked Napoléon's meetings for the week before the retreat and discovered he'd had meetings with Ciska Balanchine, Carson Karageorgevich, Atticus Doyle, Roberto Robustelli, Viktor Dahlberg, and both German twins. I had dismissed Heino and Jonas as possible suspects, but now I wondered again if they had planned to kill him together. They were so secretive and opaque....

"Nick!" Robustelli crowed as he surged into the office.

I rose and he shook hands with me as if he were a politician at the height of a re-election campaign. He welcomed me into what was now *his* office and I saw an immediate change: there were dozens of family photographs on every surface. All those faces made me feel spied upon, but at least Napoléon's fancy uncomfortable chairs were gone. I took a seat in a softly padded Eames chair that was very different.

"Herman Miller," he said brightly, gesturing at the chairs as if they were old friends. "Nice, huh?"

Roberto wore a natty black suit, neon-bright white shirt, and black-and-white paisley pocket square. The black emphasized the black of his hair and eyebrows and made him seem commanding. You could almost see him as a cut-throat lawyer or maybe even an FBI agent. But he still was wearing too much cologne. Luckily the door was open.

"So Nick, I have a big question for you."

I braced myself.

"What can the department do to help you with the Nick Hoffman Fellowship? What do you need that you're not already getting?"

I think my mouth must have been hanging open at this surprising display of concern and generosity. I'd expected Roberto to become tyrannical as chair, and here he was being accommodating, supportive. I didn't know how to respond.

"There must be something we can do, something *I* can do."

Words finally came to me. "I have a great administrative assistant, and you know there's no financial issue, since the fellowship endowment's doing so well in the stock market, but—"

"But what? Spit it out, dude."

"Well, I've tried to interest the SUM Library in hosting a small exhibit about the student who bequeathed the money to SUM earmarked for the fellowship, but no one there has shown much interest. I still have copies of some of the student's writing, and if we could get photos from his family, and they'd of course be willing, then that would fill one or two display cases on the library's main floor. We could even have some kind of evening presentation since students are always at the library after dinner."

"Well, that would be all you, of course. You knew him and the fellowship's named after you." He rocked back and forth in his chair, nodding his head enthusiastically. "I love it. You could talk about him, and about teaching, and what a great place SUM is to be a student. That would publicize the fellowship and possibly goose enrollments in the department. It's fucking genius!"

I briefly wondered if he was on drugs, then decided it was simply his joy at being in charge that was animating him. Maybe he wasn't at Columbia University anymore, but being a chair even at SUM could boost your academic career and land you a better position somewhere else—if you were looking. And he had *power* now.

"I will get this rolling ASAP, Nick. You have my word on that. Is there anything else I can help you with? No? Well, just let me know if you think of something. And by the way, you can forget that email Napoléon sent about canceling Jewish-American Literature. We need diversity in our offerings and I know you did a great job with that course—some of my students raved about how motivated and inspiring you were."

I felt my face grow hot. Being complimented by an administrator of any kind was something brand new for me.

He rose and came around the desk to pat my back.

"And let me know if anyone around here gives you trouble. I'll take them down."

I shambled out of his office and then out of his secretary's. Why was he being so amiable? Could he possibly have thought that when he dissed Napoléon to me before the retreat, in Java Joe's downstairs, that we had formed some kind of bond? I really wasn't used to any administrator treating me well—this felt almost surreal.

Celine agreed when I was back in my office and told her about Roberto's offer to help me: "Nick, ask for more PR! The

Publicity Office at SUM hasn't done enough to publicize the fellowship or publicize you. They're hot to trot when there's faculty news in the sciences but the humanities just doesn't turn them on."

"Good idea." I emailed Roberto right away about publicity and got an almost instant reply: "Absolutely!"

I turned my laptop around so that Celine could read it.

"Looks like you're the fair-haired boy for now."

"You don't trust him?"

"Can you trust any department chair? But him, he's worse, he's a loose cannon."

"Celine, maybe he just needs security and some authority to calm down."

"Hah!"

Celine left me to my notes for my classes next week, but I didn't get very far because the twins showed up, looking indistinguishable in black skinny jeans tucked into black half boots and purple T-shirts that read DAS LEBEN IST KEIN PONYHOF!

"May we speak to you?" they said almost in tandem, and then smiled robotically at their timing. Seeing them side by side, I realized how strangely luminous their blue eyes were.

"Sure, sit."

They did and I asked what the slogan on their T-shirts meant. Heino, I think, translated it: "Life is not a farm for ponies."

"I don't get it."

His brother sniffed. "It means life is not…what you would say…a bed of roses. Or perhaps more simply, Life is tough."

Heino, I was pretty sure it was Heino, brushed that off and said, "The new chair has taken it upon himself to create a new *Program of Assessment and Student-Centered Analytics* and together we have been appointed to head it up because of our expertise in Digital Humanities." His voice was high and thin with excitement now, though he was as expressionless as an actress who'd overdone Botox.

I must have looked especially blank, because he went on very slowly, as if English were not my native language, though what followed was a dialect I was completely unfamiliar with.

"It is time," he said, "for more accountability and evidence-based decision making in the department. We have been charged with conducting learning outcome assessments in a cross-functional approach that will stimulate idea and data sharing."

He paused, I guess to let the importance of that mission sink in for me.

"This will all be done electronically. Using E-analytics will surely build the department back up from its current moribund state, halt a decline in enrollments, and most importantly prove that our courses are the best delivery systems for skill-sets that will make our students extraordinarily employable."

I had absolutely no idea what he was talking about.

"We're all stakeholders, and benchmarking is important. With E-analytics we can accumulate a vast amount of data so that we can compare student cohorts in our department and across the university."

His eyes were feverish now, as if he'd seen a beatific vision.

"We will finally be able to separate efficient from inefficient teaching methods!"

His brother, presumably Jonas, chimed in. "Think of the results. Learning outcomes will be quantifiable. Students will be able to measure their knowledge attainment. Professors missing the mark will be called to account and guided toward more efficient teaching methods that foster optimal curriculum development."

They both went on like that for a good fifteen or twenty minutes while I nodded and smiled, pretending I was in a foreign country and determined not to offend the natives by mocking their customs and traditions. What I really wanted to do was tell them to fuck off and get out of my office and not talk to me about this bullshit, but I realized that an initiative like this could not have been born in Robustelli's brain. It had to be coming from higher up, from the dean at the very least, and more likely the provost or even the president. Which meant I had to tread very, very carefully. And my guess was correct when they explained that they had been guaranteed tenure for this work and a budget in the millions.

With their new venture added to the possibility of enormous grants for Digital Humanities, Heino and Jonas were set to become financial superstars in the department.

"We would be so grateful if we could count on you to include the students who will be involved in the upcoming Nick Hoffman Fellowship visits in this project," Jonas wound up. Unless it was Heino. For some reason I was having trouble telling them apart now, but I didn't really care. I had gone from feeling weirdly happy about my new place in the department's pecking order to feeling threatened by a soulless, numbers-crunching juggernaut.

"Well, I'm grateful you've invited me to be part of something so…comprehensive," I brought out as calmly as possible. "Let me get back to you, okay?"

They grinned. Well, the corners of their mouths twitched upwards a bit, and they thanked me for my time. On the way out, probably Heino said, "We are so lucky to have a new department chair. Napoléon was completely opposed to E-analytics and he said if he'd known that was one of our interests, he would never have recruited us. Fortunately for us, he's no more."

I planned my classes for the coming week in a mild state of panic. Was SUM really going to become obsessed with assessment and observation, would it now turn its "customers," AKA students, into lab rats?

Stefan laughed at my fears when we had dinner, which was defrosted chicken chili and a good bottle of Argentinian Malbec. Stefan had read a lot about E-analytics and wasn't at all worried.

"Nick, the university has to find ways to justify how much four years at SUM costs, even for in-state students. It's more bureaucracy, administration, and high-concept busy-work.

They'll promise they can streamline learning, increase productivity, and identify at-risk students better—and a whole lot more. It's a fad. It'll pass."

"But you should have seen them, Stefan. They were *possessed*."

"Isn't that hyperbolic?"

"Not at all. These guys are crazed by data." I was on my third glass of wine and Stefan had opened another bottle. "Oh. My. God. They said that Napoléon was absolutely opposed to all this analytics stuff and regretted bringing them to SUM."

"And?"

"Don't you get it? They could have murdered Napoléon because he was going to block them from building their little empire here. This E-stuff will give them status and big bucks. That's worth killing for."

Stefan was very quiet for a few moments.

"I think you may be right," he brought out slowly. "That's what you were picking up when Heino was talking to Napoléon at the retreat. Their fight was faked. They were planning to kill him and figured if they took some punches at each other, then everyone would be distracted, they'd be focused on how much the twins supposedly hated each other. That way they could get away with offing Napoléon. Nobody would make the connection."

"You think both of them did it?" I asked.

He nodded. "But how can we prove it?"

"Easy," I said. "Campus buildings stay open until eleven at night, so let's drive over and check out their office. Maybe we'll find evidence of some kind."

To my surprise, Stefan agreed.

22

"BUT ONLY ON ONE condition," Stefan said. "We need a quick cup of coffee before either one of us gets behind the wheel."

So we made some Carte Noire coffee singles, drank them down, and headed to campus feeling more clearheaded. At least Stefan was, since he was driving. In the car I chugged from a bottle of spring water to help sober myself up faster.

SUM at night was often eerie, with building lights appearing ghostly in the dark, trees no longer pretty but threatening, street lamps casting odd shadows, and a strange quiet smothering what was usually a very noisy campus. The sounds of the few cars, bikes, and pedestrians were as muffled as if they were coming from a distance. I was glad we weren't going to be walking far.

It was only when we parked in the lot closest to Shattenkirk Hall that Stefan said, "Wait—what are we doing here? Won't their office be locked?"

I grinned and pulled out a Java Joe card, which was just as good as a credit card for my purposes, and also expendable.

"I didn't tell you, but last week I left my key inside my office twice in a row. Celine wasn't around and I was too embarrassed to bother that gorgon Grace Lovejoy for her master key. Luckily I had my phone on me when it's usually on my desk, so I

Googled how to open a locked door with a credit card, followed
the instructions, and *voilà!*"

"Are you kidding?"

"Nope. It worked."

"Huh."

"Remember—the building's pretty old and the office door
locks are probably cheap."

We checked the glass-cased black letterboard in the deserted
lobby for the twins' office number. Day-to-day, I never even
glanced at it on my way in or out of the building, but I noticed
right then that Atticus's first name had been spelled sloppily, with
a numeral "1" instead of the letter "i."

Typical, I thought. He was adjunct faculty. Who cared about
getting something as basic as his name correct?

Heino's and Jonas's shared office was one floor below mine
and Stefan's, and we took the stairs, hoping no one would see
us. As usual, the stairwell smelled oddly damp, as if a pipe were
leaking inside a wall. It was so quiet on that floor you could hear
the ominous buzz of the fluorescent lighting, and some of the
bulbs flickered balefully. Empty and lifeless, this was an ideal setting for a horror movie.

We found their door with its twin nameplates, and I told
Stefan to stand guard, though I'm not sure what I expected him
to do if someone approached, and I don't know how I could have
explained being there at this time of night. Remembering what
I'd learned a week ago, I leaned against the door, took the Java
Joe card and slid it into the slight gap between the lock and the
door frame, then angled the card so that it was almost touching
the door knob. I gently pushed it in further, then bent the card
the other way and the lock released—without my card snapping
in two.

"Please tell me you haven't been studying how to crack safes,"
Stefan said when he saw I'd succeeded so easily.

"This is serious," I said.

"So am I."

I turned on the overhead lights. It was a good-sized room with newly painted gold walls and surprisingly plush aqua carpeting. I confess that I had expected their office to be less cluttered, given that they were German. All the bookcases were full of books and labeled binders, some crammed in sideways or piled helter-skelter. Both desks showed signs of being used. Each one held a nameplate; a Braun single-cup coffeemaker; a cool-looking black LED desk lamp; coffee mugs in various sizes; miscellaneous print-outs, notes, and magazines; and framed photos on their desks of what looked like cathedrals and castles in Germany.

Both desks had worktables and faced the door, and both had equal-sized windows behind them.

There was no reason I could see that Jonas should want to use his brother's desk: they were absolutely identical. I was even more convinced that their dispute about office space had been fabricated as a ruse. Unless it was some kind of weird sibling rivalry exacerbated by Heino and Jonas being twins.

"Nick, check out the art."

Hanging on the wall adjacent to one of the desks was an expensively framed print of Jacques-Louis David's *The Death of Marat*, the famous painting that immortalized the stabbing of one of the brutal leaders of the French Terror. And next to the other desk hung another beautifully framed print of some painting also from the same period, I guessed, one I'd never seen before, but whose subject was obvious: the assassination of Julius Caesar.

"These guys have knives on the brain," Stefan muttered.

"Do you think Valley's seen this?" I asked.

"Even if he has, it's circumstantial, but *I'm* convinced."

That made me feel absurdly happy, though of course we were talking about identifying killers, or one killer, at least. I imagined the scene: Perhaps both of them went into the men's room at the retreat center, and one distracted Napoléon while the other stabbed him.

Stefan was peering at the papers scattered on both desks,

and suddenly breathed in as if he'd been punched in the gut. He turned from Heino's desk.

"Nick, Look at this email!"

One of the twins had printed off an email from Napoléon addressed to both of them. It was brief, bizarre, and damning: "*I do not believe this department or any other at SUM needs the kind of Analytics you propose to institute. This is an English department, not a factory. Don't waste my time with any more requests of this nature. If you bring this matter up with the dean, provost, or anyone else, I will make sure that you suffer.*"

"Suffer how?" I asked Stefan. "What did Napoléon mean?"

"He threatened them," Stefan said simply. "And they responded."

"Let's get out of here."

We turned off the lights, closed the door, and I checked to make sure that I hadn't somehow damaged the lock. As we headed back to the stairs, we heard something unexpected: raucous laughter that seemed to be coming from the windowless conference room down the hall. I disliked having meetings there: it was a grim space badly in need of redecorating: dirty white Formica-topped table surrounded by grimy, low-backed, white leather and aluminum armchairs. Someone in the Physics department had apparently been in love with the Sixties because bad Op Art hung on the walls, making it an ideal setting for solitary confinement.

"That sounds like Carson," Stefan said. "He's got that weird catch in his throat when he laughs, like it's painful."

I listened and heard the laughter, but didn't hear anything odd about it. As a writer, Stefan often noticed things I didn't, despite his being an introvert.

I heard other voices, too, though I wasn't sure how many. We headed cautiously down the hall and as soon as we reached the open doorway, we were hailed with loud cries of "Join us!" and "Come on in!"

It was Ciska, Carson, and Viktor.

They were all gathered at one end of the table, with shot glasses and a half-empty bottle of Finlandia vodka in front of them. Viktor sat in the middle, with Ciska to his right and Carson to his left. Carson was as rumpled as ever, Viktor looked dapper and distant, and Ciska seemed wary, yet the three of them were quite chummy with each other, even ebullient, like people who'd bought a lottery ticket together, and won. Or maybe crooks contemplating a successful heist. There was something furtive about all three of them.

"Are you…celebrating something?" I asked from the door.

"Life and death. New life for us, and death for Napoléon-fucking-Padovani," Carson bellowed. There were no classrooms on this floor, and it was unlikely anyone was working late in their office, so I guess he felt free to let loose. Unless he didn't care who heard him now.

Viktor waved us in, and offered to dash to his office for more glasses, but I said we'd had enough to drink at dinner. And I wondered what it meant that he had so many shot glasses in his office. Were there parties or get-togethers at Shattenkirk Hall I didn't know about? Who showed up? For a moment I felt the misery of the new kid at school and then caught myself. The last thing I needed was after-hours boozing where I worked.

Ciska scowled at me. "It's rude not to toast the death of a dictator." Then she laughed. "No? Whatever. Suit yourself."

Carson's attention had momentarily turned inward and he was mumbling about ordering pizza.

Sensing my reluctance, I suppose, Stefan put his hand on my back and we slowly entered the room to sit a few seats down from the trio's end of the table. The oppressive overhead lights reflecting off all the white surfaces made me feel like I'd been splashed with a bucket of cold water. There was an awkward silence. Their hilarity gradually diminished just like air slowly leaking from a balloon, and the three of them surveyed me and Stefan speculatively.

"Has anyone seen Atticus?" I asked.

They all shook their heads. Ciska volunteered that Jasmine Alinejad had subbed for his classes.

Carson grunted or chuckled—I wasn't sure which. "She put the Justice League students in their place, the ones who were giving Atticus so much grief. She lambasted them for their white privilege and told them they were arrogant to think they could disrupt other people's expensive education with secondhand rhetoric. I believe she said something like 'Talking about how woke you are just makes you a *joke.*'"

"Good job," Stefan brought out quietly, sounding surprised.

Carson's mouth twitched into a grin as if someone had pressed a button.

"She's still a bitch," Ciska threw off. "I've never seen Jasmine write anything positive about other people's work, especially other *women's.* She loves going on the attack."

Well, there was nothing unusual in that. Being vicious was a good strategy to establish yourself on social media if you were an academic. Posting take-downs of other academics was guaranteed to get you more clicks from my peers because we relished seeing reputations shredded. As much as some of us mouthed platitudes about building, creating, nurturing, discovering, and sharing, others were just savages with degrees. It didn't take much for us to turn into a howling crowd in the Colosseum waiting for some gladiator to be eviscerated or have his head lopped off.

Viktor said, "Nobody knows where Atticus is. Maybe whoever killed Napoléon killed Atticus, too." It was spoken as idly as if he was wondering about tomorrow's weather.

"But why?" I asked. "What would connect the two of them?"

"Beats me," Carson said, his big, moony face a kind of blur because his eyes seemed unfocused and his hair was more uncombed than usual. "Could just be some nut job. When I was in college and worked at the campus radio station, there was somebody on staff who would take a dump in everyone's waste baskets."

We all looked at him, waiting for an explanation of what that bizarre story had to do with Atticus.

He seemed offended that we weren't getting it. "People do crazy things is what I'm saying."

"Did they catch who was responsible?" Stefan asked, and I could tell he thought it would be a great anecdote to work into a story or novel. He had that lean-and-hungry writer look.

"No. Total mystery. It started and then stopped. But then they also said the studio was haunted. Doors opened and shut by themselves. Nobody liked being there at night. Of course, ghosts don't typically haunt you by crapping in your office...."

"Adjuncts never last very long here anyway," Viktor observed, as if Carson had never gone off on his little tangent. "They're expendable."

Lolling in her chair, Ciska went on: "You know, there's always the possibility that Atticus killed Napoléon and that's why he's disappeared." She shrugged. "Not very bright to do a bunk, though."

"Do a bunk?" Viktor asked.

"Flee, run off, escape," she explained.

Carson joined in. "It's a dumb move for sure."

"What if he had an accident?" Stefan asked, but answered it himself. "Then his wife would have been called. Unless it happened someplace remote...."

Three faces greeted the idea with no change in expression. None of them seemed even mildly concerned—but then who was I to judge?

"If Atticus didn't kill Napoléon, who did?" Stefan asked boldly, as if we hadn't just been in the twins' office and discovered that email and those prints on the walls. "The three of you all had motives. Nick told me everything you shared with him."

Ciska coughed and she and Viktor looked guiltily away from each other. Carson caught their averted glances. "*What?* The two of you have been fucking?"

Ciska and Viktor both blushed. Carson grabbed Viktor's left

arm, hard. "You said you stopped sleeping with women after your wife died." He seemed very focused now and even frightening: a big, angry gorilla of a man.

Whoa, I thought. *Viktor and Carson are lovers?*

Viktor shook loose and snapped at Carson, "Did I ever promise you anything? Did I?"

Ciska seemed bemused by this revelation, and then she added more fuel to the fire: "Don't worry, Carson, he never spoke about you, and I've dumped him anyway."

"Stay out of this," Carson snarled.

Ciska held up her hands in mock surrender. Then she defiantly poured herself another shot of vodka and drank it back, staring Carson down. He was a big man, but something about her withering gaze made him shrink a bit in his seat.

Carson then turned on Viktor, as if to assuage the shame of being even mildly intimidated by a woman: "You're a fucking liar. You said you loved me. How could you sleep with anyone else?"

Viktor opened his mouth but was clearly lost for an excuse.

The evening had slipped a gear and become surreal. Ciska, Viktor, and Carson seemed pathetic and weird, like people squabbling on some ridiculous reality TV show. How could I have imagined any one of them to be a murderer? They were too self-absorbed for that.

Eyes bright with malice, Ciska filled her glass again and raised it to toast: "You know what I hope? I hope Napoléon was dispatched by a serial killer, and I hope that person's killing department chairs. Then Robustelli would be next in line."

That's when we left.

Later, when we were having some brandy before bed, with Marco snoozing on the couch, waiting for his cue to go to his dog bed in the master bedroom, I confessed that I felt I was back where I'd started: clueless.

"Why? Now you think the twins are innocent?"

"I don't know. Tonight I was feeling sure that the twins did it, *could* have done it. The way Napoléon threatened them in his email, the photos and artwork in their office, how quickly they were climbing up the ladder as soon as he was dead. But what if Ciska, Viktor, and Carson planned it together? Why the hell were they all drinking in the conference room at night? Didn't they seem guilty to you, conspiratorial? I mean with something deeper going on there than just Viktor and Carson being lovers or Viktor and Ciska having been lovers."

"Politics makes strange bedfellows and academic politics makes freaky ones. They did go to the dean as a group to try and get Napoléon fired, remember?"

"That's what we've been told, right. Do you believe that really happened?"

In a fairly good imitation of Peter Sellers's Inspector Clouseau, Stefan intoned, "I believe everything and I believe nothing. I suspect everyone and I suspect no one."

I couldn't even smile, though, because it made perfect sense to me.

23

THE FRENCH CALL IT a *merdier.* We call it a shit storm.

That's what was erupting in France, we discovered on Monday morning, over the murder of Napoléon Padovani, especially since no suspect had been arrested as yet at SUM. Editorials in French newspapers condemned the U.S. for its gun violence and "rampant lawlessness" as more than one newspaper put it— even though Napoléon had been stabbed, not shot. There were widespread calls for boycotting any products that came from Michigan and even stopping all French tourism to the entire U.S. French intellectuals were having fun excoriating American higher education in general as overpriced and philosophically bankrupt. There were calls by French legislators to withdraw their ambassador from Washington, and the French president had publicly expressed his "deep concern over troubling events in Michigan."

His French was far better than mine, so Stefan read the Gallic coverage, while I tracked American reports, analysis, and speculation, almost all of it written without any actual visits to SUM or even any interviews with faculty, staff, or administrators. I may have had bad feelings about local and campus police, but I was grateful that nobody had leaked the fact that I had discovered Napoléon's body, or there would have been a media encampment outside our house. That was a small mercy.

American lovers of conspiracy theories were churning out more and more outlandish stories on the Internet: Napoléon was a French spy who'd been killed by the CIA; rogue elements in the French intelligence community had assassinated him in a "false flag operation" to make Americans look bad and to reclaim France's rightful place in world affairs; his death was related to a drug deal that had gone terribly wrong; Israel's Mossad was killing French people everywhere in revenge for French anti-Semitism.

And the tabloid press in England, always delighted to slur Europeans, ran with a story that the killer must have been an Italian spy, not anyone French or American. "Because only a dago would use a coward's weapon like a stiletto," was the anonymous quote supposedly from a member of MI6.

That assessment of course prompted an endless back-and-forth in letters to the editor sections of newspapers all over England about whether one could be brave and kill with a stiletto, in a rising tide of unintended silliness that had the ring of a Monty Python sketch. Apparently, there was an actual British Stiletto Enthusiasts Club whose members were highly offended by any slur on the object of their admiration.

Worldwide, #stiletto was trending on Twitter.

"I wonder if those stiletto Brits were inspired by that German spy in *Eye of the Needle*?" I asked Stefan. "He was portrayed as certainly brave enough. But that would also be pretty weird.…"

"Ken Follett wrote the book decades ago. I bet there's no connection. I'm sure the society, or club, is even older than that."

"Still, that was his weapon of choice, no?"

"True enough," Stefan agreed. "But none of this adds up."

It had to. I read crime fiction with a passion and taught it, too. What the hell was I missing?

While I was cogitating, our State Department was warning American tourists in France to keep a low profile, and SUM was in full crisis-management mode, which of course meant trying to make the whole situation quietly go away.

Which was impossible.

Robustelli, our energetic new chair, alerted us that he would be summoning us to a meeting in the grim conference room— date to be determined—to discuss how we should be dealing with Napoléon's death in the classroom. As if our students were so fragile they needed our amateur trauma counseling. Or maybe Robustelli thought all of us professors needed a rhetorical group hug.

"Another meeting?" Stefan moaned. "Can't that stinker leave us alone?"

That word! I felt suddenly shocked into clarity, sharply alert, like I'd just been startled awake by a blaring smoke alarm. "What did you call him?"

Stefan frowned. "A stinker." Then he smiled fondly. "My dad used to say that about anybody he didn't like. Stinker, bum, chiseler. He didn't know it, but he talked like someone in a noir movie. Nobody uses those words anymore."

"But Roberto's *not* a stinker."

"What?"

"Roberto's always wearing too much cologne. I guess he smells good, if that's the kind of cologne you like. I'm pretty sure it's Lagerfeld. Sharon sent me a bottle once for my birthday and it was much too strong for me. It's got, I don't know what they call them, 'spice notes.' It's got a whole *concerto* of notes."

Stefan was peering at me as if I were spouting gibberish.

"Listen. When I found Napoléon's body, the smell in the men's room was super intense. I thought it was the small vase of potpourri, but why would potpourri smell *stronger* than it had the first time I walked in?"

Stefan considered that. "I don't know. It could be that you were more aware of everything, your senses heightened."

"No, no, no. *I was freaked out.* I wasn't some Marvel super-hero who got struck by lightning or blown up or something, and suddenly had all these extra powerful senses. I didn't see or hear anything more clearly, but the smell in that room was defi-nitely stronger than before and very distinctive. I'm sure of it. The potpourri was only somewhat spicy but Roberto's cologne was beyond spicy. It was a small room and the odor was overpowering, and it lingered."

Stefan crossed his arms, looking extremely dubious.

"Wait here and I'll prove it to you."

I rushed upstairs to our bathroom and frantically searched through a cabinet for the Lagerfeld I'd used only a few times. Because it was a gift, I hadn't had the heart to pitch it. I found the tall slim bottle, yanked off the cap and breathed in deeply. Napoléon's body and Roberto's face both swirled up in front of me.

Marco had bounded upstairs as if we were playing a game and he sat there expectantly, then followed me, tail wagging, as I headed downstairs more calmly, now convinced that I had identified the killer. I felt as confident as Hercule Poirot summing up to a room full of suspects.

I held the open bottle out to Stefan who sniffed at it twice.

He said, "Yes, I agree, that's what Roberto wears, but it doesn't *prove* anything."

"It's more proof than what was hanging on Heino's and Jonas's office walls that you said convinced you."

"There was also the email from Napoléon." Then he added a bit ruefully, "I got swept up by the idea of it. It was like a crazy dream."

"But this is real, Stefan."

I put the cap back on to the cologne and set it down on the counter as if I were wagering a small fortune in chips at the roulette table.

"What about the retreat when he rushed up and hugged Napoléon?" I asked. "That was all just a giant act to make people think Roberto was sucking up to him."

"But it was *obviously* fake," Stefan objected. "Nobody could have believed he was sincere."

"With somebody as showy and exuberant and loud as Roberto Robustelli, how can you tell the difference between what's fake and what's real? I'm going to call Detective Valley. I know I have his card somewhere."

"He'll think you're a crank."

"Who cares? Valley thinks everyone at SUM is a crank, or worse."

"That's not my point. He's not going to believe you."

Well, that gave me pause.

"Seriously, Nick, your sense of smell is not going to convince Valley of anything."

"Then I have to get Roberto to confess somehow."

"What you have to do is stop this. Now. Vanessa said to let the police do their job and we haven't listened to her. How do you think you can get Roberto to tell you he killed Napoléon? You think you're smarter than someone the police haven't been able to catch?"

"I'll think of something. But before that, we need to go to the retreat center."

"*Now*? At this time of the morning?"

"I have to check out the men's room."

Stefan didn't argue, but this time we took Marco with us, securing him in the backseat in his own little dog seat that was tall enough for him to look out through the windows. He loved car rides.

I thought I might feel creeped out going back to the retreat center, but I was on a mission and that protected me. When we arrived, we saw some cars parked out front, but nobody was inside the main room, which had been rearranged with lots of folding chairs in a semicircle facing the fireplace. There were cleaning and cooking sounds coming from the kitchen, so I assumed another event was in store. Despite my trepidations, the building seemed just like any other, magically purged of all the fear, disgust, and anything else horrible that I'd felt.

The crime scene tape was still up at the entrance to the hallway leading to the restrooms, and even that wasn't disturbing now. It was easy enough to duck under. I opened the men's room door with my arm so as not to leave more fingerprints than were already there (though I hadn't been fingerprinted and I didn't know if anyone else had been, either). The room was as lovely as when I'd first seen its quartz brick walls and red-and-white granite flooring that reflected the recessed lighting. It all seemed pristine and fragrant, but not excessively so.

I walked to the counter looking for the potpourri vase, which someone had apparently moved, bent over it, and then took a whiff. The scent was definitely not strong enough to have left the impression I'd described to Stefan before, and I made that very clear to him.

"Potpourri can fade," he said, playing devil's advocate, I think.

I slipped the Lagerfeld bottle from my pocket, opened it and splashed some on me, splashed a lot, in fact, while we were still in the men's room.

"An experiment," I explained.

Next I brought him back out into the hallway for several minutes, and then I said, "Go back in and see if the scent in that room isn't still lingering there, and maybe even stronger than before."

Stefan did what I asked, and re-emerged with a bemused look on his face.

"I think you should call Detective Valley," he said. "But first, wash the stuff off your face in the sink—then use the scented sanitary wipes in the car."

We left without anyone noticing we were there and I couldn't help thinking that this retreat center needed better security. *Some* security, at least.

I called Detective Valley on our short drive home and told him my theory about Robustelli.

"So you think the new chairman killed the old chairman?" he asked flatly after I explained what I believed I had verified by visiting the men's room at the retreat center.

"Yes!" I unfolded my theory for him a second time. "Isn't it at least possible?"

After a long pause, he produced just one word: "Maybe."

I pressed Valley, but he wouldn't commit to any course of action. He just thanked me for my "input." And then he added darkly, "Go to the retreat center one more time and I'll have you charged with obstruction of justice for interfering in a criminal investigation. You've got a lot to lose and that's a felony, punishable by up to two years in prison."

"Or a fine of not more than two thousand dollars," I said, proud that I had done my research on the Michigan penal code in the past.

There was silence on the other end of the phone, then he hung up.

Stefan heard the whole conversation on speaker phone, and all he said was "Well played."

"Yeah, but what's next?"

"Atticus," he said, out of the blue. "Is he still missing?"

"Why are you asking about him now?"

"It's something that Valley said."

We pulled into our driveway, clicked the garage door opener, and parked.

With the garage door down, I unharnessed Marco and let him run into the backyard. Stefan followed me and we watched Marco chase squirrels and crows out of his domain. Some trees in our neighbors' yards were starting to turn pretty early, but everything was still lush and fragrant in our yard with the sharp tang of evergreens that would give us color and texture throughout the winter, which could be bleak in Michigan, though winters had been growing milder of late.

We sat in the patio chairs close to the back door of the garage and let Marco have free time to sniff and stalk.

Stefan said, "Valley told you that you had a lot to lose, and I know that was just a threat and Vanessa would take care of us if it went beyond that. But it just hit me when he said it, that of all the suspects, Atticus had the most to lose. Think about it. He's not tenure-track, he can't find a tenure-track position because they hardly exist anymore, and if Napoléon fired him he'd have nowhere else to teach. I know there are other universities around the state he could apply to, but they're all more than an hour away and he can probably walk to campus right now. All those other schools have a glut of desperate Ph.D.s who would eagerly fill any opening."

He was right, of course, and that was one of the dirty secrets of higher education in the U.S. today: doctoral programs kept accepting students because they needed those students to teach undergraduate classes for ridiculously low stipends, while knowing that there weren't nearly enough jobs in academia for those students when they finally earned their degrees. It was a giant scam, and universities were grifters preying on students who were in love with their studies and craved to live outdated dreams of a challenging, sustaining, and fulfilling intellectual life. If legislators cared, there would have been investigative hearings long ago, but for too many of them, college was all about job training, not education in the broadest, truest sense.

Several universities in Michigan were considering eliminating humanities and social science majors like History, Sociology, French, Spanish, German, Art History, English, and anything else that didn't seem to guarantee a high-paying job right out of college. That meant cutting ties to other cultures and languages, other political systems, thus narrowing any student's field of vision—and much worse: turning college into a glorified trade school.

"I'm going to text his wife and see if she knows anything," Stefan said, explaining that they'd exchanged numbers once in connection with an exhibit a few years ago that was coming to SUM's museum from the Holocaust Museum in D.C. Stefan had a conflicting engagement out of state or he would have been a guest speaker as the son of survivors.

Stefan got an almost instant reply: " 'Still no news. But could you please come over?' "

Florice gave us her address, which was in a slightly sketchy neighborhood several blocks north of campus. Sketchy for Michiganapolis, that is, since there were more renters there than home owners. We had some time before going over, so we settled Marco in the living room and turned the TV to a calming documentary about Caribbean fish, one of his favorites, and one he never barked at the way he did when he saw most other animals.

The address Florice brought us to was a set of six shabby, bland-looking condos with ragged lawns and faded wooden siding that seemed to have been chewed on by squirrels. But when Florice let us in, she looked like she belonged somewhere far more glamorous. She was deeply tanned, wearing a caftan-y turquoise dress with matching sandals, and a heavy turquoise-and-silver bracelet adorned her left wrist.

"I took a day off, with everything that's been going on," she explained, as gracious and relaxed as someone greeting weekend guests. Her English was flawless and her Quebec accent was like a grace note.

The walls of the living room she invited us into were lined with museum exhibition posters that warmed the small, bland, spartan room with a range of colors: Kandinsky, early Picasso, Chagall, and Mondrian. There were sliding doors at one end that let out onto a flagstone patio with a small grill.

"Coffee? Tea?"

We thanked her, but declined.

"I'll reheat my coffee and be back in a moment." She stepped into the kitchen and I tried to make out the book titles in the white IKEA bookcase opposite the couch where we were sitting. "Look," I said to Stefan, "they've got some of your books."

He smiled. But I felt guilty since I didn't think we owned anything Atticus had published.

A microwave dinged and Florice was back, sitting catty-corner to us, long legs elegantly, lightly crossed. She seemed anything but troubled as she blew on her coffee to cool it off.

To me she said, "I know Atticus told you how miserable he was, how Napoléon was bullying him, how vicious he'd been, even threatening to fire him. I also know that Atticus suspected me of having an affair with Napoléon. That was simply not true. I don't like men who never doubt themselves. It's too exhausting to be around them."

Her denial was firm and clear. I studied her face for some kind of "tell" that she was lying, but she didn't glance away or look down, her calm expression didn't change. I didn't raise the rumor about Atticus watching her and Napoléon have sex because it just seemed vicious and stupid.

"Where do you think he is?" I asked.

"He's like Churchill, you know? Winston Churchill would get what he called his 'black dog.' Dark days, depression, feeling hopeless. In French we call it *le cafard*. Atticus never likes subjecting me to it, so he usually takes a hotel room somewhere in town or even in Ann Arbor. It hasn't happened like this before, when he had classes to teach." A vague unease flickered in her eyes and disappeared.

Since she brought it up, I didn't feel it was crossing a line to ask, "Has he tried anti-depressants?"

"Yes, and the side effects were awful. I think he gets depressed because his parents are so successful in Washington and he feels he's a disappointment to them."

"Why is your husband's phone off?" Stefan wondered.

She smiled. "He doesn't want to talk to anyone at times like this, not even to me. It never lasts for more than a few days. He's a writer, after all, and life calls to him again, makes him want to transform the world into words."

Stefan asked her, "Did you tell the police he was at a hotel?"

She sipped her coffee. "Of course. They haven't found him yet, but they thought the timing suspicious, evidently. And they think I'm involved somehow, especially since I don't know the hotel he's staying in. I told that detective, Valley I think his name was, I gave him some possibilities, but Atticus really could be anywhere." She finished her coffee and put the mug down on a nondescript side table.

On a hunch, I asked, "Have you checked his emails?"

She shook her head. "We respect each other's privacy too much to pry. The police wanted to, but they didn't have a search warrant, so I wouldn't let them. But Atticus has told me how much he admires both of you, so I'm sure under the circumstances he wouldn't mind if you had a look." She rose and gracefully left the room as if going off to arrange flowers or something equally pleasant, and returned with an iPad.

"Is it locked?" Stefan asked.

"No. But you'll need the login and password for his email. It's lower case," she said, and spelled out "doyle27."

"Password?" I asked.

"The password is Waterloo."

Florice passed me her husband's iPad, I opened the cover and it came on. I found the tile link to his SUM account, punched in his login and password, and *bingo*, there was his Inbox.

Then I whistled in utter disbelief when I read the first email.

24

THE EMAIL WAS FROM Robustelli to Atticus—one long run-on sentence:

> *I don't care Doyle what you think you saw at the retreat center if you tell that to anyone I will fuck you up so bad you will live to REGRET you ever took that first breath outside your mother's fuckhole and don't think your pretty wife is safe either*

Stefan was reading over my shoulder and he actually gasped at the rage and vulgarity. So did I.

"Did you find anything?" Florice asked with trepidation, her words uncertain. She was biting her lower lip. No doubt our faces must have altered dramatically after reading that cyber-eruption of venom.

I nodded, scrolling down, but Roberto's email wasn't a reply to one from Atticus—it was a separate email. When I checked Doyle's Sent folder it was empty, ditto his Trash and Spam folders. I didn't know what else to look for, or where. Maybe an IT expert could figure out what to do next, but I was stumped.

If they'd had *any* communication by email, why had he kept only this one?

I handed Florice the iPad and she read dispassionately, her face frozen. I had no idea what she could be thinking. She set the tablet down and wiped her hands on her thighs as if they'd been soiled.

"I never saw that vicious email to my Atticus before. What a horrible man." She shuddered.

There was no disputing that. But I would have expected a stronger reaction to Robustelli's threats from anyone, not just from her. What if there'd been other emails between Roberto and Atticus, but they'd been deleted?

Stefan asked, "Did your husband tell you anything unusual about the department retreat last Sunday?"

"It was all unusual," she replied with no irony. "From start to finish. He had a low opinion of Napoléon and debated whether he should even go to the retreat."

"So did we," I said, and she gave me a weak smile.

Stefan persisted. "Atticus didn't say anything about what he might have seen or who he thought killed Napoléon?"

Florice shook her head decisively. "We didn't speculate, we were just glad that Napoléon was dead, to be honest with you. Relieved." She flushed a little, clearly embarrassed to have admitted that.

My thoughts were suddenly foggy, but I pushed on, "Do you think your husband could have killed him?"

Stefan muttered, "Why are you asking that now?"

Florice didn't hesitate, and surprisingly, she didn't seem offended by my question. "The police asked me the exact same thing. And I said no, never. Atticus couldn't be responsible for something like that. He despised Napoléon, but he's not a killer. He has too gentle a heart."

I was thinking that Atticus was terrified and disappeared because of this email from Roberto, but why not show it to the police?

The doorbell rang and Florice rose to answer it. We heard a low man's voice which sounded familiar, and then Florice cried out, *"What? What? What*—I can't believe it!" and then "No, no, *no!"*

We hurried to the door and found her standing there with Detective Valley's young partner. Her face was pale and twisted in agony. The detective looked supremely uncomfortable.

"He's dead!" she shouted at us. The detective nodded.

Florice was so enraged now—I was hesitant to say anything at all, but Stefan asked, "What happened?"

"They've found my Atticus on campus, in that awful building of yours," she said as if about to sob, her breath tight, erratic. "Lying in a *stairwell.*"

She stumbled off to the kitchen. The detective closed the front door, followed Florice, and we trailed after him. She was sitting at a small white table, shoulders slumped, radiating grief and shock. Covering her face with her hands, she looked like a statue of Grief on an old-time war memorial.

My thoughts were all over the place, racing. I wondered if she had truly not known where Atticus had gone. I wondered if the story of Atticus's depression was even real—or just something she was telling people.

I pulled myself together and asked Florice if there was a neighbor or friend we could call for her. She dropped her hands but didn't look at either one of us or the detective. She shook her head slowly, heavily.

"Just leave. *Please.*"

The detective added a bit stiffly, "I can handle this," though his flushed face made me wonder if he really could. He seemed very young to be dealing with a stranger's grief.

We left, and when we were driving off, I felt like telling Stefan to keep going until we ran out of gas. Drive *anywhere,* just so we could escape that poisoned, poisonous town.

"I feel terrible that we left her all alone," Stefan said as we neared campus.

"But she asked us to get out," I answered. "Staying would have been rude, and weird. We don't know her."

We were stopped at a red light on the edge of campus and

Stefan turned to me. "Why didn't Florice look at his email her-self? Wouldn't you check my email if I disappeared and my phone was off? Why did she even call us over in the first place?"

I couldn't answer that. If she was convinced Atticus was on a kind of depression bender, why did she need to talk to either one of us, and in person?

"I think she wanted *us* to find an email or something, she just couldn't bring herself to do it," Stefan said, as the light changed and we turned right, heading to Shattenkirk Hall.

From half a mile away I could see an EMT van in front of Shattenkirk along with an array of campus police cars with their emergency lightbars flashing from red to blue to red and back to blue. Dozens of students on their way to class were now gathering outside a cordon of sky-blue wooden barricades, which read in white block letters SUM POLICE LINE DO NOT CROSS.

When we parked in the faculty lot, I saw Detective Valley emerge from Shattenkirk. Spotting us, he headed straight for us and I had the insane desire to run. The tumult, the cop cars, the flashing lights were suddenly retriggering my fear from when the SWAT team invaded our house.

Stefan must have sensed my panic because he took my arm after we got out of the car, then said to me, "You'll be fine" with absolute assurance, and led me forward. Maybe he was right, but I felt as if we were involved in some kind of risky Cold War prisoner exchange across a fogbound bridge.

Valley said, "You'll want to go inside to see your assistant."

"Celine? Why?"

"She discovered the body."

Valley clearly assumed I already knew who was dead. Had the news spread across Twitter and Facebook already? Or was it just on local radio?

I pulled away from Stefan. I felt nauseated by the swelling mass of gawkers, the lights flashing like some kind of weapon deployed by a torturer, and Valley's ever-watchful, tightly con-trolled face.

"Holy crap," Stefan murmured. "Poor Celine."

Valley nodded to an officer who opened up a path for us to go inside. He walked us to the elevators, left us standing there, and Stefan and I rode up in silence.

We found Celine sitting in her office with a kind-looking female police officer finishing her notes. The cop was tall and lean, with auburn hair pulled back in a no-nonsense bun. She was young, and looked very athletic. She patted Celine on the shoulder and left the three of us alone. Celine had a vague, uncertain air about her—as if she didn't belong there but had wandered in by accident.

I pulled a chair round to Celine to sit nearby, but not too close. She gazed at me now with dull horror in her eyes and I felt she was very far away. Her hands remained clenched in her lap, like a young student waiting for punishment by a teacher.

Stefan sat on the edge of her desk and asked if she wanted tea or coffee or anything.

"Thank you. Tea would be nice. My grandma always made me tea when I was upset—she grew up in England."

Stefan checked the electric kettle on the windowsill to see if there was enough water, then turned the kettle on and took a tea bag from the nearby box. He placed it in a brown-and-beige pottery mug that was uneven and might have been made by one of her kids.

"Are you okay?" I asked, knowing it was a ludicrous question, but feeling I had to say something. For whatever reason—and maybe precisely because it was clichéd and dumb—Celine came back.

"Yes, I think so. Thank you."

The kettle boiled. Stefan made the tea and set the mug near her. She looked at it, nodded absently as if checking something off on a mental list.

We waited for her to tell us what had happened, and after a moment in which she seemed to be telling herself something encouraging, she sat up straighter and pulled her shoulders back.

"I was walking up the stairs and it was like I'd fallen into a nightmare because I suddenly thought I was you, at that ridiculous retreat, when you discovered Napoléon's body in the men's room. I mean, I knew it wasn't Napoléon, I knew right away it was Atticus Doyle, but your story has been on my mind since you told me about it, and everything blurred together."

Before I could ask anything, Celine moved on with her account.

"His neck was at a strange angle and he was lying there mostly on the stairs, but partly on the landing, you know where it makes a turn, heading up to the second floor, like he'd tripped. I could see that the laces on one of his shoes were undone."

I looked up and noticed Stefan had been texting but he put his phone away.

"He looked so helpless I started to cry, then I called 911. I didn't try to take his pulse or anything like that. I've been around death before. I knew what it looks like. So I waited, on the next flight of stairs, trying not to look." She shuddered, and Stefan brought over a coral cardigan that was folded on top of a low long file cabinet. She took it gratefully, draping it over her shoulders. Then she sipped some tea.

"That lady officer was the first one to find me. She brought me here and took my statement."

Suddenly we heard a shriek echoing through the building. And then another that turned into a wail so eerie that it was like something out of a ghost story.

"That must be Florice," I said, and something tightened in my chest. I pictured her in the stairwell and for some bizarre reason, I remembered just then that her name was a variation of Florence, which meant prosperous or flourishing.

Now I felt surrounded by grief and pain, but somehow it wasn't retriggering anything more from last spring. Instead of feeling devastated, I found myself filled with compassion as if looking down on this scene from a benevolent height. I wanted to hug Celine, but held back. If she needed a hug, she would surely tell me. I exchanged a long look with Stefan, who seemed to have found the same inner place that I did. His face was open, his eyes glowing with compassion, and he looked like he wanted to hug Celine as much as I did.

I asked, "When you were walking up the stairs, when you found Doyle, did you notice anything different?"

Celine frowned. "Different how?"

"The stairwells always smell kind of sour and moist, don't they? I mean, they do to me."

"I've gotten used to it," Celine brought out, puzzled, and then she said, "There was something else there, like—"

"Like perfume or cologne?"

Celine closed her eyes and went as still as a medium trying to contact a spirit guide. Then she nodded briskly. "Yes. I smelled something different, something spicy, maybe. But why does that matter?"

I asked Stefan to stay with Celine, and on a hunch I headed down the hall to Robustelli's office.

When I got there, Grace Lovejoy stood up from her chair and barked at me: "You don't have an appointment!" but I stalked right past her desk and into his private office.

Roberto was busy with some paperwork and didn't look up, but he said, "You can close the door."

I'm not sure why I heeded him, but I did close the connecting door to Grace's office. Then I sat down in front of his desk in one of the chairs he was so proud of. I could smell the Lagerfeld on him now as intensely as if I were an asthmatic downwind from a chain smoker.

He looked up and grinned. He was as well dressed as the last time I'd seen him, and seemed even more expansive and welcoming. He could have been a wealthy uncle and I, his favorite nephew.

"So, Nick. Have you figured out anything else that the department can do to help you with your fellowship? I presume that's why you've come."

"Actually, I'm here because…I've just figured out…it was you…. You killed Napoléon Padovani…and you killed Atticus Doyle just now."

He grinned even more widely and I noticed that his canines were quite sharp.

"That's some wild story. I thought Stefan was the master of fiction at your house."

"You wear Lagerfeld," I said.

"Sure. So what?"

I launched into my conclusions about Napoléon's murder briskly, breathlessly, even though I tried to slow down and make it sound less like guesswork and more like indisputable fact.

His grin stayed where it was, but the look in his eyes had turned ugly.

"Nick, I'm disappointed in you." The smile had vanished. "I offered you support and now you're spouting crazy accusations. Have you seen a therapist? Because I don't think you're really over what happened to you in Parker Hall last spring. You're imagining things and you need help. *Now!*"

He was right about my not having recovered, and that stung. But so did his phony concern.

I felt stymied. What had I hoped for? That this would be like one of those scenes in crime movies where the gloating villain serenely explains how and why he committed his crimes because he's so proud of his cleverness? And does it in exhaustive detail— or admits he's the criminal and taunts the hero by saying, "You can't prove a thing. You have no evidence."

Roberto wasn't giving an inch, and I had no actual proof, only the evidence of my senses and that disturbing email he had sent to Doyle, which I realized any decent defense lawyer would argue was simply how Roberto behaved when he was angry. I could hear the courtroom spiel: "Being ill-tempered and vulgar doesn't make you a killer." And the email itself was vague enough to have any number of interpretations. I saw that now, and felt acutely embarrassed.

Roberto was smiling again. "You've been traumatized," he said unctuously, "so let's forget this little episode of yours," he said with fake geniality, "and—"

He didn't get to finish his sentence because the door opened abruptly and Detective Valley was suddenly looming there, his face and body filling the doorway, beside him that younger detective I'd seen at the retreat center. Behind them stood two uniformed campus police, and Grace Lovejoy barely visible, eyes wide, mouth quivering.

"Roberto Robustelli, I'm arresting you under suspicion of the murder of Napoléon Padovani. You have the right to remain silent. Anything you say can and will be used against you in a court of law. You have the right to an attorney. If you cannot afford an attorney, one will be provided for you. Do you understand the rights I have just read to you? With these rights in mind, do you wish to speak to me?"

The smooth-talking man who had been trying to charm me was gone. Robustelli leapt up as the two detectives came toward him and started shouting, "Are you fucking out of your mind? You motherfuckers are going to pay for this! I'll nail your asses for false arrest! You have no idea what I can do to ruin your lives forever! I know the governor!"

Valley was unruffled by his shouting as he and the other detective took hold of Roberto. Valley yanked Roberto's hands behind his back to handcuff him and the other detective frisked him. Then they got behind him, hands on his waist and shoulders, and propelled him out of the office into his secretary's, where he bellowed to Grace, "Call my lawyer!" The uniformed cops took over and walked him out of the office and down the hallway.

For all his bravado, Robustelli hadn't struggled in the slightest. I would have thought a bully like him would have resisted arrest and would have to be subdued, thrown to the ground, maybe hit with a stun gun. Wishful thinking.

"You believed me," I said to Valley.

"I believed the evidence. There were no fingerprints on the

stiletto, but there were latex glove prints. You professors think you're so smart," Valley said. "We found matching gloves in his trash." Now he was smirking. "That genius didn't do enough to hide his tracks. Then we dug deeper. It turns out he had an assault charge back in New York that was dropped."

So Robustelli's police trouble was more than just a rumor, and maybe that's why he had really left New York.

"But wait a minute," I said. "How is it possible for *gloves* to leave prints?"

Valley cocked his head at me as if I hadn't comprehended what he'd said. "Try doing some research—isn't that what you're supposed to be good at?"

I felt like a doofus, but only momentarily, because I'd been right all the same about who killed Napoléon.

"Did Roberto kill Atticus Doyle, or is his death an accident?" I asked.

Valley ignored my question.

"You first," he said, pointing to the door, and we left Robustelli's office. Valley clearly wanted me out of the way, because more cops bustled in and started methodically searching the chair's office.

Grace was at her desk again, staring at the phone and muttering something about "too much scandal." As I left, she met my eyes and said grimly, "God, I hate this place."

Behind me, I heard Valley say, "Tell me about it. Who doesn't?"

Just then my cell phone chimed. It was a text from Dean Bullerschmidt: "I'd like to appoint you the new interim chair of your department."

ABOUT THE AUTHOR

Widely known as a pioneer in Jewish-American literature, Lev Raphael is the author of twenty-five books in genres from memoir to mystery. His work has been translated into over a dozen languages and he's also the author of hundreds of short stories, essays, and blogs. He was born and raised in Manhattan but has lived more than half his life in Michigan where he's been teaching creative writing at Michigan State University. Raphael was a longtime reviewer of crime fiction for the *Detroit Free Press*; a guest reviewer on Michigan Radio and other public radio shows in Michigan; and hosted his own talk show where he interviewed authors like Salman Rushdie, Erica Jong, and Julian Barnes.

If you enjoyed this book, please review it online at Goodreads or Amazon.com. Even a short review makes a difference and would be appreciated. Word-of-mouth is crucial in publishing.

You can read what Lev has to say about writing and publishing at his blog "Writing Across Genres" [http://www.levraphael.com/blog]. Feel free to drop by and chat.

Follow Lev on Twitter [https://twitter.com/LevRaphael] or Facebook [https://www.facebook.com/levraphael].

To send him an email, go to his web site [http://www.levraphael.com]. You can also study creative writing with him online at [http://www.writewithoutborders.com].

More Traditional Mysteries from Perseverance Press
For the New Golden Age

K.K. Beck
WORKPLACE SERIES
Tipping the Valet
ISBN 978-1-56474-563-7

Albert A. Bell, Jr.
PLINY THE YOUNGER SERIES
Death in the Ashes
ISBN 978-1-56474-532-3

The Eyes of Aurora
ISBN 978-1-56474-549-1

Fortune's Fool
ISBN 978-1-56474-587-3

The Gods Help Those
ISBN 978-1-56474-608-5

Hiding from the Past (forthcoming)
ISBN 978-1-56474-610-8

Taffy Cannon
ROXANNE PRESCOTT SERIES
Guns and Roses
Agatha and Macavity awards nominee, Best Novel
ISBN 978-1-880284-34-6

Blood Matters
ISBN 978-1-880284-86-5

Open Season on Lawyers
ISBN 978-1-880284-51-3

Paradise Lost
ISBN 978-1-880284-80-3

Laura Crum
GAIL MCCARTHY SERIES
Moonblind
ISBN 978-1-880284-90-2

Chasing Cans
ISBN 978-1-880284-94-0

Going, Gone
ISBN 978-1-880284-98-8

Barnstorming
ISBN 978-1-56474-508-8

Jeanne M. Dams
HILDA JOHANSSON SERIES
Crimson Snow
ISBN 978-1-880284-79-7

Indigo Christmas
ISBN 978-1-880284-95-7

Murder in Burnt Orange
ISBN 978-1-56474-503-3

Janet Dawson
JERI HOWARD SERIES
Bit Player
Golden Nugget Award nominee
ISBN 978-1-56474-494-4

Cold Trail
ISBN 978-1-56474-555-2

Water Signs
ISBN 978-1-56474-586-6

The Devil Close Behind (forthcoming)
ISBN 978-1-56474-606-1

What You Wish For
ISBN 978-1-56474-518-7

TRAIN SERIES
Death Rides the Zephyr
ISBN 978-1-56474-530-9

Death Deals a Hand
ISBN 978-1-56474-569-9

The Ghost in Roomette Four
ISBN 978-1-56474-598-9

Kathy Lynn Emerson
LADY APPLETON SERIES
Face Down Below the Banqueting House
ISBN 978-1-880284-71-1

Face Down Beside St. Anne's Well
ISBN 978-1-880284-82-7

Face Down O'er the Border
ISBN 978-1-880284-91-9

Margaret Grace
MINIATURE SERIES
Mix-up in Miniature
ISBN 978-1-56474-510-1

Madness in Miniature
ISBN 978-1-56474-543-9

Manhattan in Miniature
ISBN 978-1-56474-562-0

Matrimony in Miniature
ISBN 978-1-56474-575-0

Tony Hays
Shakespeare No More
ISBN 978-1-56474-566-8

Wendy Hornsby
MAGGIE MACGOWEN SERIES
In the Guise of Mercy
ISBN 978-1-56474-482-1

The Paramour's Daughter
ISBN 978-1-56474-496-8

The Hanging
ISBN 978-1-56474-526-2

The Color of Light
ISBN 978-1-56474-542-2

Disturbing the Dark
ISBN 978-1-56474-576-7

Number 7, Rue Jacob
ISBN 978-1-56474-599-6

A Bouquet of Rue
ISBN 978-1-56474-607-8

Janet LaPierre
PORT SILVA SERIES
Baby Mine
ISBN 978-1-880284-32-2

Keepers
Shamus Award nominee, Best Paperback Original
ISBN 978-1-880284-44-5

Death Duties
ISBN 978-1-880284-74-2

Family Business
ISBN 978-1-880284-85-8

Run a Crooked Mile
ISBN 978-1-880284-88-9

Lev Raphael
NICK HOFFMAN SERIES
Tropic of Murder
ISBN 978-1-880284-68-1

Hot Rocks
ISBN 978-1-880284-83-4

State University of Murder
ISBN 978-1-56474-609-2

Lora Roberts
BRIDGET MONTROSE SERIES
Another Fine Mess
ISBN 978-1-880284-54-4

SHERLOCK HOLMES SERIES
The Affair of the Incognito Tenant
ISBN 978-1-880284-67-4

Rebecca Rothenberg
BOTANICAL SERIES
The Tumbleweed Murders
(completed by Taffy Cannon)
ISBN 978-1-880284-43-8

Sheila Simonson
LATOUCHE COUNTY SERIES
Buffalo Bill's Defunct
WILLA Award, Best Softcover Fiction
ISBN 978-1-880284-96-4

An Old Chaos
ISBN 978-1-880284-99-5

Beyond Confusion
ISBN 978-1-56474-519-4

Call Down the Hawk
ISBN 978-1-56474-597-2

Lea Wait
SHADOWS ANTIQUES SERIES
Shadows of a Down East Summer
ISBN 978-1-56474-497-5

Shadows on a Cape Cod Wedding
ISBN 1-978-56474-531-6

Shadows on a Maine Christmas
ISBN 978-1-56474-531-6

Shadows on a Morning in Maine
ISBN 978-1-56474-577-4

Eric Wright
JOE BARLEY SERIES
The Kidnapping of Rosie Dawn
Barry Award, Best Paperback Original. Edgar,
Ellis, and Anthony awards nominee
ISBN 978-1-880284-40-7

Nancy Means Wright
MARY WOLLSTONECRAFT SERIES
Midnight Fires
ISBN 978-1-56474-488-3

The Nightmare
ISBN 978-1-56474-509-5

REFERENCE/MYSTERY WRITING

Kathy Lynn Emerson
*How To Write Killer Historical
Mysteries: The Art and Adventure of
Sleuthing Through the Past*
Agatha Award, Best Nonfiction. Anthony and
Macavity awards nominee
ISBN 978-1-880284-92-6

Carolyn Wheat
*How To Write Killer Fiction:
The Funhouse of Mystery & the Roller
Coaster of Suspense*
ISBN 978-1-880284-62-9

**Available from your local bookstore
or from Perseverance Press/John Daniel & Company
(800) 662–8351 or www.danielpublishing.com/perseverance**